Liberty's Promise

Heidi Sprouse

Dedication

To Lise Wilson. Because of you, this sweet town has become my home, a slice of history has become a part of who I am, and Whispers of Liberty came to be.

To our brave, Johnstown colonials, and all of the Patriots near and far. You dared to dream, fight, and sacrifice to give us America, the land of the free. Because of you, we still hear the whispers of liberty today.

Acknowledgements

They say it takes a village to raise a child. The same holds true when a story is born. Thank you to Noel Levee, Johnstown's historian, the Johnstown Historical Society, Joan Fudger, and Joan Loveday for all of your gems of knowledge. A shout out to Patricia Port Locatelli for historical photos and Mysteries on Main Street for your support of local literature. You keep the history of this fine town alive.

To the residents of Johnstown for being the memory keepers of their proud, colonial heritage, past and present, you have my gratitude.

Table of Contents

Whispers of Liberty
(Preview)

December 22, 2015

"I WILL FIND YOU! I KEEP MY PROMISES!" The clamor of
battle crashed in on us. The crack of musket fire. The boom of a
cannon. A flurry of footsteps. Heavy boots crunching the faded, dry
leaves scattered across the field, bodies sprawled across the dead,
brown grass, clothed in red and blue coats. I clung to my Benjamin
for one more desperate moment, his lips sealing mine and stealing my
breath away. His voice was raw when he spoke. "As soon as I can, I
will come to you. Go now if you love me."

I wanted to cling to his body until the end, my feet sprouting roots
and planting me by his side, but I had no choice; I carried his baby
inside me. I turned and ran, stumbling and weaving my way toward
the woods, blinded by my tears. One last time. I had to lay eyes on his
face once more.

I turned to see my Patriot standing watch for my safe passage,
hand raised in farewell, and a musket exploded, loud enough to make
me jump, to nearly stop my heart. A crimson flower blossomed across
his chest, his arm fell, and Benjamin dropped. Pain, indescribable
and unbearable, coursed through me. I prayed a cannon would blast
me to bits, taking me with him.

~

Jolted awake from my nightmare, I shot up in my bed, my heart
hammering. I gasped, the scent of gunpowder stinging my nose and
lungs, chilled to the bone. I had not been plagued by my parting from
my Benjamin in a past life since he found his way back to me.
Somehow, my Patriot waded through two hundred and thirty-three
years, making a return as Ben Wilson. When we married on
Valentine's Day, he recognized me for who I truly was—Charlotte

Elizabeth Ross the First reincarnated as Charlotte Elizabeth Ross the Second. That winter's day, standing on the snow-covered field where we had been torn apart, our ghosts appeared to be laid to rest with our reunion—or so I thought.

Badly shaken, I checked the baby monitor on my nightstand. Soft breathing was the only sound. Still, the nursery pulled at me and I had to check on our son myself. I slipped into the dim room, a nightlight the only illumination, and tiptoed to the crib. Our little one, my heart, slept peacefully. Nearly a month old, he spent most of his time sleeping or eating.

I reached down and ran a hand over the fine cap of brown hair that curled over his forehead. Soft as a kitten or the down of a chick. I rested my palm on the crown of his head and sent up a silent prayer in gratitude for his safekeeping, my other hand tracing the letters lovingly carved in the crib headboard, handmade by his father. Jacob Cooper Wilson, 11-27-2015. His mouth curved up slightly—and I was snagged. It was Benjamin's smile. His father's smile.

Love wrapped itself around my heart and squeezed so hard, I couldn't move. A beat, one more, and I leaned over to kiss my baby boy on his forehead. *You have always been and will always be my greatest blessing.* The words echoed through the ages, fitting then, fitting now for our Thanksgiving baby. They would never grow old.

Eyes stinging, I took a deep breath and gazed out the window. The night was quiet, the snowflakes drifting on the air, pieces of heaven come down to earth. The Battlefield of Johnstown, the site for one of the final battles of the American Revolution, slept peacefully beneath a blanket of snow. A lone oak aglow in white lights made a sob catch in my throat. Ben and I had strung the lights the night we married. Every night since, the tree was lit, a beacon paying homage to all our brave Patriots who spilled blood on the soil below, who gave their last drop. Their last breath. Like my Benjamin.

Stop it! Stop it right now! I had to give myself a hard mental shake. Over two centuries ago, Benjamin Willson died on this unassuming, small patch of land, allowing me to flee to safety in my past life, carrying our future inside me. He'd kept his promise to find me again, his spirit coming back as Ben Wilson in the 21st century, righting the wrongs of the past. This time around, my love wasn't going anywhere.

Except to the store to get diapers and chocolate pie. Laughter bubbled up inside me at the thought as I wandered down to the living room and stood at the window, bathed in the Christmas tree's soft light at my side, eagerly anticipating his return. It was the winter solstice and Ben wanted to celebrate. A foray to town for practical necessities had to include something for my sweet tooth. Ruefully, I laid a hand on my stomach, still a tad generous after my recent delivery. I didn't need the extra calories, but my husband wouldn't utter or hear a word of complaint. *I won't deny you anything, Charlotte, not as long as I live. Life is too short.*

Headlights turned off the road below as the snow picked up in force, almost obscuring a black truck rolling up the driveway. Ben! Would I ever get over the anxiety that threatened to smother me every time he left me? Unable to wait another second, I grabbed my coat, slipped on my boots and stepped onto the porch to wait for him. Surrounded by pine garland strung in white lights, it was as if I was standing inside a torch, leading him home.

The truck door slammed shut and he moved swiftly toward the steps as the wind kicked up and the storm intensified, creating a tunnel of snow around him. For an instant, I experienced double vision, saw both my men, walking side by side. The Ben of today shivering in jeans and his navy peacoat, and the Benjamin of the Revolution bold in the blue of his militia uniform. I squeezed my eyes shut, inhaled deeply, looked again, saw only one man. My husband, two men united in one.

He hit the steps practically at a run. One glance at his face and my smile died. Ben was white as a ghost, his eyes haunted. I stepped in and hooked my arms around his neck, pressing in close. "Ben,

3

what's wrong?" His body was shaking hard enough to make me tremble. I didn't think it was from the cold. Had the past caught up with him tonight as well?

He kissed the top of my head and hugged me, his shivers running straight through me. "It's freezing out here! I think a blizzard's on the way. Get inside before you catch your death!" With one arm wrapped around my shoulders and the other around a bag of groceries, Ben nudged the door open and closed it behind us. The sack slid to the floor as his hands rested on my shoulders and his mouth took mine. I ran my fingers up and down his back and still, he was shaking. Hard.

"You're cold. Let's get you by the fireplace." I slid his coat off and hung it on a hook while Ben knelt to remove his boots. He stole my breath away, his dark hair dusted with snow and disheveled by the wind, broad back barely contained by a brown sweater that brought out the warm coffee color of his eyes, tapering down to narrow hips in jeans that fit just right. His fingers, stiff from winter's chill, fumbled with the laces and he cursed softly under his breath.

I had all the time in the world to admire him later. I sat down on the floor and rested my hands on his. They grew still. I undid each boot and eased them off his feet. Ben's palms, large, warm, and callused, cupped my face, forcing me to meet his gaze. His eyes, usually sweet as melted chocolate, were dark, troubled. He bent down and brushed my lips with his. "Charlotte, I don't like the look of you. What's wrong?"

Something must have been written on my face. Damn my eyes for stinging! My breath caught and I dipped my head to avoid his gaze, but he pressed his finger under my chin, forcing me to look at him. I swallowed hard, bit my lip, and tried to speak. A shake of the head and I tried again, managing to get control of myself. "It's nothing, really. I had a bad dream, of that day, when I lost you."

His face softened and he scooped me up as if I was no more than a child, carrying me over to a large, overstuffed recliner, one that was big enough to fit all three of us comfortably and had done so on many

4

occasions since Jacob's birth. Ben settled and nestled me in against him, pulling the soft blanket off the arm of the chair to wrap us in a cocoon and I was warm, safe. My husband had such an effect on me since the first time I laid eyes on him in the guise of a Revolutionary soldier.

His hand skimmed over my hair and my cheek, tracing my collarbone and finally resting on the button hanging on a chain, one that never left my neck. "You can't lose me. You know that."

Benjamin's button proved his words. Plucked from my Patriot's uniform on the day he died. Placed in my hand on the anniversary of the battle a year ago, in the Colonial Cemetery when I awoke from a journey across two centuries. The small disk with the letters USA proudly etched on its face was the key, sifted through the sands of time to dust off Ben's distant past. Bringing him back to me.

I closed my fingers over his. A tremor ran through him, making me quiver. "Ben, tell me. What's wrong?"

"Nothing's wrong. I just had the wind knocked out of me and had to catch my breath." He gazed at the flickering flames of the fireplace, their shadows dancing across his face. I gave him time to summon his courage, to compose his thoughts. His jaw clenched, unclenched and finally, he turned to face me. Ben would not hide from the taste of the truth, no matter how difficult it was to swallow. "I bumped into Maynard Hughes in the store. He was nearly beside himself with excitement over an artifact and asked me to give you this, another donation from the Cooper Bradley family in Cooperstown."

The town historian, well-versed in my family tree thanks to my father's enthusiasm, knew about every branch and how much anything from the Revolutionary period fascinated me. I waited expectantly while a small book in leather was placed in my palm, warm from being tucked in Ben's pocket, close to his heart. "What is it?" I asked nervously, a sudden trepidation making my heart start to skip, my mouth gone dry. My tongue darted out to lick my lip.

Ben cleared his throat. If at all possible, his skin went a shade whiter and he laid his palm on the scuffed, worn surface. His eyes closed, his face tight. I pressed my fingers over his knuckles, prompting him to say something. With a jerk of his hand, he flipped the book open. "It's a journal."

Afraid to look away from his face, it was a struggle to look down at the faded script. At the top of the first page, written in the fine, flowing handwriting of bygone days, was the owner's name and a note: *Benjamin Willson Cooper. A gift from my mother, Charlotte Elizabeth Cooper.*

I finally understood what it meant to swoon, my head light and my vision fuzzy as I began to sway. Ben shook me, hard enough to make my teeth click together. "Charlotte! Stay with me!"

It was the undercurrent of fear that I might somehow be swept away again—it had happened once before—that forced me to focus on my husband, the bands of his arms around me, the pounding of his heart thundering against my ear as my head fell to his chest. I pushed away and gazed up at Ben. I needed to be completely aware of my surroundings. "Have you read any of it?"

Ben's thumb grazed the frenzy of my pulse beating at the base of my neck; I could see his jumping as well. "No, no. I thought we would have to do this together. After all, he's mine too."

Benjamin Willson Cooper, son of Benjamin Willson and Charlotte Elizabeth Ross the First. Born in 1782. My Patriot never had the chance to lay eyes on his baby boy, to cradle him in his arms, but knew that Charlotte Elizabeth the First carried his child. Except for the early stirrings of pregnancy during my jaunt into the past and a vivid dream of Benjamin's birth, I had not become acquainted with this distant child either. His journal was an invaluable gift. We could know him through his own words, written by his hand.

I took both of Ben's hands in mine and gazed into his eyes, centering myself as his love washed over me, steadying me. "All right. Turn the page."

"You're sure? You've checked on Jake?" At my nod, Ben

6

brushed my cheek with a kiss and my stomach dropped like it did when I plummeted to the bottom on a roller coaster. My hand found its way to his as his voice carried over the snap and pop of the fire, a river of words threatening to carry me away. I held on tight.

1 June, 1812

MY MOTHER TELLS ME I AM LIBERTY'S PROMISE, what my father and so many others fought for. Bled for. Died for. My father never saw my face, never held me in his hands, never heard my first cries, although his blood runs in my veins and I bear his name.

Benjamin Willson paid liberty's price on a bloodied, war-torn field here in Johnstown, giving his life so that my mother and I might have ours. His story is written on my heart. My mother, grandfather, and step-father have made it so.

It is the man who raised me whose story I must tell. Jacob Cooper would never brag nor does he want anyone to sing his praises. He has told me often enough the way a man lives his life is legacy enough. I would have others know the man who gave my mother and me his name to avoid any stain on ours. He always loved her and in marrying her when she was with another man's child, he loved me as well.

No one except Mama, my grandfather, and Jacob know the truth. My mother slept with my father, betrothed but yet to be married, only a few days before his death. I am not truly a Cooper. No matter. My step-father does not need to share my blood to share his honor, respect, and love. Jacob may not be the man who made me, but along with my mother, he helped make me who I am. Jacob kept liberty's promise, made by a fellow brother-in-arms. He would not let Benjamin Willson die in vain. He freely gave my mother and me the haven of his home, the strength of his back, the touch of his able hands.

I owe Jacob Cooper everything. More than anything, I owe him the time it takes to put quill to paper and write his story down for all to see. I will do my best to get it right—the way he told it to me since I was a child at his knee.

2 September, 1781

THE DEAFENING SNAP OF A BRANCH, only a few feet
away, hit with a jolt. Jacob Cooper's breath caught as his heart
swelled, giving him the unpleasant sensation of rising up into his
throat and choking him. Still hunkered down in the heavy
undergrowth on one knee, he slowly turned to identify the source of
the noise. A squirrel looked him in the eye. A mad bit of chatter and
the little critter scurried away. The Revolutionary soldier's legs turned
to mush and he bit back a sudden, unreasonable rush of delirious
laughter until the boom of a musket shattered the peace and nearly
took his head off.

Biting off a curse, Jacob sprang to his feet and rushed into the
fray when most would go in the opposite direction. He was a member
of the Tryon County militia, a gunsmith and a Cooper. Coopers did
not turn tail and run.

Up ahead, there was a cacophony of shouting, grunts, and
screams as gunfire erupted from different directions. At least twenty
Redcoats took on no more than ten ragtag Patriots. Chaos reigned.

"William!" Jacob's head snapped up at the raw urgency in a
militiaman's cry. He turned just in time to see an unfamiliar Patriot
ram the town blacksmith out of the line of fire. A musket ball caught
the stranger in the upper thigh and he faltered, went down on one
knee, and collapsed.

Jacob went berserk, overcome with battle's fury, taking on their
foes. Anger, white hot, shot through his veins and he plunged into the
forest in pursuit, intent on making someone pay for every last drop of
Patriot blood that had been spilled. *If I am going to go, I will take as
many of them with me as I can.* He fired his Brown Bess, cursed the
time to reload, fired again. Lacking time and space when a
Lobsterback came on, Jacob used a knife and the hands God gave
him. Within minutes, it was over.

He leaned against a tree to catch his breath, clamping down on a surge of bile rising at the stench of death surrounding him. Killing men, even men he was forced to hate because of opposing sides on the coin of the Revolution, staining his hands with their blood, turned his stomach. Such was the price of war.

When his head cleared and he had his legs under him again, Jacob picked his way over the bodies, wincing at the sight of some of their own. William was on his knees beside the Patriot who had saved his life. The wounded militiaman was covered in soot and soil. Brilliant streaks of crimson marred his clothes and skin as his hands clawed at the dirt, digging in. William applied pressure to the wound and the stranger writhed beneath him, dark hair falling into his eyes.

Jacob dropped to his knees beside them. "William, what can I do?"

"Hold young Benjamin while I cut out the musket ball." The blacksmith's words made Jacob flinch at the mere thought, but it had to be done or the man would lose his life. He grabbed hold of his fellow Patriot's hand, slick with the hot blood gushing out of the gruesome wound in his leg. The muscles in Benjamin's arm bulged, the tendons standing out like rope beneath his skin as he gritted his teeth.

William pulled out a knife. A strand of hair like sun-ripened wheat, heavily interspersed with strands of white that had appeared practically overnight, fell into the older man's eyes. He impatiently brushed it away so he could slice off the injured man's pant leg, almost all the way to the hip. Jacob glanced around the small, bare patch of earth and found a stick.

He gripped the soldier's shoulder and gave it a hard squeeze. "Here. Bite on this." If only they had some whiskey.

"Try to keep still, young one." The blacksmith, a kindly father figure to everyone who knew him, pressed a hand to the wounded Patriot's forehead. Tormented eyes, darkened by an inner storm of terror were met by compassion in the older man's gaze.

One gasp and three words slipped out between clenched teeth. "I am ready."

At William's nod, Jacob leaned in with all his weight and all his strength. The blacksmith pinned Benjamin's lower leg with his knee and plunged the knife into the gaping wound. The blood spilled at an alarming rate as the sharp blade bit deeply through ragged flesh. A scarlet river continued to flow.

The fallen man made a terrible sound, his back arching as a cold sweat beaded up on a face gone white as winter's snow. The blood was everywhere, turning the soil black. "Good Lord, William," Jacob whispered, his voice ragged.

"I haven't quite got it, not yet. If I don't, he'll lose the leg." Another attempt and the tears were streaming down Benjamin's face. *More likely he'll bleed to death!* Jacob kept his misgivings to himself. The blacksmith had enough on his plate.

The knife slipped in William's hands that were so slick with sweat and blood. Jacob glanced up to see the older man dash a sleeve across his forehead as the perspiration dripped into his eyes. "One more time, Benjamin. One more time."

The knife went in so far, so deep, that Jacob expected the tip to come out the other side. The wounded Patriot let out a strangled scream, stick still clamped firmly in place, as William held up a bloodied ball with a great shout of triumph. Benjamin began to shake uncontrollably and his blood continued to spill. Too much blood.

William tucked the ball in his pocket and tore a strip from his shirt, binding it around Benjamin's leg and pulling it taut with the considerable strength of a blacksmith. He sat back on his haunches to catch his breath. "Jacob, will you help me get him up on Raven? I have got to get him back home to tend him."

The blacksmith's horse, black as his namesake, was tied to a nearby tree, pulling at his reins. The skirmish had made him skittish. Jacob quickly untied him, gentling him with his words and his touch. He led Raven to his owner. With William's help, they hoisted the wounded Patriot to his feet and boosted him up into the saddle where he clung to the saddle horn, swaying. In an instant, he would topple on to the ground. The man wavered, but managed to extend a hand to Jacob. "You have my gratitude."

Jacob grasped his forearm and pressed down hard. "Be well."

William patted his young assistant on the back. "You have my thanks as well. I could not have done it alone." He climbed up behind the injured man and wrapped an arm around his waist to spare him from tumbling over. "God speed and God bless, Jacob."

"I am going to see if Dodge and Stoner need any help. God keep you as well." Jacob stood still and watched them trot off in the direction toward Johnstown, the wounded Patriot slumped forward with his head hanging low. It did not sit well with Jacob. He had the sinking feeling the poor man would not make it.

Shaking off a sense of foreboding, he focused on the matter at hand and made his way toward a clash further on down the path. By the time he reached his fellow militiamen, it was all over. Jacob began the long trek home as the sun sank, marking the close of the day as it touched down on the horizon. Over thirty-six hours with no sleep, he didn't even notice the blaze of colors streaking across the sky. His head was fuzzy, like his brain was filled with cotton, yet heavy enough to fall off his shoulders. By the time he hit the door at his father's home, he could barely lift a hand in greeting. A few stumbling steps to his bed and Jacob fell face first on to the covers. He didn't even take his boots off.

4 September, 1781

"LOOK WHAT THE CAT DRAGGED IN. One would think you had drowned yourself in whiskey." Abraham Cooper stood at his workbench, set by the window to take in the full benefit of the mid-morning sun's rays illuminating his gunsmith shop. Another table was placed strategically to catch the afternoon light while oil lamps would make do when the weather or lack of hours in a day were a hindrance. He set down a gunstock in progress, intricate scrollwork underway. Jacob's father was an artist. A son could apprentice with no better man to learn his trade.

Jacob scraped a hand over his face and shook himself. "Sorry. I guess I was worn out." He stared at a stain on the wood floor. Abraham had high expectations. Failing to meet them was unacceptable. There were only the two of them, his mother dying from influenza when Jacob was only three. He had to carry his weight.

Abraham crossed the room in great strides and took his son's jaw in a firm grasp, forcing Jacob to meet a gaze of a piercing blue, like his own. Rust-colored eyelashes could not contain sparks of anger. "Don't you dare apologize to me. You fight for our cause. If you need to sleep for a week to recover, so be it. God, but I wish I could join you."

Abraham turned away and threaded one hand in his fiery curls, tugging in aggravation. Compact and muscular, his brawny shoulders hunched as the air hissed out through his teeth. If Jacob looked in the mirror, he would see a younger version of the man before him. The father had left a bold stamp on the son.

Jacob stepped forward and pressed his fingers on the nape of his father's neck. "You play a vital role here and ensure we do not falter. Someone must keep up a ready supply of firearms. Without you, we would have nothing more than knives, rocks, and our fists. I would much rather have a working musket in my hands." The knots of tension gave way as his father slid him a smile and returned to his work bench.

He picked up his father's latest project and skimmed his finger over the etchings made with painstaking attention to detail. He quirked an eyebrow. "Who wants such a luxury? Practical firearms, they are the only sensible option right now. We don't need our guns to be pretty in the militia. They just have to work and work well, as well as a Brown Bess can. We'd do better with something like the long rifle if enough men knew how to use it."

Abraham shrugged uncomfortably and took the hefty piece of wood, weighing it in his hands. "It is my own stock. I started it to occupy my hands and my mind, anything to distract me from worry. What with you sleeping like the dead and word that William made for German Flatts like his tail was on fire to get medicine for his injured Patriot, I have not been able to concentrate on anything."

"How is the militiaman? I saw him take the musket ball. A nasty wound it was, up high, in the middle of his thigh." *Saw him bleed. Heard him scream.* Jacob shied away from the images flooding his mind and focused on his father.

Abraham's face told him everything he needed to know. "Not good. Infection is raging through his body and a fever is consuming him. I fear all the herbs and learning in the world will not be enough for William to help the young lad. He is in the hands of God."

Frustration, never far from the surface since the war began, surged up inside of Jacob and threatened to boil over. He gave his father a curt nod and stalked to the door, grabbing his Kentucky long rifle on the way out. The gun was a gift from a fellow member of the Tryon County Militia who had seen the likes of Oriskany and Saratoga. Nicholas Stoner was a knowledgeable outdoorsman and guide who inspired others to follow his lead. Jacob often practiced with the weapon in his free time in hopes of rivaling Stoner's skill— or when he needed to do something to maintain his sanity.

The marvel of the firearm's weight was reassuring in his hand, something substantial. Something solid. Something that could have an impact, perhaps change the world. The rifles had only been around for about half a century. An innovative solution for the frontier, they were born on American soil. Raising it to his shoulder behind his father's shop, taking aim at the targets he had set up in the field that extended for miles beyond, the weapon gave Jacob a perverse satisfaction to know that it did not come from Mother England.

His face twisted at the thought of that small bully of a country situated thousands of miles across the sea. How could King George think he was entitled or knew best how the colonies should govern themselves? How many more men would be maimed or killed to pay the price for liberty?

With a growl that rose from his gut, Jacob prepped the flint-lock rifle, pulled the hammer back, focused on the center of the target out a good two hundred feet or more, and fired. His breath came out in a rush as he watched the custom-made lead ball, created from his own mold in his father's shop, pierce the bull's eye. Reload. Aim. Fire. Again and again, he let the light, slender beauty deliver, going beyond his expectations.

With every explosion in his hands, the wounded Patriot flashed in his mind. Scene by scene played out, from the instant the stranger saved William's life to the treacherous moment when the blacksmith plunged a knife into his leg and dug out a musket ball. Blood. Screams. Unbearable pain. Jacob relived every minute, only making his resolve that much stronger. He dug in his pocket, fingered at least a dozen more rounds and took aim. This time, Redcoats loomed before him and they all toppled to the ground.

20 September, 1781

HIS BACK, SHOULDERS, AND NECK ACHED from being hunched over his table for hours on end, repairing a mounting pile of damaged muskets for the members of the Tryon County Militia. What would they do if they were called up without notice? His fingers hurt from the tedious work of designing parts, putting them in place, handling the tools of his trade. Jacob looked out the window and his eyes were nearly scorched by the setting sun. He smacked the Brown Bess down on the workbench and his breath came out in a rush. Another day gone, getting nowhere!

I must do something, something of measure in this blasted conflict! Working behind the scenes, quietly—or not so quietly—plodding away, Jacob often felt insignificant. He wanted to face the enemy, drive them into the ground, squash them beneath his boots. Ride with the backwoodsman to put his Kentucky long rifle to the test like they did at the Battle of King's Mountain in '80, giving the Brits a sound whipping. Become a sniper like those at the Battle of Saratoga, picking off as many Lobsterback officers as he could. March with that great man, General George Washington himself. Not sit trapped within four walls doing nothing of importance.

Your father is anything but inconsequential. Abraham had taught his son everything he knew, passing on a love of guns that went to the core as well as consummate skills in metal work and woodwork. He had stressed times without counting there would be no army without the guns in their hands—and there would be no guns without gunsmiths. Jacob sighed and picked up the musket again. He fingered the trigger. Felt too much give. He forced himself to focus and correct the problem.

Heavy footsteps approached and the shop door opened with a loud creak. "Young one, I think you have had enough of this place for one day. Keep peering at that firing mechanism and you are going to blind yourself. Dodge is entertaining tonight." Abraham strode across the room, banking the fire and extinguishing oil lamps. He gripped his son on the shoulder. "Come, Jacob. That Bess will be waiting for you come morning."

Jacob's spirits lifted and his mouth quirked up in a hint of a smile despite his grim turn of thought. Brigadier general Richard Dodge was close to his own age, had a quick wit, and was decisive, bold. Jacob considered himself lucky to call the man friend. Dinner at his home would be a distraction, casting a light in the darkness. Perhaps some good would come of it. Perhaps—perhaps Charlotte would be there.

~

SHE DID STRANGE THINGS TO HIS INSIDES since the first day he saw her. When Jacob walked into William Ross's smithy at seven years old, accompanying his father on an errand, he was transfixed by a slip of a girl. William's daughter perched on a stool in the full light of the morning as it streamed through the window. She could not be any more than six, yet Jacob could not breathe the instant he laid eyes on her. The sun's rays made her hair shine like the wheat waving in the farmer's field where he ran amok on a warm, summer's day. She met his gaze and her honey-colored eyes made him fall, hard—figuratively and literally—when he took one step forward and tripped over his own boot.

His cheeks burned, and it had nothing to do with the blazing blacksmith's forge. He stared intently at the plank beneath his nose, mortified, when a flurry of footsteps crossed the floor and a small shoe came into view. Jacob looked up to find William's daughter beaming at him, making him feel like he was the earth and she was the sun. He took her hand, completely ensnared by Charlotte Ross. He still was.

The instant she stepped into Dodge's home, Jacob was sure his heart stopped. His breath caught in his throat, his mouth went dry, pressure building in his chest as if a fist was closing tightly around his lungs. The promise he had seen in the girl had been realized in the woman. At twenty-two, Charlotte was a beauty, a rare blossom. She could not be touched by the floral print on her dress in a deep blue. The hue only brought out the sunlight in her hair. The roses in her cheeks. The gold in her eyes. There was no one else he wanted more.

Jacob was not the only one who was drawn to her, a bee to her honey.

The militiaman William rescued during the skirmish in Palatine was close by her side, his hand pressed to the small of her back. Small tendrils of jealousy clouded Jacob's mind. He closed his eyes and choked down the bitter taste in his mouth. Any man would be attentive and courteous to a woman like Charlotte. However, Benjamin Willson was not just any man.

The Patriot from Boston stood ramrod straight even though his leg clearly pained him with every step, his mouth tight with the burden of his weight. His dark eyes followed Charlotte like her shadow. She tilted her head to look up at him, the blush rising in her cheeks when he smiled, a punch in Jacob's gut, forcing the air from his lungs in a rush. Curse the day William brought the stranger home to be nursed by her gentle hands!

The thought of taking Willson's place. Feeling her soothing, healing touch on his body. Her breath kissing his skin, her lips pressed on his made Jacob dizzy. Until his mind played back the moment the wounded soldier fell in vivid detail. Ashamed, he squashed his anger. Benjamin had bled and nearly died for their cause. He deserved respect. *But not my girl.*

Time to make his intentions known. Jacob approached the party of three, including William Ross, his daughter, and the Patriot. He took Charlotte's hand and fire raced from his fingertips, erupting in the pit of his stomach. Jacob bowed dramatically even as he struggled to keep his voice steady. *Breathe!* "Miss Charlotte, you are looking well." His lips grazed her fingers while he fought the urge to take her in his arms and seal her mouth with his.

The blacksmith broke her hold on him, clapping a hand on Jacob's back. "I would like to officially introduce you to Benjamin Willson, the brave Patriot from Boston. You did not truly become acquainted the dreadful day of the attack. Benjamin, this is Jacob Cooper."

"It is a pleasure." Willson nodded, his shoulders and jaw tight as he faced the challenge of mastering his pain. He urged Charlotte forward, limping heavily as he followed her into the next room. "Thank you again for coming to my aid that treacherous day," Benjamin murmured under his breath before continuing on.

A large gathering of townspeople, friends, and fellow militia members were scattered throughout the house, chatting, sharing the latest news. To Jacob, they were no more than the annoying buzz of a beehive as his gaze was drawn time and again to Charlotte. At dinner. As they lined the walls to talk war and politics. As she moved about the room, Willson was her right hand.

She glowed like a candle around Willson, drawn to him like a child to a firefly's flicker. Anger at the sight of the Patriot practically attached to her side festered like a raw and raging fire inside of Jacob.

It was as if Jacob was a pile of tinder and Willson was the spark. One touch of Charlotte's fingers on the stranger's hand and she became the wind fanning the flames into a bonfire. Jacob unleashed his fury, spouting off passionately about the war effort. "They have already taken enough from us! We cannot let them have any more, not after the Cherry Valley Massacre in '78 and just last year, that bastard, Sir John Johnson, coming through here with the Burning of the Valleys. Blocking our supply routes to Fort Oriskany and Fort Rensselaer. Leaving nearly two hundred dead. It has to stop and it has to stop *now*!"

He banged his fist on his knee as others cursed, muttered, or growled in agreement. Jacob turned his attention to Charlotte once again. Mischief writhed inside of him as she caught his eye, making him grin and wink at her.

Her companion went rigid as a block of stone, the color draining from his face as his dark eyes glittered dangerously. If Willson could throttle him, Jacob had no doubt the man would be happy to do so. He steeled himself for a confrontation and raised his chin, meeting his rival's gaze head on. *Do not expect to take her without a fight.*

Face gone a brilliant crimson, Charlotte squeezed her companion's shoulder and stood up quickly, blurting out, "How about a story?"

Within minutes, she had captured the rapt attention of the entire room, spinning a web from her imagination, something to do with a man who slept for decades and a fearsome horseman searching for his head. Jacob was spellbound. As for Willson? She was his moon and all the stars combined.

Unable to stand another second with the blood thundering in his head, Jacob murmured a compliment to William's daughter as her tale came to a close, and slipped outside. He pressed his hands against a tree and drew in one breath of brisk, autumn evening air after another. Soon chilled to the bone, it did nothing to cool the inferno in his veins. All these years. Watching. Waiting. Hoping that she would turn his way, mirror his feelings for her only to see her heart in the hands of another.

Dodge's guests began to depart, John Little and family loading into William's wagon for a ride home. As Ross' daughter bade goodbye to her host, Jacob could not resist one more try. He strode purposefully past Willson and took her hand. *Why can't you see me?* "Good night, Miss Charlotte. It was a pleasure to see you this evening."

Not content to stop there, he bowed and grazed her cheek with his lips. Her palm pressed to her face as if to capture and hold the heat of his kiss against her skin, stirring a song in his heart. Jacob whistled a jaunty tune as he walked away, but the music died when he saw

Willson set his hands on her waist to lift her on to the wagon bed. The way Charlotte gazed at the Patriot from Boston like he was her universe.

Jacob stood in the shadows and watched them rumble off into the distance, frozen until they were out of sight. He wanted nothing more than to follow them, take her away from the Patriot, sweep her off her feet. A jagged dagger of resentment stabbed at Jacob's stomach. In his mind, he saw one last glimpse of Willson's face, pale in the moonlight from the strain of his injury, head tilted to hers. Jacob's hands balled into fists and his entire body went tight.

She is not yours yet.

25 September, 1781

"LORD, JACOB! TWO HUNDRED PACES AND you have nailed it!" Talmadge Edwards shook his head as his finger brushed over the hole directly where the heart would be in a shirt stuffed with straw. The makeshift target was propped against a tree. A strand of sandy hair fell into eyes of a green more brilliant than gemstones, undimmed by the gloom of the forest or the looming shadows of war.

A true craftsman in leather work, his talent was evident as he slapped a pair of his handmade gloves against his knee. "Remarkable!"

Nicholas Stoner gestured for their fellow militiaman to step out of the way, pushing his tricorn cap back as he raised his Kentucky rifle to his shoulder. Jacob took a long draw on the communal jug of whiskey while the outdoorsman took aim and fired, just missing his mark. A soft curse slipped out as he set his gun down.

Richard Dodge stepped in close to finger the target. "I think the student has surpassed the teacher."

Stoner shrugged and took up the whiskey to dampen his competitive spirit, a rueful grin tugging at the corners of his mouth. "Perhaps. I also think someone is not getting much sleep anymore. What better way to pass his time than target practice with the Kentucky?"

Jacob grimaced and shouldered his friend out of the way, loading his rifle and leveling it. He set his jaw, held his breath, and fired. Reloaded. Took aim. Fired again. Repeated the entire process, ten times over, each time hitting his original mark. He readied to fire again when a hand grabbed his shoulder.

"Enough, Jacob. What is troubling you?" Nicholas stared him down.

The air hissed through Jacob's teeth and he snatched the whiskey from Stoner's hands, tipping his head back and drinking until a fire ignited in his gut. It did nothing to extinguish the blaze in his veins and the haze in his head that had not gone away since dinner at Dodge's place.

Dodge took away the stoneware jug, his dark eyes troubled. "I think it is a problem with a woman, the incomparable Miss Charlotte Ross. I saw how you looked at her the other night and Willson as well. He was a torch and she was the flame. I am afraid there is not a thing you can do about it, Jacob."

Nicholas slapped Jacob's shoulder. "How about a hunting excursion? I'll take you out, deep into the heart of the forest. We'll track a creature, something bigger than your anger and hurt. Something you can take down with your great skill and your long rifle. Something to bleed away your frustration."

The wiry, dark-haired woodsman was a skilled guide. If he promised to find game, Jacob would be brought face to face with one of the animals that inhabited the immense wilderness. Deer. Fishers. Wolves. Mountain Lions. Bears.

Images immediately flooded Jacob's mind of the skirmish in Palatine, the ground littered with bodies, the blood. Too much blood painting everything a vivid crimson. A red too brilliant to forget or wipe away. His gut began to churn. Breathing through his nose, Jacob swallowed hard and shook his head.

"No. I have no stomach for killing." He gestured to Dodge and took another draw of the whiskey. Powerful indeed, it slid down his throat like burning oil, pushing the tears from his eyes.

Edwards' eyebrows shot up at the rate of Jacob's consumption, prompting him to take the jug from his friend's hands and empty it out on the forest floor. The whole lot grumbled, Jacob most of all, but Talmadge firmly set his shoulders. "He will not have any more. Otherwise, Cooper will not be able to make it home and he'll have his father to answer to."

Jacob groaned and sat down on a stump, head in his hands with his fingers threaded through his mess of flaming curls. Talmadge approached and pressed the nape of his neck. "Do you want to challenge Willson to a duel?"

"Are you insane? He's a Patriot and a hero! The man saved William's life and nearly died! A duel! What are you thinking, Edwards?" Jacob shot to his feet and began to pace. He could not possibly walk far enough. Thoughts, like hungry wolves, circled in his mind, moving in closer. Headed straight for the kill and his heart was the prey.

He trudged across the forest and grabbed hold of more targets, lining them up, tree after tree to form an army of stuffed shirts. Back to his Kentucky and Jacob took aim. CRACK! One shot after another. With every shot, faces floated before him.

Sir John Johnson during the Burning of the Valleys. The nameless enemy that shot Nicholas Herkimer in the leg at Oriskany. Jacob had met the general once and was awed by an officer who proved to be brave beyond measure, refusing to vacate the field. He continued to direct his men only to die several days later, leaving them distraught, making his death that much harder to bear. Every time Herkimer crossed Jacob's mind, the anger surged up inside him, fueling his burning desire for revenge.

If only he could meet face to face with Cornwallis, leader of the British army, a trophy every Patriot wanted to win. Perhaps then, the anger that festered deep inside of him and the immeasurable sense of loss would go away. The war would finally be over, but what then? No fair lady awaited Jacob at home, although he had pictured holding a bride many times over the years.

Charlotte clouded his mind yet again, except now she was wrapped in Willson's arms, his lips pressed to hers. It was much too bitter a pill for Jacob to swallow. With a shout of aggravation, he loaded, fired, loaded and fired again until the rounds were gone. He planted his rifle between his feet, breathing hard as his eyes squeezed shut, but he couldn't escape the pictures in his head.

Jacob spotted an extra jug of whiskey Stoner had tucked behind a tree. He purposefully strode to the giant oak and picked up the jug. It wasn't hard to suck down the fiery liquid at an alarming rate. Maybe he could lose his mind, his memories, his passion for a little while. He dashed his hand across his lips, swaying slightly.

Nicholas closed the gap between the two men and glared at him, his arms crossed. "You had best ease up or you'll drop here on the forest floor. Besides, you are not fit to shoot when you get like this. You will put yourself and all of us in jeopardy."

With that, Jacob handed over the whiskey with a little more force than was necessary. Taking up his gun, he nodded curtly. "I had best be going then. Thank you for your concern." A few steps and he turned back. "Thank you to the lot of you for putting up with me."

They raised a hand in farewell and called after him, good natured as always. The shots rang out as the forest receded behind him and hearty laughter bounced off the trees. Jacob longed to turn back, share in a lighthearted moment, but his spirit was too heavy.

Still shaking with frustration, he continued the trek into town and his blood began to boil in his veins as he took in the damage left behind by raiders. The stench of smoke, imaginary though it might be, was strong enough to choke him and make him cough. Too many homes pillaged, burned to the ground, the fields cut down. Too many freshly turned graves. An overpowering rage at the cloud hanging over the colonies, sent by the British, was nearly enough to push Jacob over the edge.

By the time he reached the market square, autumn's chill, his brisk pace, and fury burned off the alcohol and cleared his mind. But his belly twisted at the sight of a tall, proud man limping beside a slender woman, her hair glowing like sun-ripened wheat in the noonday light. Jacob nearly turned around to take up Stoner's offer and get lost in the forest. How much more was he supposed to take?

Intent on giving the couple a wide berth, Jacob set out to bypass the entire stretch and slip in his father's gunsmith shop through the back entrance. His feet and his heart had a will of their own, pulling him closer with every step to Grannie Brown's stand of fresh produce and baked goods. His stomach rumbled, reminding him that he had skipped breakfast and lunch. A pastry and some cider would keep him until dinner. *Be honest. You want a taste of the honey in Charlotte's eyes. A glimpse of her sweet smile.*

Willson was sitting on a stool, his face gone white with the exertion of his walk, lines of pain drawn around his eyes and mouth. Ever tactful, Charlotte browsed the baker's wares to give her companion a private moment to deal with his pain. She reached for a basket that was well out of her reach, giving Jacob the opening he needed. He stepped in, taking up his confidence and good humor. "I'll get that for you."

It was no problem for him to snatch the item, his freckled arm grazing the young woman's as he leaned past her. For an instant, Jacob's breath was snatched away. Apparently, his nearness had an equal effect on Charlotte. She stiffened and blushed furiously, her golden eyes going wide. A heartbeat later, the Patriot from Boston stood behind her. "I can get that for her."

A breeze stirred, blowing a copper strand into Jacob's eyes. It did nothing to cool his blood as he handed the basket off to Charlotte. Somehow, he managed to grin through gritted teeth. "I know I'm not as tall as you, sir, but I can manage to help a lady in need."

The sparks from Willson's dark eyes nearly burned Jacob's skin as the Bostonian's jaw clamped shut, the muscles bulging from the tension of restraining himself. "She doesn't need your help. I'm quite fit, thank you."

"Of course." It took everything Jacob had not to spit the words in the militiaman's face. He nodded stiffly and placed his tricorn hat on his head. "Good day, Miss Charlotte. Mr. Wilson."

An abrupt turn of his heel and he walked away, all thoughts of refreshments gone, his appetite dead. He couldn't face his father, couldn't concentrate on the delicate work of his trade, not in his current state. He needed to walk off the steam rising from the surface of his brain, tame the pounding of his heart.

His feet found their way to the creek, took him tramping through water like ice. It didn't even touch the storm of churning emotions threatening to tear him apart. Jacob picked up rocks and chucked them as far as he could, but found no satisfaction. He kept stomping onward until he ran out of breath, finally hunching over with his hands on his knees, gasping to fill his lungs. His reflection made him freeze.

Eyes of deep blue snapped dangerously, glaring back at him, his fiery hair disheveled. His hand trailed through the heavy strands and gave a tug, making him grimace. He surveyed his build. Compact. Sturdy. Solid. Strong and short, compared to the militiaman from Boston. In every way, Jacob and Willson were opposites. Light versus dark. Old versus new. One more disgusted sneer and Jacob stomped on the image staring back at him, shattering it. For the first time in his life, he wanted to look like someone else. Someone who would turn Charlotte's head.

Jacob cursed. Shivering, he made his way out from the water and sat down on a large rock by the shore, head in his hands. Never one to complain, he had always been satisfied with the gifts given to him by the grace of God. Cooper. Gunsmith. American. Jacob had never given his appearance a second thought. Growing up, the girls had appreciated him and there had been no shortage of admirers, save one. He had always hoped she would change her mind. He'd given her time.

But time had run out.

The sound of voices pulled him to his feet, prompting him to take cover. Willson and Charlotte again! Could he not escape them? The Patriot was limping badly, the journey into town and back too much for him. For an instant, Jacob actually sympathized with the man. He even considered offering him aid until Charlotte shared a jug of cider. One thing led to another and Willson leaned in to seal her mouth with his. Jacob's head nearly burst as pain hammered at the walls of his skull.

He staggered away, as if a round had fatally pierced his heart. His mind had painted pictures of the two becoming intimate, but to see them sharing the air they breathed, the heat of each other's body, the touch of their hands upon each other? Jacob wished he could pluck his own eyes from his head.

Somehow, he managed to stumble home through the forest, avoiding the road. His father would not be home until darkness fell. Jacob's chest burned from the flames that had reduced his insides to ashes. If only he could numb the pain or drink himself into oblivion.

~

THWACK! THE AX SWUNG THROUGH THE AIR in a great arc. Jacob's arms, neck, shoulders, and back burned with the strain, but he kept swinging. One piece of wood after another, splitting each block into two or three with a satisfying *thunk* into the stump they used for a chopping block. As the sun rested on the horizon, streaking the sky in a brilliant explosion of colors, a fog still darkened his mind. Jacob tried to make it fade away, hoping work would be the antidote. *Thwack*! The ax lodged in a particularly thick chunk of wood, sending a vibration through his wrist all the way to his ear, making it ring. He gave the blade a mighty thrust, grunting as it popped free. One more swing and four pieces fell onto the carpet of chips on the ground.

"Keep it up at this rate and we will have enough firewood for the next ten years." Abraham stood propped against the woodshed, arms crossed. He smiled, but his eyes were troubled. Jacob set the ax down and pressed the handle into the ground, fighting to catch his breath and find his equilibrium. His father stepped forward to press his shoulder. "He cannot take what you never had. Let it rest, Jacob."

One gust of breath and Jacob turned to his father for advice as he had countless times over the years. Like William Ross, the gunsmith had been forced by fate to take on the role of two parents. He had proved to be a compass that never steered his son wrong. "What do you do when you lose all hope of being with the one you love?" A pause, staring into eyes so like his own, and he could have bitten his tongue. Such a question, when Abraham had to put his own love, Phoebe, in the ground decades ago.

For an instant, the wave of pain in his father's eyes nearly crushed him. With a blink, it vanished. Abraham gruffly kissed the top of his head. "You pick yourself up and find a reason to keep going. Every day I thank God that I have you."

16 October, 1781

JACOB TOOK EVERY JOB THAT CAME IN, repairing tools, axes and an assortment of odds and ends when they were short on gun work, which was rare. Hours melted, one into the next, the sunlight giving way to moonlight. He set up a pallet of sorts by the fireplace and caught a few hours of sleep, when sleep could take him. Every time he closed his eyes his head hurt, crowded with images of Charlotte and Willson.

"God help me!" He shot to his feet and lit the oil lamp, unable to take another minute on his back.

Lying down only made him picture the bedroom and that turned his stomach. His workbench waited for him, the tools of his trade and parts for a new gun laid out. Somehow, his fingers continued to do their job even though his heart and mind were elsewhere. Jacob forced himself to focus while the wind howled outside. A storm was coming in. Fitting. He had been caught in a tempest ever since the skirmish in Palatine.

Hoofbeats neared at a steady clip. The door swung open with a bang, bringing a cold gust of air with it. Jacob spread his hands over an assortment of parts and bent over the table, eyes closed in aggravation at the distraction. He just wanted to be left alone.

"It is getting blustery out there. I think you had best head home before it gets any worse." His father moved close to the hearth to warm himself by the fire and waited for an answer. Every day, Abraham left when it was time to close up shop. Jacob knew his father hoped he would follow. Abraham spent every evening alone, and Jacob made sure to be hard at work when his father arrived in the mornings.

Jacob straightened and picked up the stock and barrel, methodically assembling the firearm, something he could do with his eyes closed. "I think I will stay here again, finish this rifle. I have just about got it."

Abraham joined him at his side. He peered closely at his son's handiwork and his breath came out in a rush. "That's a beauty. You've finally done it, made a gun that is completely your own. May I?"

A few more pieces and it was complete. Jacob handed it over. At any other time, he would have been proud of his masterpiece. Right now, it only made him feel hollow and without purpose. His head throbbed and his eyes were gritty, like they were filled with sand. He pinched the bridge of his nose, praying for relief that would not come.

There was a quiet thud as the firearm was gently placed on the workbench and his father hooked an arm around his shoulders. "Jacob, you must stop torturing yourself. You have been going nonstop for nearly a month. You barely eat. You don't sleep. There is no joy in you anymore. You have always been filled with light and laughter, a breath of fresh air, but now it has all died. It is time to come home and find your spirit again."

Jacob shook his head. "I can't do anything else right now, Father. This is my reason to keep going. If I stop, I'm afraid I'll go out of my mind."

The thunder of hoofbeats approaching at a breakneck pace ended the discussion and for that, he was grateful. The two of them had been caught in the vicious cycle of this conversation too many times to count. A flurry of footsteps made him wary of their late-night visitor. Good news was not likely.

A loud pounding on the door, and Nicholas Stoner burst into the shop, breathless. "Jacob, there's news. Dodge is holding a meeting at his place. Come quickly!" He didn't even wait for an answer, just headed back into the night. Paul Revere was not the only one to go on a midnight ride since the war first began to rage.

Abraham's Adam's apple bobbed as he pulled his son into a rough embrace. "Go now and Godspeed. I will pray for you."

Jacob nodded and kissed his father's cheek, the rasp of his

unshaven face scraping against his father's skin. One never knew if this moment would be their last. The only sure thing about the Revolution? Uncertainty. He turned and grabbed his coat from the hook on the wall, snatching up his Brown Bess from its place by the hearth. He clapped his tricorn hat on his head and strode out the door. His father raised a hand in farewell as he glanced back one last time over his shoulder. Jacob would hold that image in his mind, a flame burning bright. Abraham would be his reason to go on and continue to fight.

~

"THERE'S A WAR PARTY ON THE MOVE. A large one, possibly a thousand!" Talmadge Edwards paced back and forth, raking his hand through his hair. The others murmured under their breath. The waiting game was finally over and they were restless, eager and fearful at the same time.

A messenger had come through town, sent word to the Tryon County Militia, and moved on to spread the news. The intent: to prepare as many as possible and not let anyone be taken unawares. The Cherry Valley Massacre, the Raid on Tillaboro, and the Burning of the Valleys were still too fresh in their minds. Too many good men, like Lodowick and Aaron Putman, had lost their lives. Too many innocents had been sacrificed. Too much destruction had befallen the Americans near and far.

Richard Dodge stood at the window, staring out into the darkness as thunder crashed and rain hammered the windows. Lightning split the sky and illuminated his face, reflected in his eyes. His skin had gone white, his jaw tight. The assembled group of men looked to the brigadier general for direction. Everyone held their breath, motionless as he turned to address them.

"Ross and Butler are at it again." His mouth twisted into an ugly snarl. "At least seven hundred. Redcoats, Indians, Loyalists. We need to round up as many as we can to intercept them, hold them at bay. They will not wreak havoc on Johnstown, not if I have anything to say about it. Who is with me?'

A shout rose in unison, fists shaking in the air, a rumble of conversation making it hard to hear anything. Richard grabbed a chair and stood on it, raising his hands for silence. "You have one day to get your affairs in order. Prepare your families and make arrangements. Right now, I need volunteers to gather more men. Young and old. I need them all."

Jacob stepped through the crowd, anger nearly crackling from his skin. With clenched teeth, he reached out to take Dodge's hand. "I will go south, get as many as I can."

A firm shake and a nod confirmed his duty. He turned and made for the door, barely taking notice as others offered to head off in different directions, including Edwards, Stoner, and John Little. Jacob's heart was already racing, his body on edge as he prepared for his first stop. The William Ross homestead.

~

SHE WAS A STATUE. The moment Jacob stepped in the door, the blood drained from Charlotte's face, turning her the color of marble. One look at her anguish and he was stricken to the core. Jacob wanted to turn back time, spare them, but it was not his choice. William was a member of the Tryon County Militia and Willson had pledged himself to their cause. The Patriot had lost everything because of the British and nearly gave up his life. The Bostonian would fight, regardless of where he was or who was by his side.

Even if it meant leaving Charlotte.

"I am sorry to disturb your meal, William, Benjamin." Jacob nodded in acknowledgement of the militiaman from Boston. Jacob's eyes met Charlotte's for only an instant, her pain too much for him to bear. He would cut off his own hand to spare her any hurt, and yet this dreadful war had forced him to be the harbinger of doom.

"The militia has been called up again. Informants have reports of at least seven hundred on the move. Redcoats, Loyalists, and Indians, under Ross and Butler. Willett is attempting to muster as many men as possible. He hopes to take them by surprise and intercept them before they wreak any more havoc on us." Jacob's breath came out in a rush. *Angry.* God, but he was angry that anyone should steal Charlotte's peace.

In a matter of minutes, his job was done. William and Willson became mired in a hushed contemplation of their plans. Charlotte sat rigid in her chair, as if in shock. Jacob wanted to go to her. To shake her for some sign of life. To fall to his knees before her, bury his head in her lap, and beg her forgiveness. Unable to do any of those things, a brief farewell was all he could manage, taking his leave to move on to the Andrews' homestead next.

With each visit, his stomach ached and his head pounded. All the while, Charlotte's ashen face and haunted eyes followed him. He might as well have taken a musket and shot her through the heart. The thought of hurting her shredded Jacob, slicing him to bits and bleeding him dry. He only wanted her happiness, even if it meant surrendering her to another man. Tonight, Jacob had destroyed her joy. As he turned his horse toward home, his mind continued to picture her, shattered at her kitchen table. *I will do everything I can to bring them home safe.* Jacob whispered the solemn vow to himself.

Another reason to go on.

~

"YOU ARE NOT STAYING HERE TONIGHT." Abraham made a statement, not a question. They'd been hard at work since the wee hours of the morning, performing last minute repairs for the militiamen. Both men were tired, their fingers, arms, and backs cramped. Both were feeling the strain of the pressure to meet the demand before time ran out. Jacob's father gestured to the door for his son as the last rays of dying sunlight created a halo around them.

Jacob's breath caught in his throat and his eyes stung. What if this was his last night with his father? He took down his coat and shrugged into it, handing off Abraham's. His fingers skimmed over his father's arm only to find two sturdy hands gripping his shoulders. Eyes of a bright enough blue to burn bore into his. Abraham leaned in and touched his forehead to Jacob's for a second, unable to say more. There was no need to speak of feelings as strong as theirs.

They mounted their horses and followed the road home, taking it slow, making it last. Neither knew when their next ride would be. As he rounded the bend that brought them to their humble cottage, a small building in a deep shade of red, Jacob had to swallow hard. This was his place, the only home he'd ever known. Warm and snug, it welcomed him as smoke curled into the sky and dusk fell, the first stars glimmering in the sky. He came to a halt and simply stared, imprinting their homestead on his mind. Jacob would carry this image with him. God willing, he would return to see it again.

He dismounted and took both horses to the barn, too uneasy to go in and sit just yet. Brushed Flintlock and Powder down. Stroked their faces and manes. Staring into the deep brown eyes of the pair of chestnut stallions tamed his emotions. When Jacob had some modicum of control, he bid them goodnight and locked up the barn for the evening.

Something smelled good when he stepped inside and the heat of the fireplace was inviting. His father had dished out plates of venison blended with potatoes and onions, one of their favorites. A hearty bread, still steaming from being wrapped in the coals, sat in the middle of the table along with two mugs filled to the brim. Jacob inspected one closely and couldn't help but grin. "Whiskey?"

Abraham gripped the edge of the table and bowed his head, unable to speak for a moment. Jacob's smile slipped away until his father managed to meet his eye and wink. "What better excuse to drink than when a man's only son is headed off to war?"

His father pulled out a chair and waited until his son did the same. Any attempts at a conversation died out after fits and spurts. In the end, they ate in silence, chewing methodically, neither cleaning their plate. Jacob stood and started to collect the dishes, but Abraham stopped him. "They'll keep. Sit."

The two men sat in chairs pulled up to the hearth, hunched over with their elbows on their knees. Jacob couldn't help but feel dejected, his spirits brought low. "If only . . . ," he blurted, then snapped his mouth shut.

"If only we could go together." Abraham finished his thought, his eyes gleaming in the firelight. "You know that I would be at your side in a heartbeat if I was not needed here in town."

Silence fell between them as they stared into the flames. Memories washed over Jacob, threatening to carry him away. Sitting at his father's knee, watching him at his craft. Learning reading, writing, and arithmetic from a primer at the supper table. Rocking by this same fire when he was only a little tyke, watching the tears roll down Abraham's face the night they lost his mother. Laughing together and telling stories. Above all else, Jacob remembered being raised in a house that stood on a solid foundation built on love.

Neither man slept well that night in the small room that held their beds. Jacob stared at the ceiling, his eyes dry and burning while his father tossed from side to side. When Jacob finally did drift off for a few minutes, the sky began to lighten. Keeping a groan to himself, he dressed quickly although he would rather stay home, go to work with his father, pretend nothing had changed. After all this time hoping for action, he was reluctant to go. If Abraham was left alone, what would become of him?

His father handed him a cup of coffee as soon as he came to the table. "Drink up and eat something. I've put together a sack of food for you. You'll not have good eating for long, I'm sure."

Jacob burnt his tongue on the hot brew and began to sputter.

Abraham slapped him on the back in an effort to be helpful, but it was no use. Neither could find their good spirits that morning.

His father took the cup while Jacob turned away to swipe a hand across his eyes. He slipped into his coat and grabbed his musket. Time to leave before he fell to pieces. Abraham squeezed Jacob's shoulder before he could open the door, turning him so they could face each other. "Be safe and come home to me. I know I haven't said this enough, but I'm proud of the man you've become and I love you."

Jacob hugged his father hard and kissed his cheek. "I love you too, Father. I am who I am because of you. I'll be back as soon as I can." Abraham couldn't speak, but he held on for a moment more then stepped back.

Jacob went to the barn by himself and saddled up with the sack of food from his father. A fine shiver ran through him, making him tremble in the early morning chill as he mounted. Powder's hooves made the most lonesome sound as he clip-clopped down the lane, away from home, to meet the enemy head on. As the sun crested the horizon, Jacob glanced back and raised a hand to his father. Abraham reciprocated, his hand like a flag he hoped would still be flying high when the fighting was over.

18 October, 1781

ONE HUNDRED MEN AWAITED JACOB in the middle of the forest, setting up camp. A ragtag bunch if he ever saw one. They ranged in age from over sixty to as young as twelve. Farmers. Carpenters. Tanners. Shoemakers. Breeches makers. Wheelwrights. Few had any type of military experience. Jacob was relieved to see Nicholas Stoner and Richard Dodge. They were young, but they knew how to fight and understood strategy.

"Cooper! This way. You can share a tent with us. We're already set up." Stoner waved him over. Jacob dismounted and led Powder to his friend, tossing his bag inside.

He turned and glanced around at the others, searching for familiar faces. A tall figure, broad of back, with an air of confidence in his bearing, caught Jacob's attention immediately and a curse slipped out under his breath. Willson was hard to miss in a crowd.

Dodge was by a campfire, talking with a group of men. Gesturing this way and that. Scraping his hand through his hair. A tensed coil about to spring. "Are they sending out scouts?" Jacob muttered to Richard under his breath. At the brigadier general's nod, he jerked his chin toward the trail. "Then sign me up."

Anything to put distance between himself and Charlotte's sweetheart. Anything to numb the ache deep inside every time he saw the Patriot from Boston. Jacob might have to fight on the same side with the man. That didn't mean he had to like it.

25 October, 1781

THE MIDDAY LIGHT STREAKED THROUGH THE BEDROOM *window, nearly setting Charlotte's hair on fire. That was nothing compared to the flames licking at his veins. Jacob shifted and pulled her close, resting her head on his chest. The scent of her soap, a blend of roses and sunflowers, made him dizzy. He kissed the top of her head and inhaled deeply. He couldn't get enough of her, would never be able to get enough of her.*

"Look at us, lazing about in the middle of the day. It's so sinful." There was a smile in her voice that made him answer with one of his own. Jacob found himself smiling all the time since Charlotte became his wife.

His hand trailed over her arm, up to her shoulder, grazing her cheek before threading through her hair. He let a strand wrap around his finger and watched it shimmer. His breath came out in a soft sigh. Jacob didn't care if he ever moved again. "It's our first day as a married couple. What else should we be doing except stay in bed?"

She rose to her knees, the sheets gathered around her body to cover her modesty. Jacob thought about unwrapping his wedding gift again until he was caught in her gaze, trapped by the honey in her eyes. Charlotte leaned over him, her hair forming a golden curtain setting them apart from the rest of the world. They could be the last two people on earth. Her lips touched down on his and a bonfire consumed him. As he rolled over, pressing his wife—he'd never get tired of that title—into the covers, her laughter was contagious, fanning the flames higher. In an instant, they'd reduce the entire house to ashes.

~

"No! Jacob shot up in a tangle of blankets in the middle of the night, gasping for air to fill his lungs. Somehow, Dodge and Stoner slept on as he lurched across the tent and threw open the flap. About twenty feet of staggering and he dropped by the creek to cup the icy water in his hands. He took a long, deep swallow and splashed it all over his face and hair. Jacob was tempted to walk into the freezing water up to his chest, anything to cool the blood boiling in his veins.

Damn his traitorous mind. Tricking his body and soul. Dangling his heart's desire within his grasp only to snatch it away. Night after night, variations of the same dream had tormented him, stealing his sleep and what scrap of peace of mind he had left. When this war ended—if it ever ended—Jacob wasn't sure he could ever look at Charlotte Ross in the same way again.

He had no respite. His only option? Saddling up and heading out on the trails, into the forest, in search of any suspicious activity. For seven days, Jacob and Powder went on scouting missions from the wee hours of the morning until after darkness had fallen. Looking for war, for anything to escape the thoughts circling around in his head.

Until the war found him.

~

"TAKE COVER! TAKE COVER NOW! BRITISH TROOPS AND LOYALISTS are headed this way! They're less than a half hour away!" After days of nothing, the messenger practically ran right over Jacob, who had dismounted for a moment to check Powder's shoe. He couldn't bear to see the horse go lame.

A young man on horseback pounded down the trail, eyes crazed, hair whipping around his face. How his hat stayed on his head, Jacob had no idea. The lad was breathless and bedraggled, covered in mud, blood streaking down his face from scratches. Branches continued to whip at him, tearing at his hair and his clothes. A curt nod in acknowledgement of Jacob and he continued at a formidable pace.

"God go with you, boy," Jacob muttered, fearful the militiaman would break his neck with his recklessness. Heedless of all danger, the messenger was intent on bringing word of impending doom to as many in their company as possible before it was too late.

Now. The moment of truth. The blood began to pound in Jacob's brain, his breath short. The waiting was over. Finishing up a quick inspection of his horse's hooves, he mounted smoothly, turning Powder's head back toward the members of the Tryon County Militia. Over the course of the past week, their numbers had swelled to at least 400. Jacob would join his band of brothers to meet the approaching threat. With a tap of his heel to the stallion's flank, he spurred the horse on at a fast clip back to the others. Everyone was scattering, headed for Johnstown to become a human barricade to Sir William's town.

Jacob burst into camp to see a young scrapper named Charlie Ross, William Ross' relation, darting into the forest at Willson's urgent shout. The boy was slight and slender as a reed. He looked like a strong wind could blow him away. Small wonder the blacksmith and the Patriot from Boston were worried about his safety. No one even had time to breathe when at least twenty British regulars were on top of them. The fight was on. Here. Now.

Jacob dismounted, dropped on one knee, and bit off the end of a paper cartridge. He spat it out and primed the pan, rested the butt of the stock on the ground, all the while inwardly cursing the precious seconds that were slipping through his fingers. Loading took too much blasted time!

Powder horn handy at his waist, he quickly poured some down the muzzle, dropped the cartridge in, and rammed it home. A clock inside his head ticked off precious seconds. The hammer pulled back and he fired, taking one Lobsterback down with the blast of his musket. Twenty more seconds to repeat the repeat the whole process stretched out like seven of the longest days of his life. Time! He needed more time!

Jacob's ears were ringing and his eyes were burning as the stench of black powder seared his nose and singed his lungs, making him cough. He could barely see through the smoke, but could make out Benjamin Willson fighting valiantly by William Ross' side.

Their bond gnawed at Jacob's insides. He'd always thought of William as a friend, an honorable man whom he held in the highest esteem. A man who would have made a good father-in-law. The Patriot from Boston had stolen Charlotte's heart and her father's, yet he wasn't even one of their own. An outsider! What right did Benjamin Willson have, to count himself as part of their company?

The rational part of Jacob's mind recognized Benjamin for what he was—the embodiment of a true Patriot, liberty's torch burning brightly inside him. Born and bred in Boston where the flames of the Revolution started burning, scorched by the loss of his mother to the Tories and the loss of his father on Breed's Hill, he'd publicly vowed one night at the campfire to avenge their deaths and fulfill liberty's promise if it took his last breath. Watching Willson now, a fearsome opponent as he threw himself into the fray, was proof enough. Benjamin was a man of his word.

Add the Patriot's unwavering loyalty to William, remaining by his side when all hell broke loose, and Jacob had to squash his resentment, push it aside, focus on the fight. Vaguely, he was aware that Willson, the blacksmith, and several others were caught up in the heat of the skirmish while Jacob faced his foes. When his Bess proved too awkward, he took it up as a club and brought it crashing down on a Redcoat's head. The soldier dropped, blood spilling from his temple onto Jacob's boot. He nearly began to retch.

"NO!" Jacob's head snapped around at the sound of Willson's raw cry, the dead man at his feet forgotten. The Patriot from Boston tried to intervene on William's behalf in a scene that was déjà vu all over again, so like the first time he saved the blacksmith's life. Benjamin attempted to thrust Ross out of harm's way when a musket ball caught Charlotte's father in the arm—or was it the chest? In the smoke, clash of battle, and chaos, Jacob couldn't tell as a crimson stain blossomed, growing larger by the second.

In the space of a heartbeat, barely enough time to draw breath, William fell to the ground. Benjamin's face appeared to split down the middle, shattered. In that instant, Jacob took back every negative thought or misgiving he'd ever had about Willson.

The Bostonian fought like a banshee, taking down two Redcoats as they came on, intent on one goal: reaching the Lobsterback that hovered over William's prone body. Willson pulled out a knife, lips curled in a grim snarl, and slit the soldier's throat.

Stunned, Jacob gave himself a mental shake and resumed the fight, clearing a path to the blacksmith and Benjamin. It was over within minutes, the woods gone still as the silence grew, pressing in on all sides until its weight was suffocating. The forest floor was littered with bodies, the majority in red coats. Willson knelt by William and tore off a strip of his shirt to wrap it around the wounded man's arm. Jacob's legs nearly buckled in relief. The arm. Not the chest.

"Is he all right?" Jacob dropped down beside the two men and gripped the older man's good arm with no response. The blacksmith's eyes were closed and he'd turned a ghastly shade of gray.

Benjamin tore off another strip and yanked it hard, murmuring an apology when William groaned. "God willing, he will be. The ball went clean through, but he's lost a great deal of blood and I'm sure it hurts like the devil."

The blacksmith raised one hand, slowly reaching out for Benjamin. Jacob caught his fingers and held on. "Char— " William's voice was a hoarse whisper, so low both men had to lean in close to hear him.

Benjamin's eyes sprang wide in alarm and a curse slipped out between gritted teeth as he cut off the older man. He turned and gripped Jacob's arm, his fingers digging in hard enough to hurt. "Charlie! You've got to find him. He'd just a boy and he's William's kin. I'd go, but I must stay with William."

Clearly, Willson was torn by the desire to be in two places at once. Jacob nodded curtly and climbed to his feet. "I'll find him. Be safe."

He took off in the direction the boy went. Talmadge Edwards passed him by, leaning over his horse's neck to urge his stallion on. Jacob called out after him, "William's been hit. It's not fatal, but Willson could use your help." The glove maker spurred his horse on with a kick to his flank and an urgent shout in answer.

With no time to spare, Jacob ducked his head and pushed his way through the undergrowth. Following the lad was easy. He'd left a trail of broken branches and footprints along the way. A complete novice would be able to locate the youngster. About one hundred feet off the beaten path, the footing became treacherous with a steep incline.

Jacob nearly fell head over heels down the slope. He grabbed hold of a tree and scanned the area below. Charlie was sprawled at the bottom, leaves in the boy's hair, chest heaving as the young one panted frantically. Even in the gloom of the forest, his face was white as a ghost.

"Charlie!" Jacob called down, taking a deep breath to steady himself before carefully picking his way down the hill.

The boy grabbed his hat and shoved it on his head just as Jacob reached him. He hunched over and pressed a hand to his side, fighting a stitch from the hard run. "Sweet Jesus! I thought I'd never find you. Benjamin sent me. When he told you to conceal yourself, I don't think he wanted you to fall off the face of the Earth. You wouldn't believe how worried he is about you, since you're such a little tyke and green around the ears. Willson's seen a lot more than me, more than anyone should see. That and your being William's nephew are part of the reason he's keeping such a close eye on you."

Jacob blew out a great gust of air, sucked in, and straightened up. "Lord, but I did run fast."

For the first time, he took a close look at Charlie Ross, having avoided contact with William and Willson to that point . . . because it was simply too difficult. The youngster was small. He looked like his clothes were swallowing him up. His skin was pale, from the fall or fear, and he stared hard at the ground, trembling like a leaf caught in a fierce storm. Only a boy trying to fill a man's shoes, too delicate for the demands of a soldier.

Taking pity on the lad, Jacob offered Charlie a hand in greeting and to aid him to his feet. "By the way, I'm Jacob Cooper. I've seen you at a distance but have been too busy to introduce myself."

The boy shot up and yelped, favoring his right ankle. Twisted it in the fall, more likely than not. Jacob wrapped his arm around the injured boy's waist to offer support and became still as a statue. His hand had inadvertently brushed against something on Charlie's chest, a soft swelling of a mound, hidden beneath his large, brown coat. Something that shouldn't be there.

Mouth gone dry and heart rammed into his throat, Jacob moved as if in slow motion, his hand inching its way up to push the boy's hat off his head. He took hold of the young one's chin, shivering at the soft texture of his skin, and tilted the boy's head so they could look each other in the eye. The face of his dreams stared back at him.

Her eyes were wide as a doe's caught by a hunter in the forest, the glory of her sun-ripened hair shorn to above her shoulders to aid in her effort to masquerade as a man. Jacob felt light-headed, as if all his blood rushed to the pit of his stomach—or spilled out on the ground at his feet. "Charlotte?! What are you doing here? Are you out of your mind? You should be safe at home!"

A white-hot poker of anger jabbed at his insides, setting him to shaking. Jacob itched to place his hands on her slim shoulders but thought better of it, fearing what he would do to her. The very idea of her putting herself in danger, marching with their company, risking her life, was horrifying. He wanted to throttle her.

Wonder of a woman that she was, Charlotte Ross reminded him again why he had loved her since the first time he laid eyes on her, a passion that had only grown stronger with time. Once a burbling creek, it was a raging river as she bit her lip and lifted her chin to face him down. "I had to come! They are all that I have, Jacob! I couldn't sit there while they were out risking their lives. I just couldn't! I need William. I need Benjamin because . . . ."

Something died inside of Jacob and its name was hope.

"Because you love Willson and he loves you." Jacob's voice was dull, his jaw moving woodenly. "I could see that the night the two of you came to Dodge's. Your bodies were practically humming each time you looked at each other."

He inspected her one last time and nodded abruptly, cutting off the raging torrent of emotions rushing through him. Time enough to feel later. Right now, he had to think. To act. "Well, we'd best get you back to him, but I don't think carrying you will look good. Sit down."

Jacob yanked at a frayed corner from his shirt, tugging off a strip for binding. He knelt down and took Charlotte's foot in his hand. For the span of a heartbeat, he closed his eyes, imagined that she was his. With a hard swallow, he managed to wrap the cloth around her ankle, pulling it tight. She let out a small gasp, but did not complain. "Okay. Give it a go now."

She stood up and gingerly stepped forward, a wrinkle of pain passing over her face before it went smooth. *God, what a woman!*

"I'm all right. Thank you." Charlotte paused, a softness creeping into her eyes. Her hand drifted upwards and grazed Jacob's cheek. His eyes closed as his body ached for her. "I know you wish things were different between us, Jacob. I'm sorry."

He heard the catch in her voice, saw her lip tremble, and couldn't bear to cause her any more hurt. Jacob took her hand and kissed it, pressing her palm against his heart, the closest they would ever be. "Your friendship will have to be enough, sweet Charlotte."

They made slow progress up the steep incline, her hand holding on to his shoulder for support. Jacob resisted the urge to pull away. Her touch burned, like a brand, searing its way through his clothes, down to his skin. They were both breathless for entirely different reasons when they reached the top.

Charlotte paused to rest and her eyes widened in fear. "Why didn't Benjamin come?" At Jacob's uneasy silence, she grabbed hold of his arm, her nails biting into his skin. "Tell me!"

He took a deep breath and forged ahead. "It's your father. He's been wounded." Charlotte shot forward, a tiny cry escaping between clenched teeth as she put too much pressure on her injured ankle. Jacob ducked under her arm to help her on her way. One glance at her face and a fist squeezed around his heart.

"Now don't look that way! A musket ball just grazed his arm, but Benjamin refused to leave him while someone tended to his wound. Your young man is quite loyal." They took a few more steps and he gave her hand a squeeze. "He's a good man, Charlotte. I wish you only blessings."

The truth was a double-edged sword. In wishing the couple well, Jacob shattered his dreams as he severed any chance of a relationship with Charlotte. They did not speak again, intent on reaching William. A few breathless moments, more like an eternity, passed and the remnants of the struggle came into view. Bodies scattered. Blood staining the carpet of autumn leaves, the undergrowth, the trees. Faces twisted in terrible grimaces. Eyes gazing with an empty stare at the painfully blue sky above. Jacob fought the sick feeling in the pit of his stomach and focused on Charlotte's father.

The blacksmith was seated on a rock, Willson holding him steady while Talmadge Edwards added another bandage in an effort to stop the bleeding. One hard yank and William was as white as the cloud hovering overhead on an otherwise tranquil day.

"Papa!" Charlotte cried out and ran to her father, heedless of her ankle or anything else. She knelt beside him and placed her hand on his knee. William wrapped an arm around her and kissed the crown of her head, his body sagging in relief that his daughter was safe. Unable to control his emotions, Benjamin turned away and drew his sleeve across his eyes. Her absence had cost them both dearly.

A ghost of a grin tugged at Talmadge's mouth. "I always did think your daughter was a remarkable woman, but then you are a remarkable man." The leather craftsman did not appear to be surprised in the least about Charlotte's ploy. Fortunately, the rest of their company was gone.

William closed his eyes and rested his head against his daughter's, a tear slipping down his face unnoticed. "My Blessing. You are all right." He appeared to shake himself and looked up, offering Jacob his hand. "Thank you for bringing her back safe to me. I see our secret is out."

Benjamin stepped forward and gripped Jacob's shoulder. "How can I repay you?"

"Take care of her." Jacob's voice was hoarse as he stepped back, making way as Willson took Charlotte in his arms, sealing her mouth with a kiss.

Their bond was so strong, the strength of their emotions powerful enough to tear Jacob apart. *This must be what it is like when the flint hits the flash pan.* William's groan of pain was the only thing that kept him from losing his mind as he turned to offer his assistance to the blacksmith in his effort to gain his feet. Talmadge reached him first, catching him before he dropped. Benjamin let go of Charlotte and turned his attention to the injured man. Jacob could breathe again.

Charlotte grabbed her father's lapels, steel in her gaze as she told him fiercely, "You can't fight like this, Papa! You must go back home and rest, heal. You will only be a risk to yourself and others."

Willson supported her argument. "Listen to her, sir. Take Raven, and go back to the house. Charlotte and I will join you as soon as we are able. We'll be slower on foot." He pressed the older man's shoulder, urging him insistently, almost to the point of desperation. "Please, William. After all you've done for me, do this for us."

Jacob's mind began to wander as Charlotte, Benjamin, Edwards, and the blacksmith decided on their course of action. One thing was clear. Jacob would not, could not go with them. He would go in the opposite direction, as far away from the source of his heartbreak as possible.

As Talmadge and William mounted and departed, making way for Johnstown, Jacob forced himself to be civil. He extended his hand in farewell to Benjamin and Charlotte. "Some of our company went the other way. I'm going to see if they need any help. God keep you both." Allowing himself one last glimpse of Charlotte's face to give him strength, Jacob fled.

Frozen from the inside out, Jacob ran until his feet began to falter like a mortally wounded man. He numbly walked the last few paces to his horse, mounted, and prodded Powder in his flank, urging him into a hard gallop. Five minutes down the trail and the pain rushed in, a wildfire raging so fiercely he nearly doubled over. Charlotte had made her choice, gone so far as to become a soldier for Willson, putting her life on the line. One could not compete with such devotion, nor would he try. As Jacob leaned over Powder's neck and held on tight, his eyes burning with the maelstrom inside, he didn't care what happened to him or if his feet ever walked on Johnstown's soil again.

Behind him, a cannon boomed, back in the direction of town. A volley of shots fired. Absolute dread coursed through his veins and stabbed at Jacob's heart. He pulled up short, yanking on Powder's reins and turning him around. "H-yah! Home, boy! Take us home!"

A sharp kick from his master's boot made the stallion set off at a fearsome pace with a powerful push of his hind legs. Jacob let him have his head and hunkered down, his knees squeezing the great animal's sides, heading them straight toward the heart of the action. Jacob had to get back, back to Johnstown, for one reason and one reason alone—to see that Charlotte Ross made it home safe.

Some thirty minutes or more later, Jacob and Powder ended their fast and furious ride when another cannon boomed, making the earth shake. The stallion rose straight up on his hind legs, pawing at the air, as Jacob desperately clutched handfuls of his mane in an effort to remain in the saddle. An innocent meadow had been transformed into

49

a battleground.

A large company of British regulars, more than he could count, surged in and the Tryon County Militia rose to the challenge. Musket fire rang out, smoke choked the air, but Jacob could barely make out Benjamin and Charlotte embracing in the distance. His stomach clenched in an instinctive reaction. How much more must one man endure?

He dismounted and hugged Powder's neck, unwilling to risk him in the heat of battle. "Run, boy. Go home!" Jacob started making his way across the field, the reassuring sound of his horse's pounding hooves receding into the distance. Jacob was almost within reach of the young couple only to see them break apart. Relief nearly made him stagger.

The scene played out before him like one of Shakespeare's tragedies his father had forced him to muddle through as a boy. Charlotte ran for the woods and turned back for one last look at her beloved. Jacob couldn't breathe. Couldn't look away. The mad drumming of his blood thundered in his ears.

Benjamin raised his hand in farewell at the exact instant a musket roared, sending a tremor through Jacob's body. Horrified, he stood, frozen in place, watching a crimson stain bloom on Willson's chest. The injured man's arm dropped and his body toppled to the ground. Time stopped.

"NO!!" Charlotte's ragged cry echoed the silent scream in Jacob's brain. She took a step toward the field even as John Little, injured as well and gripping his wounded arm, reached their fallen brother's side. He dropped on his knees beside Willson.

Spurred into action as more muskets crackled around him, Jacob bent low and put on a burst of speed, hunkering down close to the ground. Shouts and screams rang in his ears, but he had to get to her, couldn't let anything stop him. Precious seconds later, he took hold of Charlotte and pulled her into his arms, dragging her kicking and screaming to the woods. She fought him every inch of the way, the tears rolling down her face.

"Get out of here, Charlotte! He died for you! Do not let his death be in vain!" Fury lashed at him, cutting him to the quick. The senselessness of it all, that more had to give their lives on this day, shook him badly. Above all else, that the woman who was his everything could be sacrificed for their cause was more than he could stomach. Jacob would be damned if he'd allow that to happen.

Getting a firmer hold of her, he half-carried, half-dragged Charlotte further into the depths of the forest, putting more of a buffer between them and the clash of battle. They'd made it perhaps twenty feet when Jacob stopped long enough to clamp his mouth on hers, the strength of his love nearly bringing him to his knees. Sympathy warred with sorrow in her eyes.

It took everything Jacob had to let her go. To keep himself from seeing her to her door. Seeing her safe. "Forgive me. In case I die, I had to taste your lips at least once. Now run! Run like Hell is nipping at your heels!"

He pushed her away and forced himself back to the battle, intent on stopping anyone who might pose a threat to her. One other goal drove him. To see that Benjamin Willson was buried with respect. "God be with you, Jacob!" Charlotte's voice echoed in his mind, giving him the courage he needed to go the distance. *God be with you, Charlotte. May He hold you in the palm of His hand. If I make it off this field, I make this vow. I will.*

The fighting raged on, the ugliness that was war not about to stop to mourn one man's death. Jacob peered through the dust and cluster of men, lost in the struggle. Smoke. Grunts. Screaming. Shouts. The pounding of footsteps. The cannon that set off an earthquake with every explosion. The battle went on around him, but his focus remained on the Patriot from Boston and the pain of regret welled up inside him. Here lay a good man. Rival or no, Benjamin Willson did not deserve his fate.

One hundred feet away, John Little had turned himself into a human shield, his body covering Willson's. Jacob had to bridge the gap. Had to make sure Benjamin's body was taken care of, that the Patriot was not defiled in any way. Jacob made a run for it to reach his brother-in-arms. Closer. Nearly there now.

CRACK! He was knocked off his feet and driven into the ground by a blast of a Brown Bess close enough to deafen him. Black boots marched on, a red coat flashing by in the corner of his eye, not even bothering to assess the damages.

Jacob laid on his back, dazed, the world spinning around and then the pain struck. It was a monster with teeth and claws, digging into his right shoulder. Jacob's left hand reached out and fumbled for the wound, trying to make sense of it. His fingers just grazed the edge of a gaping hole and his sight blacked out for an instant. He pulled his hand away to find it dripping with blood while a red river gushed down his chest and his arm.

Jacob clamped his jaw shut and breathed through his nose, inhaling once—twice—again. One more time and he pulled himself into a sitting position. His stomach pitched and he nearly passed out on the dead, dry grass littered by a scatter of leaves that skittered in every direction, carried away on a strong wind. He wanted nothing more than to lie back down. Close his eyes. Let go.

Benjamin. You must get to Benjamin. For Charlotte.

By the grace of God, the sounds of the struggle abated, forces retreating from the field. Somehow, Jacob staggered to his feet, an ungodly groan rising like the sound of an entrapped animal. He grabbed hold of his shoulder in hopes of stopping the bleeding. That bit of pressure forced him to hunch over and be unceremoniously sick. As soon as he could catch his breath, his feet managed to carry him until he dropped beside John and Benjamin's body. The large, blond militiaman looked up with sorrowful eyes, unashamed of his tears. "There was no hope for him, none at all. I tried, but there was nothing I could do."

He was shaking, the blood running from the wound in his arm.

Jacob patted him weakly on the back. "I know—I saw . . . . You need to take care of yourself, John, before you join him. You've a wife and a little one at home. They need you."

Jacob's shirt was already torn from helping Charlotte only an hour before. Wincing at the memory, and the streak of pain that nearly flattened him, Jacob struggled to rip off another strip. He fought through the agony to wrap the strip around John's arm, but he couldn't pull it tight. He growled in frustration. Tried again. His injured shoulder argued with him, his fingers too clumsy to follow his mind's orders. *Work, damn you! Just work!*

A firm hand gripped the nape of his neck. "We'll do that, Cooper. You need tending yourself."

Nicholas Stoner stood over him, Richard Dodge silent at his side. Both were crimson-stained, but it wasn't their own blood. Thank God. Their clothes were muddied and torn. Worse for the wear, they were the best thing Jacob had seen in a long time. He sagged back on his heels, swaying like a sapling in a windstorm, vaguely aware as they bound his shoulder and took care of Little.

Richard gripped Jacob's arm and studied him, hard. "You need to get that ball out of your shoulder and take to your bed before you bleed to death or infection sets in. We'll help you to get home."

Together, Jacob's fellow militia members eased him to his feet. Stoner took great care with his wounded arm, but Jacob couldn't help crying out. He bit down on the inside of his cheek with resolve and tasted blood. He would not let them know how much his shoulder hurt him or they would refuse to fulfill his request. "Wait. Willson. I must see him buried. For Charlotte and William's sake, and because it is his due."

Richard shook his head, eyes wide in disbelief. "Are you insane, man? You can barely stay on your feet. We'll take him to the church and make sure the pastor does right by him. Let us take you home."

They tried to draw him away from the body on the ground, a stunned John Little still keeping watch. Jacob planted his feet. "No.

Give me his jacket at least. Charlotte will want a keepsake." He drew himself up to his full height and stared his friends down. They would not sway him.

"Did you ever see such a stubborn man?" Nicholas threw his hands in the air. "It must be that Irish side that gives him his flaming hair and fiery temper."

"And a skull as thick as stone." Dodge muttered.

When Jacob still didn't budge, silent communication passed between the two and they knelt by Willson's prone body on the ground. Richard made the sign of the cross and gently closed his eyes, leaning down to kiss Benjamin's forehead, before they worked together to ease his coat from his body. Once a brilliant blue, the uniform was now marred by a horrid, red stain and a hole in the chest. The militiamen worked together in grim silence, none of them ashamed when their tears mingled with the blood of their dead. None of them would look at this patch of land in the same way again.

"Here. Now will you let us take you home?" Stoner asked in exasperation. They were all punch-drunk with exhaustion, eager for this day to come to a close. The last thing they needed was an argument with one of their own.

Jacob swallowed hard and forced himself to pull it together. "I've got to make sure Charlotte is safe at home, that I see this coat is in her hands. You take care of Benjamin—and John. That will be a Godsend to me."

They grumbled. Neither of his friends liked it, but in the end, they agreed. No one wanted to abandon Benjamin's body. There was no telling what might happen if he was left behind. Richard stepped forward and pressed Jacob's good arm. "God go with you, Jacob. Take care of that shoulder before it takes care of you."

Nicholas hooked an arm around his neck and kissed the top of his head roughly. "Don't you dare let anything become of you. I'd never forgive you." He abruptly turned away and focused his attention on attending to their dead and the living. God willing, John Little would survive his wound.

Jacob forced himself to set one foot in front of the other, wishing that the Ross homestead was much closer. The only thing that kept him from falling to the ground was the bloodied, damaged coat he held in his clenched hand. Benjamin Willson had given everything he had to their cause. His parents. Himself. His life. Surely, Jacob could walk a mile or so to bring closure to the woman they both loved.

The sky was growing darker, or was it his eyes? Charlotte's lane loomed before him. It might as well stretch to the other side of the ocean, the distance seemed that impossible to travel. He leaned against a tree, his good shoulder propped against the rough bark, and stared dumbly as red droplets splashed down on his boot, forming a puddle within seconds. Jacob's stomach churned and the horizon tilted. A few, hundred paces, that's all. *You can do this and then you can sleep. Forever.*

Jacob breathed hard through his nose and picked up his head. One step. Another. Moving at a snail's pace. His toes dragged in the dirt, making odd tracks, a thin, ribbon of red joining them. *Please God. Let me make it to her door. Let Charlotte be there, safe and sound inside.*

What if she wasn't? His heart thumped painfully in his chest and Jacob moved more quickly than he thought possible. The last dredges of his strength pulled him up two steps onto the porch and his fist thumped against the heavy oak. The blood thundered in his ears, his heartbeat a trip hammer when there was no answer. *Please, dear God. I beg of You and all that is holy.*

Jacob pressed his forehead against the door and raised his fist one more time, making one last effort to knock. The door slowly opened and he grabbed hold of the door jamb to keep to his feet. Otherwise, he'd be a heap on Charlotte's floor, so thankful to see her. Her eyes were red from crying, her face a ghastly white. Her sorrow was a tangible thing that had drowned out all the joy in her. Her hand clapped over her mouth in horror as her eyes traveled from Jacob's face to his shoulder and the burden he carried. The tears were quick to fall. He didn't know if they would stop before drowning them all in an ocean.

"Forgive me, Charlotte." His voice was faint, as if it came from far away. Jacob wasn't even sure he spoke. "I could not bring Benjamin home. The others, Dodge, Stoner, they brought him to St. John's. This was all I could manage." Jacob handed her the uniform, such a pitiful substitute.

Charlotte swayed for a moment and steadied herself by hanging onto the doorknob. She closed her eyes and he could see her throat working. Any moment and her sobs would shake the timbers of the house to the ground, flattening them all. Her hand reached in the pocket, and pulled out a braid. Like the wheat in the fields around them. A medley of gold, brown, and yellow. Her braid. Her fingers trembled so she nearly dropped it. He thought he'd be sick at her feet.

A black curtain fell over his vision and he gladly tumbled into oblivion.

"Jacob!" Her frantic cry echoed in the dark recesses of his mind and her surprisingly strong arms caught him as he fell, a source of both immeasurable pain and pleasure. He knew no more.

27 October, 1781

HIS SHOULDER THROBBED WITH EACH BEAT of his heart and his body was on fire, consuming him from the inside. Standing with his feet in the coals of the hearth while the flames licked at him from head to toe couldn't be any hotter. Shaking hard enough to make his teeth chatter, every movement sent a bolt of agony that extended from his shoulder down to the tips of his fingers.

A cool hand touched his forehead. "Steady, Jacob. Steady." Charlotte stood over him, her eyes warm and caring. *God, take me now.*

William sat at his side, holding his arm down firmly. "You're in good hands, Jacob. My Blessing tended Benjamin and me. She'll bring you back to good health too."

Jacob found himself in William Ross' bed, the fire built up to a great blaze, heating the room to a furnace that rivaled the blacksmith's forge. Both Charlotte and her father were flushed, beads of perspiration dotting their foreheads and dampening the hair at their temples. All for the wounded militiaman in their bed. Déjà vu all over again.

"I should go, should not be a burden to you." Jacob attempted to sit up, pain streaking though him, making him breathless. William eased him back down, wincing at the movement of his arm. The effects of the older man's injury lingered.

"Be still and do not speak of such nonsense again! A burden! You are one of our own. You are our friend." The blacksmith's voice dropped low as he dipped his head. "You helped to save my daughter's life when you made her leave that bloodied field. You will stay with us until you are well."

Jacob closed his eyes and began to drift until Charlotte lifted the bandages off of his wound, making him painfully aware of her touch. She murmured quietly, doing her best to offer him comfort as her deft fingers prodded the wound and swabbed it with a cloth dipped in steaming water. His back arched and his teeth clenched.

"I'm sorry, Jacob," she whispered, her tears threatening to fall. She covered the hole in his arm with another poultice of herb-filled, dampened cloths. By the time Charlotte was done, his head was spinning.

"What about—my father?" He asked on a gasp.

William held up whiskey. At the slight tilt of Jacob's head, the blacksmith stood, wrapped a strong arm around his back, and held the jug to his mouth. Jacob took great gulps of liquid fire. He feared the whole jug wouldn't be enough. As William eased him back down, he attempted to focus. "My father—does he know where I am?"

"He's been here already. I told him not to worry himself, we'll take care of you. What with the mountain of weapons brought in after the battle, he's hardly had a moment to breathe. We do not know when the militia will be called up again. Abraham is working around the clock to meet the demand. Your father would have taken you home, but we told him he was needed and you required someone to watch over you." The blacksmith stood and patted Jacob's hand. "Do not worry. There will be time enough to take up your burdens on another day. Rest now."

Jacob tried to do as he was told, waiting for the pain to ebb, but it only grew. His entire body was tensed, ready to break at any instant. He breathed through his nose and waited for relief that would not come.

William studied him closely, brow furrowed in concern. "I know you are in pain, but be thankful you were unconscious when I removed the musket ball. It was in deep. Lodged in the bone. I really had to dig for it. We were fortunate. Some of the herbs remained from Benjamin's injury. That and whiskey will pull you through."

The room began to fade in and out. Even in so much pain, blessed unconsciousness still came for him. Charlotte was the last thing he saw as she wiped his forehead with a cloth dampened in the bowl of cold water on the stand. If anything saved him, it would be the woman at his side.

28 October, 1781

JACOB'S BRAIN SIZZLED WITH FEVER. Lights, colors, and strange images flashed when he closed his eyes. It seemed like he was drifting away. His body no longer felt like it was his anymore, just a shell that could be left behind. His eyes slowly opened and stared at the hearth without truly seeing it. Charlotte sat by his side, humming softly. The glow of the fire appeared to form a halo around her, making him wonder if an angel had come for him. His mind meandered, back nearly 20 years, to the first time he saw Charlotte. Framed in sunlight, her hair lit up like a candle, Jacob had likened her to an angel then.

There was a rustling of heavy skirts beside him and the sound of water splashing. A cool cloth was placed on his forehead. It felt so good, Jacob thought he'd weep. Charlotte laid her gentle palm on his cheek next, and the tears began to spill.

She gasped and pulled her hand away. "Oh, Jacob! You're on fire!"

She stood quickly and filled a stoneware mug with water from the pitcher on the stand by the bed. Her strong hand came up at the nape of his neck, setting him to shivering, and Jacob drank greedily, down to the last drop, moaning with the constant throbbing in his shoulder that only seemed intensified. As she eased him back down on the pillow, he shifted and a poker jabbed at him, making him cry out. One look at the wounded expression on his nurse's face and he clamped his jaw shut. He would not cause her any more pain.

Charlotte leaned forward and took his hand, tears rising in her eyes. "I wish I could do more for you, Jacob."

She faded in and out of view as he hovered on the brink of consciousness. Her fingers trailed through his hair, pulling him back from the edge. Jacob smiled weakly. "You being here, by my side. Your caring ways. I couldn't ask for more."

The smile died and his eyes drooped shut as the pain washed over him and threatened to carry him away. "Jacob!" Charlotte called out urgently. "Stay with me!" A little shake and his eyes snapped open. *Hang on.* Had to hang on—for her.

The hand from his good arm fumbled with the covers and reached for her. It took the last of his reserves, but he managed to entwine his fingers with hers. "Just—just sit here. That will do."

Charlotte perched on the side of the bed and began to stroke his hair. Her voice trembled as she spoke. "So strong, Jacob. You have always been so strong. I noticed it the first time we met, that day when you came to Papa's smithy. You carried yourself like one of the adults. After all, you'd had to be like an adult at such a young age with losing your mother. You tripped and fell, yet you didn't utter a sound. When I offered you my hand, you nearly crushed it. All through the years, I marveled at the power in your hands, your arms, your back. I'd see you walk through town, watch you fire a musket, eye your handiwork, and be struck with awe. Do you remember that day you carried me home all the way from town during that horrible windstorm? No more than fifteen I would say. You didn't think twice, didn't utter one word of complaint. You've always been a wonder."

"You are the wonder, Charlotte." Jacob felt like he was slipping under the surface of a pond, gazing up at a wavy world above him. The light started to fade. He heard his name as if it came from thousands of miles away and the darkness took him once more.

~

SOMEONE WAS PRAYING, MURMURING WORDS OF FAITH. Over and over. Jacob opened his eye a crack. Night had fallen and the cabin was dimly illuminated by the fireplace and one oil lamp turned down low. Although the room was cast in shadows, he could still make out a figure seated at his side, elbows leaning on the bed, face in his hands and shoulders hunched. Someone with coppery hair and a broad back. His father.

Jacob shifted and let out a hiss as something jabbed at his shoulder. A white-hot poker of pain coursed deep down, to the bone, streaking to his hand. Letting the arm go would be a welcome alternative.

"Papa! What can we do for him? The wound. It's not improving, festering and oozing, like Benjamin's. If he doesn't lose the arm, he'll never use it at this rate. If Jacob can't be a gunsmith, he'll be like half a man!" Charlotte's hands clenched over the rag she'd been using to cleanse his shoulder.

Jacob forced himself to stay conscious, catching sight of William leaning against a chair, blood seeping through the bandage on his arm, while he swiped his other sleeve across his sweaty brow. "We must cut out the infected tissue. Wait longer and we're sure to have more trouble on our hands. Get the whiskey, boiled water, and my hunting knife."

She did his bidding. All the while, Jacob's mind hinged on his shoulder. He couldn't bear much more. Jacob lost himself to Charlotte's touch as she rested her palm on the crown of his head— until the blade dug in, biting deep into the skin. He screamed. His father took hold of his good hand and lent him his strength, burying his head in Jacob's arm. He could hear Abraham's sobs.

"The whiskey! Give him the whiskey, Charlotte!" William shouted urgently.

His daughter held Jacob's head, pushed the hair out of his eyes, and tipped the jug to his lips. He managed a long draw. Sweet heaven and then dragging him back down to Hell again when the alcohol was poured on the wound. Jacob retched, the pain was so fierce, but swallowed hard and choked the bile down.

"Just—just let me go, Charlotte, I beg of you. Let me go." Jacob whispered raggedly, throat raw from shouting.

She set the whiskey aside and cupped his face in her palms, her eyes boring into his. "I've lost my love. I'll not lose my best friend."

With that she leaned in and pressed her lips to his. If Jacob died, at least he'd already experienced paradise.

"That's it. Let's give it one more go!" Once more turned to twice more. The knife plunged in until William removed all of the deteriorated tissue. Jacob's vision blurred, the scene merging with that day when Benjamin was shot—and he tumbled over the edge of consciousness.

One day ran into the next and Jacob lost all concept of time, sleeping more than not. The fever made him alternate from chills that made him shake so hard his teeth chattered and the bed shook to a blazing heat that threatened to vaporize him.

In a rare moment of clarity, Jacob became aware of his father standing over him, hand on his forehead, blue eyes dark and troubled. William's words floated in the air as if through a tunnel. "Nonsense, Abraham. You must work. Jacob needs someone's care throughout the day and night. Keep him here. He's past the point of crisis. He just needs time."

Abraham murmured a reluctant consent. He bent and kissed Jacob's cheek, the stubble of his beard scraping against his skin. "You know I love you, my son, but you are in good hands here. William and Charlotte can care for you better than I can. Be well." His voice became choked as he strode to the door and took up his coat, clapping his hat on his head. "If the state of his health changes or you need anything, anything at all . . . ."

William crossed the room and placed both hands on his shoulders. "I will come for you. Fear not, Abraham. Jacob's young, strong. He will be well."

The gunsmith nodded, a shadow crossing over his face. "For what purpose? To fight again? Messengers say the war is over, but I'm not sure that will ever be the case. Peace is tenuous at best, like my son's health. Good night, William, Charlotte."

He lifted his chin toward the chair where she sat by the hearth. Abraham stepped outside, a cold draft blasting through the room, snatching Jacob's breath away as the blacksmith shut the door tight.

The war was over? Why didn't that good news fill him with joy? Jacob shifted, pain making him bite the inside of his cheek to keep from crying out. Lying there, helpless in bed, watching the mournful expression on Charlotte's face as she stared at the flames with unseeing eyes, he knew the answer to his question. For Charlotte, William, and Jacob, the war would never be over. It had only ended for Benjamin, taking him with it.

4 November, 1781

CHARLOTTE'S CANDLE HAD BEEN SNUFFED OUT. Always a source of light—in the honey-glow of her eyes, in her smile, her laughter—all traces were gone now. Benjamin's death left Charlotte altered, possibly irrevocably. Pale. Dead inside.

When she wasn't caring for Jacob or tending William's healing wound and household, she sat. Charlotte gazed blindly into the hearth, rocking herself more often than not as if she could not bear to be still, her arms wrapped around her middle. She didn't sleep. Jacob could hear her smothered sobs in the night or see her lying on her back, staring wide-eyed at the ceiling. She didn't eat. On the rare occasions that her father persuaded her to take something, his daughter covered her mouth, ran outside, and the sound of her retching made Jacob's stomach tighten in sympathy.

He woke up before the dawn, unable to fall back to sleep, worry for Charlotte running a ragged circle in his mind. As William quietly dressed in preparation for his return to the smithy, Jacob slowly rolled over on his good side. He clamped his mouth shut against the moan that threatened to escape. Curse his traitorous body! When would it be his own again?

Always attentive, Charlotte was at his side, face tense with concern. "You're in pain. I'll get the whiskey."

Jacob caught her hand and drew her back to the bedside before she could leave. He grazed her cheek with his palm. "You are stronger than any whiskey ever could be, Charlotte."

She became completely still, like the does with their young that Jacob came across from time to time while hunting in the forest. He never could take the does, for fear of leaving the young orphaned, something he understood well from firsthand experience.

The color drained from Charlotte's face, the pulse fluttering wildly beneath her chin. Jacob grew still as well. His heart thumped painfully in his chest. He wanted to trail his fingers down her jaw. To her neck. Feel that life force firsthand. Press his lips to that mad beating and take her in his arms. Make her forget her pain for a little while. Forget Benjamin. Impossible.

The tears, never far from the surface, spilled and Charlotte pulled away. "Don't Jacob! Oh, please! Don't!"

She turned and ran outside, the door swinging shut heavily behind her. The daily retching grabbed hold of her again and Jacob longed to go to her and comfort her. He could do neither, a prisoner in his own body, too weak to do much more than sit up.

William sat down at his side and pressed his arm. "You must be patient, Jacob. She will recover in time."

Jacob swallowed hard, trying to shut out the sounds that carried through the solid walls, his stomach twisting in fear. "What is it, William? What is wrong with her? Shouldn't we send for a healer? She gets ill every day. I fear that Charlotte will fade away."

The blacksmith's jaw set as he took pause. Mulling over his thoughts perhaps? With a slight nod, he took Jacob's hand. "You need to understand something. Charlotte and Benjamin were betrothed. God did not give them enough time to marry. Knowing how precious every minute was that they shared, they found a brief moment to light a spark of hope for the future." He stopped and Jacob's heart began to hammer. Any instant and it would strain through the fabric of his shirt.

William leaned forward and met his eye. "Charlotte is with child, Jacob."

His sadness, immeasurable in its depth, washed over Jacob and the blacksmith roused himself. He stepped outside and Jacob could hear him speaking softly to his daughter, followed by her weeping. William attempted to comfort her, to be a balm to her wounded heart, but Jacob doubted much could help. She was bleeding to death before their eyes.

~

REST WAS ELUSIVE THAT NIGHT. Charlotte wept in the darkness, her sobbing a soft, mournful song that stole Jacob's sleep. Night after night, he'd listened to her crying, thought it was her unshakeable grief that made her carry on so. Now he knew better.

Jacob could not comprehend what a burden she had to bear. Carrying a baby. Knowing her baby would never know its father. Night after night, she keened for Benjamin—and so much more. For her unborn child. For her uncertain future. So much at stake.

Jacob tossed and turned through hours that seemed to drag on for an eternity. Dry-eyed, his gaze became pinned to her shadowy figure on the other side of the room as the firelight gradually died down, leaving only the red glow of the coals. As the darkness slowly surrendered to the first signs of daylight, Jacob knew what he had to do.

~

THE SOUND OF HOOFBEATS FADED INTO THE DISTANCE as William departed for work. Charlotte was outside. Jacob could hear her muffled sobs. He forced himself out of bed and staggered to the door. The room spun and he had to hang on to the handle to steady himself before he could venture out. He didn't have far to go.

She was on the top step, her knees gathered up to her chest, head bowed. Jacob dropped down beside her, uncertain whether he could get up again or not, and tentatively wrapped an arm around her trembling shoulders. "Your father—he has told me. About the baby."

Charlotte gasped and straightened quickly, scraping her hands across her face. She started to pull away, but he wouldn't let go. "Let me be your husband, Charlotte. I can give you my name, my hands, my shoulders, and my back. When I am able, I will build you a home."

She shook her head, a blush of embarrassment rising. "No, no. I couldn't ask that of you, Jacob, to marry a woman who carries another man's child. It wouldn't be right, not with the way you feel for me. I cannot offer you the same in return and that is too unfair to you."

Her words cut him to the quick. At least she was honest, painfully so. Jacob swallowed the hurt and took her clenched hands in his. "I would not have there be any stain on your reputation or your child's. Benjamin would not want that."

She shook her head and gazed down at the ground. He pressed a finger beneath her chin, forcing her to meet his eye. "I would not want that. You mean too much to me, Charlotte. Even if I cannot have your sunlight, I am content to stand in your shadow. Please. Let me do this for you."

One tear slid down her cheek and her face cracked. She fell against him and Jacob did the one thing he was capable of. He caught her.

9 November, 1781

THUMP! THUMP! JACOB AWOKE WITH A START, cutting off a curse as his shoulder jerked, stirring the monster within. Healing was an excruciatingly slow process. Thankfully, he spent most of his time sleeping. Otherwise, he dreamed with his eyes wide open, following Charlotte's daily routine, waiting for the day that her feelings would grow for him. Unwilling to let go of sleep just yet, he slowly turned over and started to drift when someone pounded loudly again. With a sigh, he hitched himself up and scraped at his face. Darkness had fallen and they'd already had their evening meal. The others would be turning in soon. It was a strange time for a caller.

William crossed the room and opened the door. Nicholas Stoner practically fell in, breathing hard in his haste to deliver his message. He scanned the room with wild eyes and latched on to Jacob. "We need your help! An angry mob is on its way to Sir William's! They want to burn it down. Dodge is there now, trying to hold them off, make them see reason." He grabbed the knob and bent over, holding a stitch in his side.

"Then we must go."

Jacob came up fast. This time he did curse as his legs swung over the side of the bed. Gritting his teeth, he stood and almost toppled back into the covers. With an exclamation of alarm, Charlotte was at his side in an instant. She ducked under his arm and offered her support. He nodded in gratitude.

William met Jacob's gaze with a level stare. "You're not strong enough, Jacob. Stay here. I'll go with Nicholas." He grabbed his coat and hat off the hooks by the door, snatching his Brown Bess next.

Not to be deterred, Jacob set his jaw and pulled away from Charlotte. His progress was slow, but he reached the hearth and picked up the gun over the fireplace. With grim determination, he joined his fellow brothers-in-arms at the door. Shoulders set, his body screaming with every movement, his chin jutted forward. "I'm going."

"So am I." Charlotte had already slipped into her cloak and held his Kentucky long rifle. It had been quietly waiting in the corner for the day that he was well enough to fire it again, a gift from his father on one of his daily visits.

There was no point in arguing with the woman. When Charlotte set her mind to do something, she did it. One only needed to look back at her short stint as a soldier to understand. William and Nicholas went to the barn and quickly hitched the wagon. They all loaded up, Charlotte and Jacob sitting in back. It shamed him when the others had to help him to climb into the bed of the wagon. Each bump made him feel as if his shoulder was about to come apart from his body. At that moment, an amputation was a welcome prospect. At least it would put out the fire burning in his wound.

Charlotte took his hand and propped herself against his good shoulder. Lending him her strength. Her comfort. She'd gone completely white since Nicholas burst through their door. Thinking back to Jacob's own messages in the night, he thought it likely she'd had enough of such deliveries.

Jacob turned and grazed the side of her head with a kiss. "It will be all right. We'll sort it out."

His confidence was shaken as Sir William's came into view. A large group of townspeople, at least one hundred, were gathered round with torches, a ready source of fire to ignite a bonfire that would rage through the night if no one stopped them. A lone figure stood at the top of the steps of the great estate with his hands raised, his military jacket pulled on in haste to lend him an air of authority, imploring them. Richard Dodge might as well be one sapling trying to hold off a hurricane.

With a great shout William picked up the pace, full speed, and sent the team of horses charging straight toward the building. There were roars and protests as the crowd parted like the Red Sea. Mission accomplished, the blacksmith pulled up directly at the steps. He and Nicholas jumped down quickly.

For Jacob, it was another story. His face burned in mortification as Charlotte climbed down with no aid from anyone and reached up a hand to help him. He had no choice but to accept, his strength failing him. The earth seemed to shift under Jacob's feet and his stomach dropped. Much more movement and he'd pass out, flat on the ground. As their group mounted the steps, muskets and rifle in hand, an ugly muttering stirred in the crowd.

Dodge nodded at them, face awash in relief, but the battle wasn't won yet. "People, go on home now. The war is over!"

Word, painfully slow in its progress, had traveled throughout the Colonies, sharing the triumph of Cornwallis' surrender in Yorktown on the 19th of October. The taste of victory was bitter. If only the news had come sooner. Johnstown, Jacob's shoulder, Charlotte's heart, and Benjamin could have been spared.

The crowd only became stirred up even more at Dodge's plea. One farmer yelled about his home that had been burned down. A merchant ranted that his business was in ruins with no money to be had. A militiaman gestured to his missing arm. Jacob's wound throbbed in sympathy and he felt sick to his stomach. Without William and Charlotte's care, he would have suffered the same fate. No. For this group of people, the war would never be over.

"Sir William took too much from us and kept it for himself. Let's take it all from his ancestors!" Someone shouted in the crowd. Others grumbled about the fighting, all they'd lost, the struggles they were suffering now. A loud thunder of approval proved the mob was getting restless.

"The Brits are still in New York Harbor! They could come back. Let's leave them nothing, make sure there is no welcome mat!" Fists came up in the air in agreement and stones started to fly through the air, pelting the building. Glass shattered. The men on the steps ducked.

Jacob pushed his own anger and resentment aside. He stepped in front of Charlotte, shielding her. Taking his lead, Dodge, Stoner, and William closed ranks around him, creating a united front, each raising their muskets to face down the riled mob. More missiles took flight, one hitting Jacob's wounded shoulder. He almost dropped on the spot. Swaying, Dodge and Stoner caught him and held him steady.

A curt nod and he forced himself to raise the Brown Bess, stiffness and an aching that went to the bone nearly doing him in. Jacob fought through it and fired the musket into the air. The butt rammed against his shoulder and nearly made him vomit with the pain. "Is this what you want? More shots fired? More anguish? My time in the Tryon County Militia has shown me enough death and suffering for five lifetimes. I want to build a brighter future for Johnstown, not tear anything else down. Haven't you had enough of destruction?"

Something gave in the crowd, their voices dropping. These people were his friends, neighbors. There was a quiet murmuring and the men slowly dispersed, the crisis averted. Jacob sagged with the release of tension and the world began to spin. He lost his balance, there was a moment of darkness, and he found himself on the steps. On his back. Staring up.

William loomed over him, face creased in concern. "Jacob, you must get up, get home, and get strong. How can my daughter have a wedding without a husband?"

How life could change in blink, on the brink of tragedy in one instant, riding on the crest of hope and optimism the next. Richard and Nicholas helped Jacob to his feet, smiling and laughing, congratulating him for his good fortune. They pounded William on the back and dropped kisses on Charlotte's cheek. With the potential disaster squashed, they welcomed an occasion for joy.

Jacob studied Charlotte as they shared good wishes with her, saw the color spill from her face, the shadows creeping up in her eyes. His heart fell. This wedding was not cause for celebration for his future bride. Her love would never sleep in her wedding bed. Benjamin Willson slept in the cold, unforgiving ground.

15 November, 1781

"JACOB COOPER, DO YOU TAKE MY BLESSING, Charlotte Elizabeth Ross, to be your wife?" William's voice came from far away, echoing in Jacob's mind and his legs nearly buckled. Weak from the lingering effects of the fever, infection, and his wound, Jacob could barely stand and had wasted considerably. Glancing at his bride, and his father-in-law to be, he saw the toll the war had taken on them as well. *What a sorry lot we are.*

Not even a month since the battle and they were all recuperating. Surprisingly enough, William, the oldest, was mending best. Charlotte had proven to be a good nurse with Benjamin and did so again with her father and husband to be, but who would care for her?

You will. The words rang out in Jacob's head although no one in the room had spoken. A shadowy figure hovered at his side. He'd seen the tall, dark-haired Patriot often since Benjamin fell on that dreadful field and Jacob's heart ached with regret yet again. It was such an irony that Charlotte nursed the militiaman from Boston back to health only to see him give his life in the Battle of Johnstown, so far from his home.

Jacob felt like someone was pressing his arm, reminding him of what he had to do, would've done regardless. He tilted his head in a nod. *I will care for her—and your baby.*

William reached out and rested a gentle hand on Jacob's good shoulder. "Jacob, stay with me. Do you take my Charlotte to be your bride?"

As the town's blacksmith, it would not be the first time that Charlotte's father had performed a common-law marriage. Typically, he'd do so in his smithy, pounding a hammer on the anvil to celebrate their vows. For Charlotte and Jacob, standing before the hearth in the Ross cottage would have to do—if the groom could remain on his feet long enough to do so.

74

"I do." Jacob squeezed Charlotte's hand. It was like ice.

It was her turn next. He could barely hear her as she repeated his words. William linked their hands and gave them a sad smile. "You are husband and wife. God bless you and keep both of you."

He made the sign of the cross and rested his hands on the crown of their heads. Gently, Jacob tilted Charlotte's face to his and grazed her lips with a kiss. He felt Willson standing behind them. His bride's face was pale and bloodless. The pain, stealing the light in her honey eyes, took his breath away.

Jacob tucked her in his arms and rested his chin on the sun-kissed wheat-colored spill of her hair. "I will care for you until the day I die. I promise this to you." *And you, Benjamin.*

"I've had enough promises to last a lifetime. You're here now. That is enough."

Charlotte stepped back, one tear trickling down her cheek. Jacob wiped it away with his thumb and her sorrow crushed him. His knees gave. He would have pitched to the floor, but his bride and father-in-law caught him, helping him to the bed, and easing him down. Charlotte sat and took his hand, but her eyes were lifeless, her fingers cold.

Jacob had always wanted Charlotte and now she was his, but at what cost?

Be careful what you wish for.

~

GOING TO SLEEP WITH HIS BRIDE THAT NIGHT WAS A QUIET AFFAIR. Jacob simply had to slide over. He'd taken up residence in the bed and wondered if he'd ever get up again. Charlotte dressed behind a folding screen, covering her modesty with a long, simple gown of white cotton. She lay down beside him in the darkness and turned away. Inevitably, her weeping shook the bed, even though she tried to muffle her sobs in her pillow. Jacob's heart hurt.

An ocean might as well have stretched between them, the gaping distance between their hearts that wide and her sorrow that deep. He turned on his side, wincing as the pain streaked through his shoulder. He ignored it, his hand hovering over her hair, trembling as his fingers began to stroke the tumble down her back.

"Let me be your haven, Charlotte," he whispered hoarsely. "Let me calm your fears and ease your sorrow. I ask nothing more of you. I know that you cannot give me what you do not have."

"I do not deserve you, Jacob Cooper." She turned to him and buried her head in his chest. The warmth of her body and the slight swelling of her belly pressing against him filled Jacob with a desperate aching. He pulled her in close and let his breath out slowly with a hitch.

"You deserve so much more. I'm sorry Benjamin cannot be here—but I will do my best to shelter you through life's storms. It is the least that I can do."

Jacob had watched over and waited for Charlotte for most of his years. Standing by her side for the rest of his days was enough. It had to be enough. For her sake. For the child that belonged to her and the Patriot from Boston.

He shifted, wincing at the movement, and pressed a kiss to her forehead. "I am sorry I was not well enough for a wedding at St. John's. Forgive me."

Charlotte turned to stone in his hands, holding herself so stiffly that she could've been carved from granite. When she raised her head to meet his gaze, he saw sparks fly from her eyes in the firelight. Jacob feared he'd be reduced to dust. "I will not ever set foot in St. John's again. That is Sir William's church, understand? Anything that reminds me of him is a reminder of everything that's been taken away from us. Everything we've lost. All the suffering. Marrying there would've felt like a funeral. The likes of Sir William cost my Patriot his family and his life. They almost stole you away from me too. I cannot stomach anyone who wore a Redcoat, ever!'"

She burrowed in against him, clinging to him, her head leaning against his shoulder. Jacob welcomed the pain with the pressure on his wound. It was only a drop in the bucket compared to Charlotte's— or Benjamin's.

Slowly, he could feel her unwinding, the knots that had held her rigid throughout the day finally letting go. Charlotte let loose a long sigh and her eyes slid shut. He listened to the slow, easy song of her breathing and allowed it to lull him to sleep. There'd be time enough to take up their struggles tomorrow.

~

BODIES WERE STREWN ACROSS THE GROUND, so many, too many to count and the grass, his clothes, his hands were stained with crimson. Jacob could barely set his foot down without stepping on one of them. They wore red. Blue. Homespun. What did it matter? All of them shared the common denominator of death, unseeing eyes staring at the painfully blue sky above, mouths twisted in agony.

The bile rose up, hitting Jacob's mouth and he stumbled to a tree, heaving until he thought his stomach would turn inside out. He dropped to his knees by the body of a militiaman and a cold, dead hand grabbed his arm.

As Jacob stared in horror, struggling to pull free, the flesh fell away revealing only bone. He looked up to find Benjamin staring at him, sorrow in his eyes. *She was mine!* The mournful cry rang out in Jacob's mind and then Willson's face disintegrated.

"No!" Jacob sat up in a rush, heedless of his shoulder or anything else for that matter. His heart was beating erratically, the blood thundering in his ears, and he couldn't breathe. He pushed the covers aside and rose on unsteady feet, wavering as he stumbled across the room to the pitcher of water. His hands shook as he poured a mug, sloshing its contents over the side and down the front of his shirt as

the coolness slid down his throat. It did nothing to calm his rattled nerves.

Jacob leaned on the table with both hands, pressing down in an effort to steady himself, to slow the mad fluttering of his heart. Releasing a pent-up breath, he took hold of the whiskey jug and made his way to a chair by the fire.

Since the Battle of Johnstown, nightmares had plagued him, filling his mind with visions of the dead. Sometimes, those he killed. At others, those he called friends. The worst were when his mind was crowded with Benjamin.

Jacob took a long, deep swallow of the fiery liquid, set the whiskey down, and drove the heels of his hands to his eyes. The pressure did nothing to erase the mental images he grappled with night after night. He wondered if the guilt—for the lives he'd taken, for sleeping with the love of Willson's life and mother of his child, for simply being alive when so many others were not—would ever stop eating away at him.

"Dear God, please. Make it stop." His ragged whisper slipped out. Jacob shuddered and rested his elbows on his knees, his shoulders hunched. The weight of it all was too much to bear.

Soft, blessedly cool fingers pressed lightly on the nape of his neck and began to stroke his hair. "Shh. It's all right." Charlotte moved in front of him and pressed his head against her body. "You'll be all right now." A ripple ran through him, shaking him, and she knelt, taking his hands in hers.

Her finger grazed his simple wedding band of iron. Although William was still weak from his injury, he insisted his son-in-law would have a ring. As for Charlotte, she wore Benjamin's gift, forged by his own hands only days before his death.

"Nothing can ever be all right again." His voice was hushed, the burning in his eyes causing the tears to spill. Jacob had never been one to cry.

War changed a man.

Charlotte cupped his face in her palms. "Whatever do you mean, Jacob? Every day, you grow stronger. The war is finally over. We will build a new life, all of us."

He shook his head and a shudder ran through him, making his shoulders shake. "Nothing will ever be all right because I am here and Benjamin isn't. I know what you and William wanted. I am but a poor substitute. It is your Patriot who should be with you now, watching the changes that are happening every day until he holds your child in his hands. It is I who should not be here!" Silent sobs wracked his body and set him to quivering.

"Don't you ever speak to me in such a way again." Charlotte took hold of his shoulders and gave him a hard shake. The pain was worth it to see her eyes glitter as the flush rose in her cheeks and her chest heaved. Such a marvel. She never looked more beautiful.

She sat down on his lap and looped her arms around his neck. "Jacob Cooper, you listen to me. Benjamin's death hurts deeply and I am sure that a part of me will always long for him, but that cannot be changed nor would I ever want to exchange you for him. Would I wish that you could both be here? Yes, but I will be forever grateful to have you by my side. You have fought this war as well. You care for me like no other. You are my friend. If anyone is fit to help me through this terrible time, it is you. Now, let me help you. What can I do?"

He leaned back in the chair and nestled Charlotte against his chest, his arm wrapped around her. "Stay here with me and save me from my dreams. Every night I dream of those I have killed, those who died before me, of Benjamin. So many have paid too high a price. I have not paid enough."

Her hand tightened its grip and her lip began to tremble. "You've paid a dear price, Jacob. Your injury, taking on another's child, marrying me out of friendship."

More than friendship. He pulled her in, pressed her head to his shoulder and welcomed the pain that was a distraction to her sorrow, to what was in his heart, before he drowned in it. "I would do so again for you. I don't regret a moment."

She rested her hand on his chest and began to circle round and round. "Then the least that I can do is to stay as long as you need me."

When Jacob awoke, stiff and sore in the morning light, Charlotte was still on his lap, a faint blush in her cheeks as she slept peacefully. Staring at her, at the gift he held in his hands, the load on his shoulders lifted. As long as he had her, Jacob could believe in new beginnings.

25 November, 1781

WATCHING HER, JACOB WANTED TO SPRING FROM HIS BED. Take hold of her. Shake some sense into her. Charlotte was rarely still, circling the confines of the small cabin like a moth beating at the window glass, trying to escape. She swept, dusted, and scrubbed—the same spot, the same bed, the same cup. If she would not be still, Jacob thought he would scream.

One thing brought her to a halt. Her stomach rebelled, forcing Charlotte to flee outside. Moments later, she returned, pale and shaken to gather the wash in a basket, only to go back outdoors where Jacob could hear the splash of the bucket.

Somehow, he found the strength that had been sorely lacking in the month since a Lobsterback's musket ball turned his world upside down. Jacob stood on legs gone weak and inched his way to the window. He propped himself against the sill and stared out into a blindingly bright day to see Charlotte desperately plunging and scrubbing.

From time to time, she swept an arm across her face as the tears rained down. Stretching on tiptoe, her hand appeared to flutter in the breeze as Charlotte pinned up every item on the line her father had hung for her. When the last shirt was poised in the air, her sorrow got the best of her. She sank to the steps, head in her hands. Jacob felt her pain, so deeply he barely made it back to his bed before she came in. Her first stop: his bedside. Always. Charlotte Ross put herself before others.

"Is there anything I can get you, anything you need?" She asked softly, sitting on the edge of his bed.

Jacob reached out to wipe a tear away with his thumb, a hint of a smile tugging at her mouth. "You can allow your heart to mend."

"I don't know how." Her head tilted down as her hands began to work the fabric of her dress between her fingers.

He covered them with his hand. For an instant, they clenched tightly together and went loose. His gaze unable to look anywhere else but at her, he sighed in frustration and closed his eyes. Not enough. Jacob had not done nearly enough for her.

His only recourse? To lend her his warmth, his comfort. He shifted and sat up, drawing her into his arms to calm her. His body trembled with the effort. The blasted weakness! When would his strength return?

Her forehead creased in concern as her gaze scanned his face. "Your forehead is covered in a cold sweat." She *tsked* and wiped his face with a handkerchief kept on hand in her pocket. "You've not been up, have you? If you need the privy, I'll help you." He shook his head. She frowned. "I don't like the look of you. Your color is terrible. I wish I didn't have to tend your wound."

Taking his cue, Jacob lay back on his pillow. His fingers took hold of a bit of blanket and tightened into a fist as she gently lifted the bandages, cleaned it with scalding water from the bowl at the side of the bed, and added a poultice of herbs. Her face was tight as she covered up his shoulder and patted his arm gently.

"You're making progress. I'm sorry that healing is so long in coming. I fear Papa may have cut you too deeply. Benjamin . . . . " She bit off her words, unwilling or unable to continue.

There was a darkness in her eyes that had not gone away since that day on the battlefield, dousing the fire that drew Jacob to her from the start. He had to find a way to light a spark once again.

He sat up and snatched her hand. "Charlotte, I know how much Benjamin mattered to you and I don't expect you to avoid speaking of him."

She sat down on the edge of the bed and stared at their clasped fingers. Charlotte would not lift her head or meet his eye. "It was a long, difficult road to recovery for him as well, but I am confident you will be well and whole soon. You must be patient."

Jacob shifted and pressed his palm to the side of her face until she allowed him to see the honey in her eyes. "You must be patient too. You feel like this shadow will always hover over you, but the sun will shine on you again. I promise you this."

She gave him a ghost of a smile and grazed his cheek with a kiss. "If anyone can bring out the light, it's you, Jacob Cooper."

Tentatively, he reached out and rested his hand on the slight swelling of her stomach. "You carry the torch inside of you. It has already been lit by you and Benjamin. Don't be afraid to let it shine."

10 December, 1781

THE HOUSE SHUDDERED, BUFFETED BY INTENSE WINDS. Jacob glanced out the window and winced at the wall of white that was falling down at a steady clip. The winter storm had hit suddenly, shortly after William left for the smithy for the day. Within an hour, several inches had fallen already. It showed no signs of stopping. Neither did Charlotte.

She was shoveling a path to the barn with a vengeance, her cloak billowing around her, the wind snatching her hood from her head. The long strands of her hair became a wild tangle and her every step forward was a battle. Undeterred, trembling in the frigid air, Charlotte staggered forward. The wind was so strong, it pushed her back and nearly knocked her from her feet. Stubborn woman!

Jacob cursed under his breath and shrugged into his coat, his stiff shoulder arguing with him. The bone-deep ache that was his constant companion was made worse by the damp and the cold. He ignored it with a vicious thrust that had him pounding the wall with his fist. A moment to win back control of himself and he set his tricorn hat on his head.

One step outside and the storm almost shoved him back inside. Setting his jaw and gathering his resolve, he plowed ahead. Charlotte continued, the wind bending her like a sapling in a wind storm, even as the snow continued to bombard them at a frightful rate. The path was filling back in as soon as she cleared it, but Jacob knew what drove her. Worry for her father.

The storm fought Jacob. He fought back, reaching Charlotte's side and putting out his hand. "Give me the shovel." She opened her mouth, prepared to protest, until his finger pressed to her lip and his pointed stare aimed for her midsection. "You've more than yourself to think about. You've been out here long enough. Give me the shovel, Charlotte. Please."

Her displeasure was plain in her pinched expression, but she gave in and went inside. Jacob forced his shoulder to move, beating down the pain, and reached the barn. He went inside to let his hands thaw, checking on the animals and waiting for the fire within to die down. A few heart beats, a deep breath later, and Jacob stepped back outside. One would never know a shovel had touched the pristine path that stretched before him.

There had to be at least a foot of snow, evidence that the storm was substantial. Jacob took up his shovel and struggled to reach the house, his gaze drawn to the lane. He cast up a silent prayer for William. Hopefully, his father-in-law was safe at the smithy, buttoned up tight for the night.

The last few feet to the cottage were a battle. Jacob pressed on the door with all his weight, slamming it against the wall as he stepped inside. Charlotte jumped then rushed to his side to help him shut the door and drop the bar to latch it tight. She helped him tug off his damp coat, brushing her hand along his jaw as he gritted his teeth together. His shoulder was not used to such abuse.

"Sit by the fire, Jacob. You're a block of ice." She didn't have to tell him twice.

He sank into a chair, a fine quivering running through his body. Charlotte moved swiftly, grabbing a blanket off the bed and wrapping it around him. A moment later, a steaming mug of tea was placed in his hands. She stood behind him and set her hands on his shoulder, kneading at the sore muscles until his whole body sagged. Only when he stopped moving did Jacob realize how much his body hurt.

"You have been doing too much." Charlotte scolded softly, taking his empty cup away.

Jacob grabbed her arm and forced her to stand still. His hand slid down to clasp her wrist while his other palm rested on the slightly swollen mound of her belly, growing a bit more day by day. "It is you who do too much. You must always put the little one you carry first before the rest of us."

"If I don't keep busy, I fear I will go out of my mind." She covered his hand with hers for a moment, closing her eyes tightly before pulling away. Charlotte picked up her sewing basket by the side of the bed and carried it to a chair, setting herself to mending odds and ends. Jacob shook his head. At least she wasn't doing something strenuous.

At odds with himself, he began to walk restlessly about the cottage. Unwilling to lie down and desperately in need of a purpose, Jacob eyed William's Brown Bess over the fireplace. The firing mechanism had stuck a tad that day at Sir William's. Finally, something he could fix.

Jacob crossed the room and took the gun down, carrying it to the table where they ate their meals. He pulled up a chair and laid out his tools. His father had brought a bag of essential items, strong in his faith that his son would return to his calling one day soon. That day had come.

The job was a simple task; one he could do in his sleep before the Battle of Johnstown changed everything. Jacob picked up his tools, intent on taking the musket apart, but his hand was too clumsy. Pain streaked down his arm and the gun slipped from his hand, clattering on the table with a thud. Jacob thumped the table with his other hand and pressed his forehead to his fist.

Charlotte set down her mending and went to his side. "Jacob, what is it?"

"Useless! I'm completely useless! What good will I be to you, your father, or my father if I cannot do my trade? All those years of apprenticeship, thrown away, all because of a Lobsterback!" He smacked the table again, making her jerk.

She stroked his hair in an effort to calm him. When that was not enough, Charlotte went to her sewing basket and pulled out several rags. She knotted them, forming a ball, and set them in Jacob's hand. "Start working your hand with this, squeezing it, tightening and loosening your fingers. You've got to build up your strength and flexibility, get those muscles working again. Your recovery has been long and hard. You can't expect to be yourself overnight."

She closed his fingers around the wadded cloth, the warmth of her touch affecting him more than anything that Charlotte said. Jacob brought her hand to his mouth and grazed her knuckles with a kiss. "Thank you, Charlotte. You always choose the right words."

She stayed long enough to make him think that perhaps the tides of emotion were turning in his favor. Long enough to look him in the eye and gift him with a smile before she slipped away and returned to her sewing.

The hours dragged on and the snow continued to pile up outside their door, the storm growing in ferocity. Darkness fell and the temperature dropped, the air slipping through the cracks and poking them with icy fingers. Charlotte had long since given up any pretense of calm. Her panic was growing. Still no sign of William. She wandered to the window after cleaning up from dinner, her hands clenching into fists.

"What if he's out there stranded?" she murmured under her breath.

Jacob left his place by the fire and tucked her in his arms. "Your father has good common sense. He's at the smithy, I'm sure, buttoned up tight, cozier than we are. If there's any place to be on a bitter night like tonight, it's next to that forge. Come morning, when the snow stops, he'll come back home. Safe and sound." Jacob prayed he spoke the truth.

Charlotte trembled in his arms. "If I lose him, I have nothing left." Her words were a slap in the face. Jacob turned away, his insides torn wide open. She shifted and placed her hands on his face. "Jacob, I didn't mean that the way it sounded. If anyone can understand how I feel, it's you. Papa is the only person in this world who has known me since my beginnings. Like you and your father. Imagine if it were Abraham out there on this stormy night."

He pressed his forehead to hers. "I understand. You have to have faith that he will be home soon."

Dinner was a strain. Neither ate much, only managing a few spoonsful of soup and a chunk of crusty bread. Side by side, Jacob cleared with Charlotte and settled with her by the fireplace. From time to time, she dabbed at her eyes, a tear escaping. Jacob shifted his chair closer to hers and took her hand, forming a lifeline. She held on tight until sitting was no longer an option.

Charlotte lunged from her chair, oblivious of the sparks flying from the crackling fireplace or the warmth in the cottage, the shadows in her eyes crowding in. She went to the window and took up her post, staring out into the inky darkness. Snow pelted the glass and the wind howled, making the whole house shiver. Charlotte trembled with it, her arms wrapped tightly around herself.

Jacob went to her side and took her shoulders in a firm grasp. "It's like waiting for a pot to boil. Your fretting isn't going to get your father home sooner. The hour is late. Come lie down and rest your head. Lay your worries on me for a while, Charlotte."

He felt her body give as she sagged against him. Jacob took her hand and led her to the bed. He helped her to ease her dress over her head and pulled her nightdress from the chest at the foot of the bed. Gently, he slipped it on and nudged Charlotte to sit. Her brush sat on the stand beside the bed. Jacob picked it up and pulled her hair down. She closed her eyes as her curls fell to her shoulders and he drew the brush through the heavy strands.

For a little while, the rest of the world went away, the only sound their breathing and the snap of the flickering flames in the hearth. Charlotte began to sway. Jacob set the brush down and eased her to her pillow. Her eyes slid shut and she surrendered.

He laid his hand on her golden curls, shining in the firelight, and bowed his head. *God keep her and the babe safe.* The prayer was his nightly ritual before bed and the first thought he offered upon waking each morning. His breath let out in a long sigh. *Dear God, also, please watch over William.* Jacob removed his boots and stretched out beside her, too tense and tired to undress. For the longest time, he watched the steady rise and fall of her chest until it hypnotized him to sleep.

~

WITH A JOLT, JACOB SHOT UP IN BED, HEART POUNDING. The bed was empty beside him, the cottage blanketed in darkness except for the soft glow of the dying coals, and an indescribable dread filled him. Thinking it was unease over William or the fact that they were trapped by the storm, he threw back the covers and set his legs over the side of the bed in search of some sort of release. A muffled sob made his head snap around to find Charlotte in a chair by the hearth, holding something in her arms. For a flash in time, he saw Benjamin Willson, the blood streaming down his jacket, his dark hair fanned out against Charlotte's chest as she rocked him, silent weeping shaking her.

Jacob blinked and relief nearly flattened him. It was the Patriot's coat, clutched in Charlotte's arms. Her tears streaked down her face, wetting the jacket in her lap and the braid in her hands. Jacob trod softly to her side. Slowly, he eased his way down to his knees and placed his hands over hers.

"Charlotte, it is not healthy for you or the baby to grieve so. Benjamin would not want this for you, would not want you to suffer so. Please. Come back to bed."

She nodded, handed the jacket to him, and set her fingers in his. Jacob pulled her to her feet, set the jacket down long enough to turn back the covers, and helped her to slide in. He opened the chest at the foot of the bed and carefully folded the uniform, setting it inside at the bottom. He turned and saw Charlotte staring into the fireplace. So haunted, sending chills up his spine. Again, he felt a presence at his side and his heart grew heavy. *I'm trying, Benjamin. What more can I do?*

Keep loving her. The words were spoken inside his mind. The air shifted, making the hair flutter around Charlotte's face. She closed her eyes and let out a sigh as another tear trickled down her cheek. Jacob lay down beside her and rested his hand on her hip, his thumb grazing the gentle swelling of her midsection. He circled round and round. Finally, her eyes closed, her body went loose, and the woman he loved slept. Not good enough. Not nearly good enough, but it was a start.

Unable to find any peace for himself, Jacob put on his coat, boots, and hat before stepping outside. The wind took his tricorn from his head, stealing it away. Another gust like that, and he would be lifted from his feet. A curse slipped from between gritted teeth. There had to be close to three feet of snow on the ground and no path to the barn. There was no help for it. Jacob would have to forge a way.

Setting his back into it, his shoulder screaming with every thrust, he made progress at the pace of a snail. What must have been an hour later, he fell inside and dropped onto a bale of hay. Winded, the breath completely sucked out of him, Jacob couldn't have lifted another shovelful of snow to save his life. Bonnie nickered to him while Belle let out a soft moo. His mouth turned up at an attempt at a grin and he pushed his way to his feet.

"Hello, girls. You're in the right place tonight." He checked their water, brought in some snow to fill their troughs, and gave them each a pitchfork full of hay. "I don't know when I'll be in come morning. I'm done in. Sleep well you two."

Giving them both a pat, he opened the door, prepared to brave the storm. The cottage could've been a mile away; he was that worn out. On unsteady feet, Jacob began the return trek. He was only halfway there when a terrible moan froze him to the spot. He turned slowly, half expecting Benjamin Willson. Instead, it was the figure of a man, crusted in ice and snow, trembling so hard his teeth chattered.

"Jacob—help me," came a hoarse cry and another moan as the man's body began to sway.

"William?!" Jacob lunged forward and caught his father-in-law just as the blacksmith's knees buckled. "Where is Raven and what in God's name are you doing out in this monster of a storm?" He half carried his wife's father to the porch.

"The snow—the snow finally let up in town. I was worried about you and Charlotte." He struggled to get the words out, stammering with the cold. "I didn't want to—put Raven—through such harsh conditions—so I went at it—alone—I almost lost my way. Thank God I found you." He moaned again as they struggled up the steps. "So cold. I have never—been—this cold in my life—and my feet—how they ache."

Frostbite! With a grim sense of purpose, Jacob dragged the blacksmith across the threshold, slamming the door behind him. Charlotte jerked awake and sat up, eyes wide with fear.

"Papa!" She ran from the bed and threw her arms around him, pulling back with an exclamation. "Oh, Papa! You are frozen! We must get you warm before you catch your death!"

Jacob threw logs on the fire, building up a hearty blaze while Charlotte led her father to a chair. She rushed to grab a blanket and wrap it tightly around him before kneeling on the floor to strip off his wet stockings. One glance at his feet and she gasped. His feet were a brilliant red in some patches, white and gray in others.

"Papa! Your feet! They are like ice!"

Jacob knelt beside her and inspected for himself, his jaw clenching at the sight. "It's frostbite. I've seen it in the militia. We've got to warm the skin, slowly, or he could lose toes." *Or worse.* Horrified, Charlotte looked to him for guidance. He took hold of her arm and gave it a squeeze. "Fill a bowl with warm water. We'll soak them and get the blood flowing again."

While she did his bidding, Jacob gripped the older man's hands. "William, I need to get you out of your wet clothes. You need to be dry to get warm."

Shaking fit to fall apart at the seams, his father-in-law nodded and slowly stood on legs gone weak. Jacob helped him to wrestle the damp clothing off his body. Anticipating his thoughts, Charlotte was at their side with a dry night shirt. Together, they dressed her father, and eased him back in the chair. While his daughter held him tightly with the blanket to keep him warm, Jacob set William's feet in the warmed water. Time to wait.

As the minutes slowly dragged into an hour, shudders continued to wrack William's body and the color of his feet went through dramatic changes. First blue, then purple, then mottled.

His face twisted and he leaned forward, elbows driving into his knees and his hands forming fists. "Ah, how they burn! It is as if my feet are buried in the coals!"

"Hush, Papa. Hush." Charlotte pressed a kiss to his cheek and buried his head in her chest.

His arms came up around her and he held on tight. Jacob gently lifted William's feet out of the water and toweled them dry. He began to massage them one at a time with a soothing touch in the hopes of getting the blood flowing freely again. The blacksmith let out a terrible groan.

"I'm sorry, William. I do not mean to hurt you. Pain is the first sign of healing. Be thankful. If you felt nothing, I might not have been able to save your feet." Jacob looked up at eyes that were so like his wife's, the honey glow dimmed by torment, and yet the sweet man smiled. Like father, like daughter, putting his pain aside for others.

William rested his hand on the top of Jacob's head, a fine quiver continuing to travel through his frame. "Like My Blessing, you are a Godsend to us both, Jacob. Your strength is carrying all of us, giving us something solid to lean on when it feels as if our world is crumbling. I am forever grateful that we have been able to call you friend. You have proven to be that and so much more." His eyes closed as his face twisted in a grimace and his hands dropped to his knees, holding on so tightly his knuckles went white.

Charlotte knelt before him once again, her tears sliding down and wetting his fingers as she covered them with her hands. William's face smoothed with an effort and he drew her into his arms. "You mustn't carry on so, My Blessing. All will be well. In the capable hands of both you and Jacob, I have no other choice."

That made her laugh softly. She rose to her feet and took her father by the arm. Between the two of them, they managed to help William to the bed. The covers continued to tremble with the chill that simply did not want to let go. Charlotte sat by his side, gently stroking her father's hair until he slipped into a heavy sleep born of a crushing fatigue.

Nearly too exhausted to stand, she did not put up a fuss when Jacob picked her up in his arms and carried her to their bed. He fell in beside her, sleep coming for him on a wave and dragging him under. He didn't think anything could pull him back up to the surface.

A nasty bark of a cough proved otherwise, arriving with the dawn.

~

WILLIAM'S HACKING SHOOK THEM ALL FROM THEIR SLUMBER. Within hours, the coughing attacks worsened and the blacksmith raged with fever. Jacob's worst nightmares had come back to haunt him. Influenza darkened their door.

For what seemed like the hundredth time, Charlotte held her father's head and helped him to drink a mug of cold water. He drained it quickly, consumed with thirst as the fire in his body continued to burn. No sooner was the last drop gone then the coughing took hold again until he couldn't breathe. His daughter held a handkerchief to his mouth and when she pulled it away, it was smattered with blood. She glanced up at Jacob, fear in her eyes. It was a fear he understood and knew well. His mother had been stolen away from them by the influenza.

"What can we do?" She whispered.

Nothing. There was really nothing they could do to stop the progress of the illness. They could care for William, give him their support, but the sickness would have to take its course.

Wearily, Jacob took up the stoneware pitcher and filled the cup half way, topping it off with whiskey. "Exactly what you're doing, Charlotte." And pray, placing William in the hands of God.

As the afternoon gave way to night, William worsened. He complained of a pounding in his head, his joints ached, and vomiting took hold. The fever raged and would not let go. Unable to go to the well what with the deep snow, Jacob brought in snow in the jug and set it by the fire to give his father-in-law water, dribbling slowly through his cracked lips. To cool his body, they melted the snow in the kettle, doused rags, and wiped the blacksmith down. When that wasn't enough, Jacob packed his father-in-law in snow. Drenching the bed. Drenching his clothes. Drenching his body and both of his caretakers.

As William drifted off into a fevered, fitful sleep, Charlotte crumpled into a heap in the chair by his side. She buried her face in her hands and her shoulders shook with weeping.

Jacob went to her and tucked her in his arms. "You need to rest. You are completely done in."

"But Papa . . . ." Her words trailed off as Jacob picked her up and nestled her against his chest. Much too light of a burden to bear.

He kissed the top of her head. "He sleeps. Hopefully, we will see a turn for the better come morning."

Jacob laid her down and stretched out beside her, sheltering her with his arms. He closed his eyes and watched the dance of flickering shadows inside his eyelids. As his wife slipped into slumber, his thoughts turned to his mother. To William. *Dear God, make him well.*

~

"JACOB." SOMEONE CALLED HIS NAME AS IF FROM A

GREAT DISTANCE. Sleep did not want to give him up easily. He shifted and turned on his side. "Jacob." Again, his name drifted in the air, faint and soft. He reached out and set his hand on Charlotte's hip only to snatch it away. She was on fire. "Jacob. I'm so thirsty."

He laid his hand on her cheek and bit off a curse. She was flushed, her glassy-eyed stare nearly stopping his heart. Jacob lunged from the bed and grabbed a stoneware cup, filling it from the jug, his hands shaking so badly the water sloshed over the side. He brought it to her and set a hand behind her shoulders to lift her up to drink. Charlotte swallowed it all swiftly and he laid her back down.

She gave him a ghost of a smile until a fit of coughing chased it away, the rattle deep down in her chest cutting Jacob to the quick. Just like his mother's. *Please God. I beg of you. Please don't take her from me.*

Jacob felt like a sailor shipwrecked on a deserted island as the backbreaking, heart-wrenching work of saving two lives began. He couldn't leave them to go for help, too fearful of what might happen in his absence. Hour after hour dragged on with no marks of improvement for either patient. He plied them with tea and water, cold cloths, and packed them with snow, a laborious process that left him frozen and weak.

Pushing his own needs aside, Jacob lifted Charlotte from the bed and set her in the chair by the fire. He fumbled with the wet bedding and replaced it with dry covers, stripped her wet nightdress and pulled on another, then gently eased her back down on her pillow. The heat from her body felt like a torch in his hands. The entire process had to be repeated with William. By the time Jacob had his father-in-law settled in bed, his head was swimming.

He propped himself up and pressed his forehead against the wall. Running on empty. Not much more to give. Wanting nothing more than sleep to take him away. To make this all a dream.

Something nagged at the back of his mind, forcing him to straighten up. The animals. They hadn't been tended to in some time.

He took up his coat and stepped outside. The storm had finally abated, but the skies were still a heavy, oppressive gray and the entire world was muffled with snow. Jacob stomped his way through a foot or so. He had no energy to shovel again. When he reached the barn, he nearly wept at the sight of Bonnie and Belle, quietly waiting in their stalls. As if it was a normal day and all was well with their souls.

He brought in more snow for their troughs, mucked out their stalls and gave them clean hay, milking Belle last. Jacob leaned on the cow's warmth and gave her a pat. "Thank you, girl." The milk might be the only nourishment he could give his patients.

Back to the cottage and he built up the fire. His steps began to waver as he turned away and a chair caught him. Just a few minutes. He needed to rest for only a few minutes.

Sleep snatched him away.

~

"JACOB. JACOB, WAKE UP." A HAND SHOOK HIS SHOULDER. With a start, Jacob came up out of a heavy slumber to find someone with eyes like his staring down at him, copper hair lit by a halo from the crackling blaze behind him. Abraham.

Jacob's whole body sagged and he lurched from his chair to embrace his father. "Thank God you're here. I have had nothing except water, some herbs, tea, snow, and my hands to bring them relief. I have never felt so inadequate in my life."

"You have your faith and you have more heart than any other man I know." His father gripped him by the shoulders and gave him a hard shake. "You have me." The older man's gaze was bright and he blinked, dragging a sleeve across his eyes.

"What brought you here?" Jacob asked wearily, beginning to wobble. He gripped the arm of the chair to steady himself.

"I was worried when William didn't come back to town for Raven after the storm died out. I half-expected to find him as a frozen block of ice on the way here." Abraham shuddered and took Jacob by the nape of his neck. "I've tended your father-in-law and Charlotte. They're both resting. It is you I am worried about right now. Are you well?"

"Yes, just more tired than I have ever been." Jacob slowly stepped away from his chair, his whole body stiff, when his legs gave out, pitching him to the floor.

Abraham caught him and looped his arm over his shoulders. "You've worn yourself thin. That's it. To bed with you and get some rest. I'll not have you share your mother's fate. Don't worry yourself. I'll take care of William and your wife." He settled Jacob beside Charlotte and kissed his forehead. "God keep you, Jacob. Sleep well." Jacob wanted to argue, to get up and see to everyone else for himself. His body wouldn't let him.

He was cloaked in darkness, wrapped up tight, unable to move with no idea how much time had passed. A weight pressed against him, but Jacob couldn't open his eyes. Sunlight warmed his face and beat on his eyelids. A hand took his, small and soft, pulling him from sleep. He turned swiftly to find Charlotte gazing at him, her eyes no longer clouded with fever, her fingers cool as they grazed his cheek.

Jacob wept.

24 December, 1781

THE NIGHTMARE WRENCHED HIM AWAKE, on the verge of tearing him apart. Jacob sat up, hands pressed to his knees, gasping for breath as he fought to rein in his heart. He was so tired of sleep being a fight. Of everything being a fight.

Unable to sit still and unwilling to disturb the others, he swung his legs over the side of the bed and stepped down on the hardwood floor. Its chill made him shiver. Jacob shrugged into a pair of pants, boots, and his jacket. He stepped outside and the bitter cold immediately snatched his breath away. The porch caught him as he dropped down on the step and stared up at the North Star.

The lingering traces of his dream crowded in. Jacob dropped his head in his hands and let the frigid air have him. Perhaps if he was cold enough, his heart and mind would become frozen. Numb. Keep him away from visiting that bloody battlefield again.

The door creaked behind him and clicked shut with a quiet thud. Footsteps approached and arms wrapped around him. "Trouble sleeping again?"

Jacob shifted over, making room. Charlotte sat beside him and set her palm on his knee. He covered it with his hand. "Every night, it's like I'm walking on thin ice. I'm desperately trying to get to shore, but it keeps getting further and further away. One step the wrong way and I fall through. I am so afraid my dreams will drown me."

"I will be there to pull you back up to the surface and make it safely to dry land." She spoke so softly, he could barely hear her, but her words eased his heart. Charlotte stood and offered him her hand. "Come back to bed, Jacob, and I will try to keep the dreams away."

Jacob brought her hand to his lips. The flush rose in her cheeks, her eyes glistening in the moonlight. He wanted nothing more than to pull her into his arms. To seal her mouth with his. Feel the butterfly's flutter of her heart against his chest.

His code of honor would not allow him to act.

He cleared his throat and told her gruffly, "I know you have nightmares of your own. Many a peaceful night has been shattered by your cries, no matter how you try to hide them."

Charlotte made a poor attempt at a smile, blinking hard when her tears threatened to fall. "You always help me to pick up the pieces. Let me do the same for you."

She stared up at him and he could not deny her anything. Jacob would move heaven and earth if she asked it of him. Taking a few steps to their bed was nothing. Charlotte lifted the covers, waiting for him to slide in.

She rested her head on his shoulder and he could breathe easily again. "Merry Christmas, Jacob."

He pressed a kiss to her tousled hair. "It is because I have you beside me. Sleep well, Charlotte." Come morning, her head was on his chest and she was cradled in his arms. Jacob could think of no better gift on this blessed day.

15 January, 1782

A COLD BLAST OF AIR TRAVELED THROUGH THE
TAVERN, its icy fingers making everyone shiver and hunker closer
to their tankards of ale, cider and whiskey. Jacob took a long swallow
of his ale, hoping to light a fire in his innards and his shoulder. The
damp and the chill made it hurt like the devil.

Heavy footsteps sounded behind him and a hand clasped the
offending joint, making him sink his teeth into his bottom lip.
Nicholas Stoner let go and sat on the stool beside him, slapping his
hat down on the bar. "Sorry. The shoulder still pains you, does it?"

Richard Dodge settled in beside Stoner and reached across to
shake Jacob's hand, nodding with understanding. "I broke an arm as a
boy and it still aches any time the temperature drops or it storms
outside. I can only imagine since you nearly blew your arm off at the
hinge." He motioned to the tavern keeper to get his attention. "A
whiskey for Cooper. I think he needs more than ale tonight. Make that
two more for Nicholas and me." His mouth quirked in a grin. "In
sympathy, of course."

A mug was placed in front of Jacob. He reached for it with his
right hand, fumbled with the handle and switched hands, unable to
hide the grimace on his face. Nicholas' forehead creased in concern.
"How's the grip?"

"He only gets butter fingers after pushing himself too hard."
Abraham, seated on his son's left side, gave Jacob's neck a good
squeeze. "Which is every day."

They all fell into the easy conversation of old friends. Another
round of drinks was passed around, courtesy of Jacob's father. No one
noticed the grumbles of discontent at first, until some loud shouting
and cursing made it impossible to ignore a group of farmers,
merchants, and townspeople who had all avoided joining the militia.
They had no problem complaining about their lot in life.

"The blasted Revolution was a waste of time," one man called out, his words slurring as the ale sloshed over the side of his cup the instant he slammed it down. "There's no market for our goods, no imports, no money. The Continental Congress has done nothing for us. We'd be better off with Old King George!"

Jacob couldn't keep quiet. He turned to face them down with a cold, level stare. "There's an abundance of freshly turned graves in the cemetery. I'm sure those who slumber there would tell you otherwise."

A farmer stood up and slammed his fist on the table. "The Brits are still here in New York Harbor. They could come return any instant with reinforcements. Do you think they'll just give this country back to us? They'll plow us under just like those sorry souls that sleep in the graveyard."

Jacob stood up and planted his feet, jaw raised in challenge. "If they dare come back, my brothers and I will be prepared to send them packing or put them six feet under in the ground. What will you do? Find more poor excuses to avoid a fight? Go home and hide behind the skirts of your wives and mothers? You want to reap the benefits of liberty, but you are unwilling to pay the price. You turn my stomach."

Abraham, Nicholas, and Richard gathered around him, arms crossed, shoulders set. If anyone thought of standing up to the Tryon County Militia, they reconsidered at the show of force.

Disgusted and weary in spirit, Jacob turned and grabbed his tricorn hat off the bar. "I've had enough for one day. I'm going home."

Nicholas caught Jacob rubbing at his shoulder and clapped him on the back. "At least you have Charlotte to bring you comfort when you get home." His eyebrows wiggled suggestively.

Jacob frowned and pulled away. "It's a marriage based on friendship and nothing more."

Dodge nudged his arm. "Many a marriage has been built on a weaker foundation."

Jacob bade them all a good night and stepped out into the night, transfixed by the sight of his breath floating into the darkness. Sometimes, he wanted to drift away and be set free from the trap of his emotions.

His father joined him and spoke quietly. "Give her time, Benjamin. Charlotte and Benjamin had a love as deep as the ocean. Be patient. She will be ready to set sail again and will take you with her."

They walked in companionable silence to the gunsmith shop to get their horses and part ways. Jacob raised a hand in farewell, the sound of Abraham's horse's hooves receding into the distance. The journey home did nothing to put him in a better state of mind. As the sun touched down on the horizon, day giving way to dusk, Jacob's tension mounted. He couldn't go inside, not yet, otherwise Charlotte would bear the brunt of his frustration.

Once Powder was rubbed down and tended, Jacob gave attention to the other animals as well. Mucking stalls, pitching hay, and lugging water still weren't enough to give him a sense of release. He went outside and kicked up snow, circling aimlessly, until the chopping block grabbed his attention. Splitting wood. That ought to wear him down, take off the edge.

William had stacked a large pile of logs beneath the eaves of the barn, taking care to protect them from the elements for a ready supply of dry wood. Jacob hefted a large piece and placed it on the stump that served as the perfect place to cut the firewood down to size. Taking up the ax, he made a sweeping arc through the air and brought it down with a satisfying *thunk!*

The pain bloomed in his shoulder and he welcomed it. Anything to take his mind off the thoughts that cluttered up his head. Three small, manageable chunks of wood fell to the ground. Time to repeat the process.

Jacob fell into a steady rhythm, the sweat beading up on his forehead, heat burning through his body. He shed his jacket and his hat, shaking his hair from his eyes, making the pile mount at his feet. With each swing, fire streaked from his shoulder to his fingers. He'd likely regret his fervor.

"You're going to pay come morning."

He stopped mid-swing and whipped around to find Charlotte leaning against the barn, her cloak wrapped tightly around her. So beautiful it hurt, with her hair loose for a change, forming a curtain around her face. The setting sun cast her in a rose-colored glow, lighting a flame in her eyes. It was nothing to the bonfire in his veins.

"More likely in the middle of the night. I don't sleep well anyway. Might as well have a reason." Jacob turned around and took up where he left off. Five more and the ax slipped from fingers gone numb. He cursed and grabbed at his shoulder.

"You've done enough for one night. Come inside." Charlotte approached and set her fingers on his arm. She deftly began to rub at muscles gone tight, the heat penetrating to the bone. The sizzle of her touch was too much.

Jacob jerked away. "I've got to stack the wood first or all of my efforts will go to waste when it gets wet."

One excruciating armload after another, he formed a neat pile, but his strength was running out. A log slipped from his grasp, followed by all the rest, and he nearly exploded.

"Let me help." Charlotte stepped in and bent over to take a few pieces in her arms. He yanked them away from her.

"Have you lost your mind? I'll not have you hurting yourself in your condition. Your father would never forgive me if anything happened to you or the baby." *Neither would Benjamin.*

Jacob finished the job, ignoring her hurt expression. When the last bit of wood was balanced with all the rest, he leaned on the side of the barn and dropped his forehead on the cradle of his arms. So tired. He was so tired.

Quiet steps approached and she rested her hand on the nape of his neck, continuing her massage. Continuing the torture. "What's wrong? Tell me."

"It's a useless lot of cowards at the tavern, moaning and groaning about their fate. They want good King George and all his Lobsterbacks to fix everything. As if it's going to all get straightened out like magic, overnight! It took years to get here. It's bound to take years to set it right, but we've all got to work together to make it happen. Why can't they see it?"

Charlotte moved in front of him and took his face in her hands. "Because they are not all as strong and brave as you." She rose on tiptoe and kissed his cheek. How his face burned. "Please come in. Let me tend your shoulder, give you something hot to drink. Papa will be home soon. We'll eat and shut out the woes of the world for a little while. It will keep until the morrow."

He grabbed his hat and coat, allowing her to take his hand. Charlotte led him inside where he hung up his clothes and accepted her cloak. As she turned away from him, his breath caught at the sight of her outline. Her body was becoming more rounded, her face fuller, a welcome change after the weight loss caused by morning sickness and grief. When he made no move to follow her, she faced him and took his hand again.

"Look at you. You're so tired you can't even set one foot in front of the other." She settled him in the chair and began to work his shoulder again. At her touch, he closed his eyes and let loose a groan that came from his toes. It had nothing to do with pain.

Her hands stilled, her voice trembling. "You do too much."

He covered her fingers with his, marveling at how small her hands were, yet how strong. "Not nearly enough. Never enough."

No matter what Jacob did, he could never be the husband Charlotte wanted. He couldn't be Benjamin Willson.

She said no more. Charlotte understood when to speak and when to let silence reign. With a swish of her heavy skirts, she moved in front of him and sat down in the cradle of his arms and lap. Jacob leaned in and rested his head against her chest. If anything could heal him, it was the woman by his side. Stronger than steel, strong enough to hold their tiny household and the entire United States of America together.

~

HER MOANS TORE HIM FROM SLEEP. For one terrible instant, Jacob thought Charlotte was giving birth. He rose up on his elbow and touched her. She was cold as ice, her face twisted in pain. She began to toss from side to side then sat up with a gasp. One look at him and she muffled a cry. She jumped from their bed, grabbed her robe, and slipped on her boots, making great haste. The door opened, letting in a rush of bitter air, spitting with snow. Charlotte plunged into the night.

"Whatever is the matter?" William called from his side of the cottage. Jacob could see his shadowy figure, sitting up, peering through the darkness.

"She had a nightmare. I'll see to her." He hurried to pull on breeches, boots, and his coat. The bitter chill took his breath away as he stepped into the night. His lungs burned if he breathed in too deeply. The wind tugged at his hair and clothes, slipping icy fingers down his neck, making him shiver. His teeth were chattering within seconds.

Clamping his jaw shut, Jacob followed the trail of Charlotte's footsteps to find her at the corral, hanging on to the fence so hard Jacob feared she would have splinters in her fingers. He rested a hand on her back and spoke gently, afraid of spooking her as they stood under the moonlight. "It's over, Charlotte. Whatever had you in its grip? It's over."

She shook her head and spun around to look at him. "It will never be over. Can't you see, Jacob?" Her hands moved to her bulging belly, her fingers splayed across it. "My reminder of Benjamin is growing inside of me. With every kick, every shift, every mark this

105

little one leaves on my soul, the wound only grows deeper until I fear I will bleed to death from it. Night after night, I see Benjamin's face. Night after night, I watch him fall on that battlefield. I should've gone with him, Jacob! I should have gone with him!"

Her sobs rose and she sank to her knees, oblivious of the cold and snow, rocking herself back and forth. He knelt with her and held her in his arms. "Don't ever say that! You know Benjamin wanted you to live. Everything he did, the price he paid, was in hopes of giving you something better. Your dying would mean everything happened for no reason in his eyes. In my eyes. Don't you know how much you mean to me? To your father? How much pain you cause when you talk in such a way? You are ripping me apart, Charlotte, one, merciless piece at a time."

Jacob's words ran out and he dropped his forehead to the spill of her hair. Shaking. Shaking so hard he didn't think it would be possible to ever stop. She lifted her head and her gaze met his. Her hand grazed his cheek, lighting a trail that blazed all the way to his heart.

"I'm sorry. I would never want to hurt you." She stood slowly, her fingers threading through his. "Let's go inside, back to bed."

They fought their way back to the cabin door, buffeted by fierce winds, snow whipping around them. Jacob slipped into bed and tucked Charlotte in his arms. His wife was made of a nearly invincible mettle, but there were times when she needed a respite. He would give her whatever she needed. He had vowed to do so when she became his wife. When she became his friend so many years before.

She shivered for a long time, making the entire bed shake, and finally fell into a sleep of exhaustion. No more nightmares would torment them that night. If they did, Jacob would hold them at bay.

14 February, 1782

COLD. WHEN WOULD THE BLASTED COLD GO AWAY?
Jacob's shoulder talked to him more than ever when the temperature
dropped or the snow fell on a day like today, and he didn't like what it
had to say. Cursing at it and rubbing at the joint that grew stiffer by
the minute while holding Powder's reins with the other hand, he
struggled to see his way through the white sheet that was coming
down. The warmth of the Ross homestead, something hot to drink,
and Charlotte's smile beckoned to him. He couldn't get home soon
enough.

His fingers brushed against the small parcel in his breast pocket,
reassured he hadn't lost the package. It was Valentine's Day.
Charlotte deserved a token of his affection, even if it was only a little
gesture.

More. Jacob wanted to give her so much more. Her heart's
desire. The whole world, but would have to bide his time for the day
when she was ready.

If that day should ever come.

He rounded the bend and his breath let go in a rush. Almost there.
Just down the lane, to the barn, and through the mounting snow to the
door. His mind began to play out a fantasy of being wrapped in
Charlotte's arms, tucked in their bed, her breath kissing his skin, her
hands trailing over his body until he caught sight of her coming from
the barn. She fought against the fierce winds, snow stinging her eyes
and turning her hair white as she lugged a bucket of milk with two
hands.

Jacob bit off a curse and urged Powder on by a nudge to the ribs,
intent on relieving Charlotte of her burden when she suddenly came to
a halt. The milk sloshed over the sides as the bucket slipped from her
fingers and dropped to the ground, her hands clutching her stomach.
Jacob jumped from his horse's back and tied him to the fence.

A quick sprint to close the gap between them and he was at her side, grasping her arm. "What is it? What's wrong? Is it the baby?"

Her teeth were clamped down on her bottom lip, her eyes about to overflow as she met his gaze. Terror stared back at him, stabbing at his heart. "It hurts. Dear Lord, it hurts! A terrible cramping!" Her words were cut off as she bent at the waist, her breath stolen away.

Jacob lifted her in his arms and fought his way to the door. A blast of icy air pushed them over the threshold and slammed the heavy oak against the wall. He shut it with his foot and crossed the room to the rocking chair William brought home for Charlotte at Christmastime. Her body was tense as he set her down and began to knead at the tight muscles in her neck.

"Now, just sit here and rest. Breathe in and out. Try to relax. You've got to stop doing such heavy lifting. Leave that to your father and me."

She nodded, her eyes sealed shut as her hands continued to hold on to the growing mound of her belly. Jacob stepped in front of her. He knelt down and rested one hand on her knee while fishing in his pocket with the other.

Startled, Charlotte's eyes shot open as he pressed the cloth wrapped package into her hand. "What's this?"

The heat flared in Jacob's face. He cleared his throat and glanced down at the floor. "It's Valentine's. I couldn't let the day go by without a sweet nothing of some sort."

She slowly unwrapped the parcel to reveal a band of iron that was molded into the shape of a heart, covered in delicate scrollwork. "Jacob, it's lovely. Calling it nothing does not do it justice. Where did you get it?" Charlotte turned it over and skimmed her fingers over the engraving. She took pause when she found the words. *To Charlotte. Love, Jacob.*

Jacob shrugged. "William helped me forge it in the smithy and I did the engraving in my spare time at the gunsmith shop. I know it's not much, but you have such a big heart with enough room to love all of us. You deserve a gift today and every day."

She grabbed his hand on her knee and gave it a squeeze. "It's beautiful. Thank you." Her smile was genuine until she cried out and squeezed his fingers so hard the bones rubbed together.

"More pains?" His grip tightened on hers and he gave her an anchor, something to hold her steady in the midst of her fear.

She nodded, her face twisting. "Oh, dear Lord! Jacob, what if the baby comes now?"

He sprang to his feet and grabbed hold of her shoulders. "Don't think anything of the sort. I'm sure you're just overdoing it, probably pulled a muscle or something. Where's your father?"

Jacob ran a hand through his hair, glancing out the window at the fierce snowstorm that had kicked it up to a higher intensity. If the baby came now, he couldn't go for help. *Too soon. It is much too soon. Please help her, Lord.*

"He's at Talmadge Edwards' place, said he needed help with a project." Her words were cut off as she pressed a hand to her side, a deep flush blooming in her cheeks. Of all the times for her father to leave them privacy in his effort to help them build a bridge from friendship to something more.

Jacob rested a palm against her face, meeting her gaze with a level stare as he fought to remain steady. "Listen. I want you to sit here and try your best to rest. I'm going to fill the tub and have you take a warm soak. That might unwind those muscles that keep tensing up." He really had no idea what to do, but Charlotte looked at him with such trust in her honey-colored eyes that Jacob had no choice but to do something.

He began with the laborious task of dragging the large wooden tub used for bathing and washing from the barn. The next step? Filling bucket after bucket with snow, melting it over the fire, and transferring it to the tub. All the while, Charlotte rocked. From time to time, her hands gripped the handles of the chair or her swollen belly and she whispered something, her eyes pinned to her midsection.

Jacob suspected she was praying.

His arms were trembling with weakness as the last bucket was poured into the steaming tub. Jacob turned to see the tears streaming down Charlotte's face. That gave him a jolt. "Is it worse?" He asked, glancing at the chair for any signs of blood. Lord help him if the baby came now. Lord help them both.

Charlotte nodded. "The cramps keep coming in waves, closer together." Jacob didn't know how labor worked for mothers, but he'd watched his father's animals over the years and knew they went through contractions, a tightening and loosening of their abdomens that eventually pushed the young animal out. *No, Lord. Please. Not now.*

"Lie back in the tub and maybe that will make the pains go away." She looked up at him and didn't move, the unspoken hovering between them in the air. Jacob pulled her up from the chair and led her to the steaming water. "Yes, you're going to have to get undressed before me. You are my wife, Charlotte. It's all right for me to see you, especially in an instance like now."

Another pain hit, one that snatched her breath way, ending any arguments. She turned her back to him and allowed him to unbutton her dress before lifting it over her head. Several layers later, fumbling with laces and petticoats, Jacob almost grabbed the scissors to cut off her clothes. How did women wear such truck? All the while, the blush was creeping up Charlotte's chest all the way to her hairline and she wouldn't look him in the eye.

Jacob's hand chose that moment of all times to lose feeling as he struggled with her corset. He breathed out hard through his nose, shook his arm, and gave it one more go until finally his wife was clothed only in the glory she'd been born with. At any other time, he would have marveled at the sight but there were more pressing matters at hand—like keeping that baby inside of her and wiping the fear from her eyes.

Another pain doubled her over and Jacob simply picked her up and set her in the tub. Her head fell back and she leaned against him as he wrapped an arm around her shoulders to brace her. Jacob picked up a cloth, a bit of a rag, and used it to rub it over her back, her arms, and her midsection. He concentrated on massaging her, listening to her breathing, and watching her hands. For the longest time, her knuckles bulged, white from balling her fingers into tight fists. Gradually, they relaxed and she rested her palms on her belly. Her entire body went loose and so did his. Jacob nearly sagged to the floor. *Thank You, Lord.*

"It's better now. Thank you, Jacob." Her voice brushed against him softly. He met her gaze and the golden glow of her eyes was blinding. Charlotte reached out for him and took both of his hands in gratitude. They stared at each other until Jacob feared he would topple over the edge and never come back up.

She mesmerized him. The flush in her cheeks. The flutter of her pulse at the base of her neck. The warmth of her skin on his as she nearly burned him at her touch. He sucked in deeply, finding his courage. A rush of air escaped him. Jacob could not resist. He leaned in closer. Their lips touched.

This. Waiting a lifetime for this moment. Jacob didn't know how long it would last, but he would hang on. He lifted her out of the water and wrapped a blanket around her. His hand threaded through her hair and his mouth found its way to hers again. Jacob lay her down on the bed and stretched out beside her. He drew her in, his breath warming her face as his fingers trailed down her jaw. To her collarbone. Her ribs. Forgetting himself, his hand grazed her breast.

The effect was like a lightning bolt struck as she jerked away from him. "No, Jacob. No! I can't do this! I cannot betray Benjamin's memory." Charlotte turned away, her chest heaving, the tears streaming down her face. "I'm so sorry."

He rolled on his back, hand over his eyes, listening to the rush of blood in his ears. His head began to pound. The sound of her crying grated on him and the anger began to build. So close. To take a step closer to her heart. To simply touch her. To see the walls between them crumble. Paradise dangled before him, only to have it snatched away. She shifted and laid a tentative hand on his.

Jacob shot up and told her gruffly, "It's all right. I've got to tend the animals for the night."

He couldn't bring himself to look at her, crossing the room to yank on his boots with a violent tug. He didn't even bother with a coat, the heat of his fury lighting a blaze inside of him. Jacob slammed the door behind him, the noise giving him no satisfaction. He stomped across the yard and untied Powder. His horse nuzzled his ear as if sensing his owner's turmoil. Jacob took a moment to bury his head in the stallion's mane. He wanted nothing more than to scream until he had no voice.

The horse stood patiently until Jacob began to shiver. The night wasn't getting any warmer. He led Powder inside, brushed him down, and closed him in his stall. Jacob concentrated on the task of watering and feeding all the animals. Nothing could touch his rage.

His feet carried him back and forth, wearing a track in the floor, his pent-up frustration threatening to boil over. He was a good man, an honorable man, but how much could a man take trying to bridge the gap between himself and Charlotte?

How could he compete with a ghost?

One more time across the barn and Jacob ran at the wall, slamming his fist into the solid planks. Standing there, with his chest heaving and head bowed as he cradled his hand, the bloom of pain was nothing to the ever-widening crack down the middle of his heart.

28 February, 1782

"WHAT'S THE MATTER WITH YOU? CAT GOT YOUR TONGUE?" Nicholas Stoner's breath came out in a cloud as they fought their way up a steep incline. A grin tugged at the corner of Jacob's mouth, but he didn't feel like laughing. In truth, he was in a foul mood. Jacob had his doubts about a hunting excursion now, at this time of year, but had stopped caring much about anything. His friend had pried him out of the Ross homestead to lighten his spirits.

"No. Keep going before I lose my footing and slide down to the bottom." Huffing and puffing, out of shape after his injury and long recovery, Jacob wasn't sure he would make it to the top.

Nicholas pulled ahead of him. Jacob would be damned if the hunter and trapper would leave him behind. A desperate lunge and the two men found themselves at the top of a rise. Jacob leaned against a tree and his breath caught at the view below. A blanket of snow covered the landscape, the trees sparkling in the early morning light, the sky overhead a blue that was so intense, it hurt to stare at it for too long. Like Charlotte. How could the world look so beautiful when it was falling apart around him?

Nicholas clapped him on the back and practically knocked Jacob off his feet with his exuberance. The man packed a lot of power in that wiry, muscular frame. "Stop glowering like that. The fighting is over after all this time and the bloody Brits will get the heave-ho soon, if we listen to the Continental Congress. The Articles of Confederation show promise for straightening out the mess we're in. You've got an amazing woman waiting for you and a child on the way, not to mention your livelihood. What do you have to be so miserable about?"

Jacob waved him off. "Are we here to hunt or not? If I wanted to sit and yammer on about gossip, I would've went to a quilting session with the old women in town." With that, he turned and marched off toward the thick of the forest with no idea of where he was going. This was Stoner's territory.

"All right. If that's how it's going to be, keep your thoughts to yourself, but let me lead the way or we'll find ourselves stumbling about in Canada." A few great strides and Nicholas' shorter legs caught up. Jacob had to grudgingly give him his respect. What the trapper and guide lacked in stature he made up for with sheer nerve and pure grit. "I do not want to meet up with a mess of angry Indians because I crossed over where I don't belong. I don't think you want to either."

Jacob wasn't so sure. Perhaps he'd clear his head, find a sense of purpose again, put his feelings for Charlotte away while he lived in the wild, off the land. If the natives let him live. If they didn't, at least it would put an end to the images that filled his head, the ache that filled his heart, and the intense longing that tugged at his insides. Day in and day out in the Ross homestead, getting worse by the minute. Frustrated and bitter, he shut down his thoughts and concentrated on putting one foot in front of the other.

They walked in silence for a solid hour, as they had since they left town. From time to time, Nicholas signaled to stop, taking pause to read any signs left on the ground. The man was uncanny, at one with the wilderness around him. The Adirondacks were his refuge, embracing him many times over the years, giving him peace. Jacob hoped to find a small respite as they ventured farther into its depths. A cathedral of pines and gentle peaks rose around him. For the first time in months, Jacob could breathe again.

Another hour passed as they trekked into the heart of a forest with no end in sight when Nicholas' hand extended across Jacob's chest, forming a barrier. He pressed a finger to his lips and pointed to the snowy ground. Paw prints, from something considerably large, headed off toward a rocky outcrop.

"Do you think it's a bear—or a wolf?" Jacob whispered, anxiety creeping in.

He had confidence in his marksmanship and believed they had good odds between the two of them. Jacob also knew that life rarely went according to plan, especially when it came to wild animals. Civilization was far away. No one would ever know if tragedy befell the two men.

"Bear, most definitely, and probably a miserable one at that, just coming out of hibernation. There's little to eat right now. Even your sorry hide might appeal to him." Mischief sparked in Nicholas' dark eyes until he caught Jacob's sour expression. He reached out and grabbed his shoulder, giving him a little shake. "What is the matter with you? You haven't been yourself for weeks." Try months. Or years.

Jacob's answer never came. As he mulled over his response, there was a crashing in the forest, a sound like thunder, and a great wall of black hair broke through the stand of pines before them. Both men froze. Jacob had the impression of beady, little eyes, a lip curled in a snarl, too many teeth, and vicious claws. An uninvited guest, the beast was the last thing either man wanted to meet up close and personal—or fight. In a heartbeat, the bear turned on Nicholas.

Cursing up a storm, Stoner dropped to one knee and loaded his long rifle. Jacob did the same, even as his fingers trembled. *Let's go on a hunt,* he said. *It will be good for you,* he said. It was supposed to be something harmless, a fine buck or doe, not some furious, starved creature that wanted to tear apart anything in its path. Nicholas' gun went off first but his aim was off and the bear was upon him, plowing him down underfoot.

Jacob fired and hit a tree of all things. Taking a page from the book of his war experiences, he improvised, using his long rifle as a club. Shouting like a mad man, a description that wasn't far from the truth as his sanity hung by a tenuous thread, Jacob whacked at the massive animal again and again.

With a great roar of disapproval, the bear rose on his hind legs. As Jacob stepped in and swung his rifle yet again, Nicholas rolled out

115

of the way, leaving a brilliant trail of blood in his wake. A grunt escaped him and he was up, crouching low, a growl of pure rage rising as Nicholas plunged into the fray with his gun. Evidently, two crazed opponents were too much for the animal. Letting out one last howl of protest in a flurry of movement, the mass of black hair receded into the distance, leaving both men breathless in its wake.

Nicholas sank down onto his hands and his knees with a moan, blood continuing to gush from the side of his head. A curse thrust its way between Jacob's gritted teeth. He pulled off his coat, ripping his shirt over his head next, and tearing it down the middle to press it against his friend's wound. Upon closer inspection, he could see the furrow of claw marks that ran from the top of Stoner's head, down the side of his face, and across his ear.

His friend made a poor attempt at humor. "How bad is it? The damage can't be much worse after Saratoga."

His laughter was feeble as he began to sway, his color fading fast. Stoner had been at the Battle of Saratoga with Benedict Arnold when a fellow soldier had his skull blasted to bits by a cannon ball. Nicholas had been in the wrong place at the wrong time as the fragments lodged in his face, his head, and robbed him of the hearing in his right ear. It would appear that he had the misfortune of poor timing once again.

Jacob fought to keep his voice steady as he applied pressure to the wounds, getting a groan in response. "You'll live if that's what you're wondering. You've got some nasty scratches that will need to be tended to. They're bleeding like a bastard."

Nicholas waved him off. "That's nothing compared to before." He pulled himself up on to his knees and pressed a hand to the side of his head, his face twisted in a grimace. "It feels like that beast nearly took my head off. My good ear is still ringing from the blow."

Jacob stood up and offered him his hand. "I'd say our hunting excursion is over. We'd best get back so Anna can tend to you."

Stoner's sweetheart and wife waited for him with a baby girl.

While he was off to war, she had married another only to lose her husband in battle. Although she had a child from another man, Nicholas loved her too much to leave her to fend for herself. Much like Jacob and Charlotte.

Jacob shook off thoughts of the comparison and nudged Nicholas' shoulder. "Come on now."

His friend nodded and stood. One step forward and his right foot gave, pitching him to the ground. A blistering streak of curses made the heat rise in Jacob's face as Stoner gripped his ankle.

"I must have wrenched it when that bear went over me like a boulder. I can't walk on it!" More curses rang out and his fist banged on the ground in useless protest. The heavens chose to open up at that moment as snow began to spit at them from all directions.

Perfect. Jacob sighed and gazed about their surroundings. "There's nothing for it then. I'll cut some bows to make us a shelter and get a fire going. We'll have to spend the night."

His friend didn't argue, a fact that sent a bolt of fear through his heart. Nicholas Stoner did not give up easily. Eying the blood seeping through the cloth on the side of the woodsman's head and his color that was fast approaching gray, Jacob got down to business. Within short order, he'd made a lean-to of sorts hanging off of some boulders, shielded by a wall of evergreens. Once Nicholas was settled inside, his back propped against the rocks, Jacob found some fallen trees. He broke branches into manageable pieces and built a pile. The wind and damp conditions didn't help matters any, but Jacob was more stubborn than most and eventually had a fire burning just as the sun met the horizon. He gazed out and shivered. It was going to be a long night.

"You all right?" He nudged Stoner softly in the arm. Jacob didn't like the look of him. The trapper's eyes were closed, his mouth forming a grim line, and the cloth in his hand was completely saturated with blood.

Nicholas opened one eye and glared at his friend. "What do you think? The scratches burn like you wouldn't believe and my head is pounding. To top it off, my ankle throbs like the devil. You might as well put me down like a horse that has gone lame."

From somewhere in his reserves, Jacob found a rusty smile. "Sorry. You'll have to suffer. Anna would never forgive me."

Thoughts of Stoner's wife made him think of his own. No matter how things stood between them, Jacob longed to see Charlotte's familiar face. She would be worried about him, what with dinner on the table and the snow piling up at an alarming pace. The two men had not planned on spending the night in the woods. Next time, Jacob would be prepared for anything.

Silence fell between them. Jacob looked up from the fire to find Nicholas staring at him, his eyes troubled. "I'm sorry to be keeping you from Charlotte. Thank you for helping me. I had meant for this trip to help you."

"That's all right. That's what brothers-in-arms and friends do. They're there for each other."

Jacob gave him a smile and turned his attention to the fire, feeding the blaze as needed. He would have to be attentive throughout the night, not only to generate heat, but to hold the predators at bay. As the snow continued to fall, a howl rose in the distance. The hair sprang up on the back of Jacob's neck. Nicholas looked uncomfortable too as a chorus of cries answered the first.

"Wolves?" Jacob muttered between gritted teeth.

His companion nodded, his expression grim. "Whatever you do, don't let the fire go out. Give me my rifle."

Jacob obliged and watched in awe as Nicholas loaded within seconds. He laid the rifle across his knees and stared out into the night, his eyes darting back and forth. As time crept by, his eyes drooped, his body swaying, about to topple over.

Jacob steadied him. "You should lie back a while and rest your eyes. I'll wake you if I need to."

The corner of Nicholas' lip went up for an instant only to twist as he pressed the side of his head. "It's not my eyes I'm worried about. I feel as if my skull is about to split open. Perhaps if I sleep a bit, that will help."

Jacob helped him to stretch out on a bed of pine boughs, staying close to provide heat and security. Nicholas went under within seconds, proof of the strain of his injuries.

The howling rang out in the night again and again, getting closer. Jacob shivered and pulled his coat tight. He threw more branches on the fire and pressed his body against Stoner's. Nothing would get to his friend. It would have to go through Jacob first. As the hours dragged by and he longed for morning, the night grew quiet. Jacob found himself beginning to drift, his chin dropping down on to his chest when a ragged scream made his head snap up so fast, he heard his neck crack.

Nicholas was sitting bolt upright, his face covered in a cold sweat, and he was shaking. Jacob took his friend's arm. He could've been holding on to a block of ice, he was that frigid and stiff. "Nicholas, you're safe with me in the forest. Is the pain getting worse?"

Stoner's eyes fluttered shut and he shook his head, stopping himself at the movement and pressing his hand to his head. He drew his fingers away to find them slick and red. The bleeding had resumed.

"No, no that's the same. It is the nightmares again. When will the war let us be?"

Jacob let the air hiss through his teeth as he stared into the crackling flames. "I wish I could give you an answer. I still have fearsome dreams. Filled with those I have killed, friends we have lost, Benjamin Willson's death. The last is the worst. I see him with the blood pouring out of his chest and his mournful eyes haunting me because I have Charlotte and he doesn't."

Jacob poked more wood on the fire, rubbing at his arms as a fine shivering ran through him. "It is only fitting, don't you think? We lived. At least we can pay them tribute by remembering them in our dreams. A wretched sleep is a small price to pay for so many who sacrificed everything. What did you see tonight that stole away your rest?"

None of them talked about the war or what happened unless they were gathered together with others from the militia and they were drunk. Jacob wished he had some whiskey now to keep his teeth from chattering and make his friend numb. Nicholas stared at the fire.

It would appear that he had nothing to say until the words began to spill from his mouth. "I saw Oriskany, right after the battle. You know I was there not long after General Herkimer was mortally wounded?" Nicholas shook his head. "What a leader he was. When his men tried to take him off the field, he insisted on being brought to a tree where he was propped up against it on his saddle. His leg must have pained him terribly, but he refused to leave the fight. I often think about Herkimer, how awful it must have been with his infected leg, worsening by the day. They didn't even try to amputate until some ten days after he was shot and then the poor man bled to death. Such suffering."

Nicholas' words trailed off as he gazed into the flames. Jacob waited. The telling did not come easily as he well knew. He had not uttered a word to anyone about the things he'd seen since his time in the American Revolution, but his soul bore the burden of every death, whether the blood was on his hands or not.

Stoner's head started to droop. With a start, he jerked his chin up and resumed his story. "Oriskany was a terrible sight. The dead lying all about and the stench so overpowering we could not help them. My nightmare was filled with visions of those who were sacrificed and then it merged with Saratoga and that bloody moment when Tyrell..."

He pressed his palms to his eyes, but Jacob knew the pictures were still there. He took Nicholas by the nape of his neck and gave it a squeeze. "Get it out, all of it. Say it so it cannot torment you any longer."

Nicholas took a deep breath and plunged ahead with his memories. "Tyrell was the one who was wounded by a cannon when I was at Saratoga. The ball pulverized his head, blasted it to bits. There was blood, gore, and pieces of his skull everywhere. All over me, in my face, my hair, my ear, lodged in my head. When they found me, I was lying with my forehead propped on his thigh. What was left of him. I can't stop seeing what was left of him!"

Jacob began to rub his back, murmuring softly. What more could he do? There was no erasing the past for any of them. "Your face must have been bothering you. I'm sure that spurred on your dreams. Once it is better, your nightmares won't plague you so badly."

Nicholas was white, shadows like bruises under his eyes, mouth tight with the strain of whatever still had him in its grasp. He nodded slowly. "You are right. Yes, of course, you are right." He closed his eyes and began to sway.

Jacob put an arm around his shoulders. "As the days and years pass, the memories will not be so vivid. As with all things, they will begin to fade because time is the great healer."

Nicholas stared at Jacob for several heartbeats. "I sincerely hope that you are right, Jacob. For my sake—and for yours. Why don't you sleep a bit now? I couldn't if I tried."

There was no use protesting, not with the stubborn jut of Stoner's jaw. Reluctantly, Jacob lay back on the pine boughs. Surprisingly enough, sleep came for him, but it was by no means an easy sleep. His head was too crowded with personal images of war. What had happened to Nicholas. Charlotte. She and William had to be frantic. No matter what was between Jacob and Charlotte, he did not want to cause her more pain. As shreds of darkness finally faded and the first tendrils of light made their way through the trees, sleep released its fragile hold on him.

Nicholas was gently shaking him. "Let's go. Anna and Charlotte must be beside themselves with worry. Besides, my stomach is carving its way into my backbone."

Jacob sat up and scraped his hands across his face, threading his fingers through his hair. He slowly rose to his feet, overcome with stiffness, and went off a ways to relieve himself. When he returned, Nicholas was standing. His face was pinched, his skin nearly black beneath his eyes, but he gestured to get started, his gun in hand. They took several steps and he began to curse.

"It's no good!" Stoner muttered, grabbing hold of a tree.

Jacob reached in the bag slung over his shoulder and pulled out the remnants of his shirt. "Let me bind the ankle. That should hold you until we get to William's. We'll take a horse from there."

"All right then. Hurry up, will you? My stomach is grumbling so loudly that bear will be back for breakfast!" It was said in jest, but both men looked over their shoulders, reliving the events that took place the day before.

Jacob knelt down and quickly tied off the ankle, the tension coursing through Stoner's body so fiercely he could snap in an instant. "Try it now."

Nicholas took a step and gave him a grim smile. "I'll do. Let's get on with this, shall we?"

They continued to forge a path through the deep snow. As the walking became more of a trial for Stoner, Jacob slung his arm over his shoulder to lend him his strength. It was nearing sunset once again when they caught sight of the Ross homestead.

Charlotte was standing on the porch, her face turned toward the horizon, painted in the glory of reds, oranges, and yellows of the dying day. As they neared the house, Jacob could make out the tears glittering in her eyes and the smile on her face. She gave out a cry and waved frantically, calling out to her father. He burst out of the house and they made their way to the wayward hunters, William taking hold of Nicholas' other arm.

Charlotte pressed her hands to Jacob's cheeks. "Bless the Lord that you are home! We feared something awful happened to you."

Every part of Jacob screamed to take her in his arms and kiss her until she was senseless, but the memory of Valentine's Day and how she pushed him away was still too raw. He pulled back and the pain flashed in her eyes, making him regret it instantly.

He gave her a shaky smile. "Something awful did happen. Nicholas was attacked by a bear. Do you think you can tend to him before I bring him home to Anna?"

Charlotte immediately focused her attention on the injured man, caring for him with her gentle ways in the same way that she did for everyone. Jacob and William settled Nicholas in a chair by the hearth at her insistence. She quickly gathered supplies and washed his wounds with a cloth dipped in hot water poured from the kettle. His hands tightened until his knuckles were about to erupt through the skin, but he did not make a sound.

Charlotte finished with a rinse in some type of herbs and brought him a cup of tea laced with whiskey. "Drink this, Nicholas. I am so sorry for your ordeal."

He found a tired smile for her and took her hand. "Thank you for all you have done, Miss Charlotte. Jacob is a lucky man to have you."

Standing back with his hip propped against the stone hearth, soaking in its heat, Jacob had to admit the truth of his friend's words. No matter how much of Charlotte he had, he was blessed beyond measure. He stepped forward, intent on taking her in his arms and showing her his gratitude when a loud pounding on the door shook the small cottage.

"Who is it?" William called out.

"It's Richard Dodge. Please let me in, William. It's a matter of great urgency." Charlotte's father immediately complied, ushering their friend and brother-in-arms inside.

Richard's dark eyes scanned the room and immediately pinned Nicholas. He crossed the room and knelt by his chair, gripping his knee as he did. "Nicholas, I've terrible news. It pains me greatly to tell you that a band of Indians raided your father's place in Tribes Hill."

123

Nicholas drew himself up and reached out to grab hold of Dodge's shoulder. "Is he all right?"

Everyone could see the answer written on their comrade's face. Richard shook his head and swallowed hard, his jaw clenched so tightly the muscles bulged. "I am sorry to say that he is dead, Nicholas. The vicious monsters scalped him."

All of the color drained from Stoner's face and his eyes darkened with pain. He stood up slowly, his voice wooden. "Take me there. Now."

Jacob hurried to get his coat off the hook, only hung up minutes before. "I'm going with you."

"As am I," William called out, grabbing his coat. He turned and kissed Charlotte on the crown of her head, both cheeks, and her mouth. "My Blessing, we will be home as soon as we can, but we must go with Nicholas in his time of need."

Jacob went to her next, tipping her face to his so that he could graze her lips with a kiss. He saw his pain and sorrow for their friend mirrored in her eyes. "I love you."

She nodded and told him faintly, "I love you too. Be careful."

The words were said freely. There was no reason to be cautious. The damage was done, the beasts long gone. All they could do was take care of the dead.

~

"DOES IT HURT YOU TERRIBLY? IT LOOKS AWFUL." Nicholas' wife, Anna, dabbed at his face, swiping her sleeve across her eyes from time to time in an effort to stem her tears. With a jolt, Jacob realized how similar Stoner's wife was to Charlotte. Although Nicholas was her old flame, she married William Scarborough while Stoner was away at war, had his baby, Mary, and lost her husband at the Battle of Johnstown. Nicholas offered her a safe haven, taking her for his bride. They created a home together. One of mutual affection.

Jacob longed for the same. With a mental jerk, he focused on his friend.

Nicholas stared into the fireplace, his eyes dead. He'd said little since they'd gone to his father's farm, dug a grave on the land that he loved, and buried what was left of Henry Stoner. Jacob suspected that a part of his son went with him into that cold, lonely plot. It begged for a marker. There was a desperate urge to do something, but nothing could bring Nicholas' father back.

The baby began to cry in her cradle, pulled up close to the hearth to keep the little one warm, yet Stoner's wife continued to tend to her husband with fingers that trembled.

He took hold of her hand and gave it a squeeze. "Go take care of Mary. Just bring me the whiskey, please."

She leaned over to drop a kiss on his lips before swiftly moving across the room to grab a stoneware jug and two tankards. She set them down before Nicholas, her hand trailing down the uninjured side of his face. There was such pain in her expression, pain for her husband.

On her way to the cradle, she pressed Jacob's arm. "Thank you for bringing him home safe."

Jacob stood and took her in his arms, offering her what strength and ease of spirit he had to give. "It is nothing he would not have done for any of us."

Anna gave him a tremulous smile in return, but it quickly slipped away as she bent down to take her infant in her arms. The baby's crying covered her own as Stoner's wife buried her face in her daughter's blanket. A soft humming rose as she paced back and forth before the hearth, gently rocking the infant. It was unclear who she was trying to soothe.

Nicholas leaned forward, his hands pressed to his knees, the anger coming off of him in hot waves. "I must do something!" He practically exploded, echoing Jacob's thoughts. "I want to go after them. Make them pay. Kill them all! I feel as if all of this, all the fighting has been for nothing! I thought this would be our time of peace after our long time at war. My father had a farm—a farm, for God's sake—and still, death and destruction found him. Was any of it worth it?"

Jacob rose from his chair and crossed over to grip Nicholas' shoulder while he glanced at Anna, rocking her baby girl by the fireplace. Her face was turned away, but her shoulders shook and tears made tracks down her cheek. "You have your home. Your wife. Your child. Much worth living for."

Nicholas grew still and the tension eased beneath Jacob's grip. The only sound was the snap and crackle of the wood on the fireplace, the baby's soft cooing, and Anna's muffled sobs. Stoner raised his head and pinned his brother-in-arms with a level stare.

"As do you." His meaning was clear. It was time for Jacob to stop wallowing in self-pity and dissatisfaction.

"Let us drink then. To the memory of Henry Stoner." Jacob poured two cups of whiskey and took a long swallow, wincing as the fiery liquid burned a trail to his stomach.

Nicholas stared into the fire. "Drink to all those who have sacrificed for this cause." He drained his cup and poured some more. Watching his friend's face, following the map of scars from the Battle of Saratoga and his most recent wounds, Jacob knew. Sacrifices were still being made.

Every minute that they drew breath.

7 March, 1782

"EASY, NICHOLAS. YOU'VE ONLY BEEN ON THE MEND FOR A WEEK. You're not fully healed." Jacob grabbed his friend's arm as he began to sway. "Perhaps you should lie down in the wagon bed." Visions of the woodsman pitching head first into the road sent a chill down his spine.

Nicholas shook his head, grimaced at the sudden movement, and took a firm grip on the edge of the seat. "Just try not to hit every bump along the way, will you?"

He closed his eyes and breathed hard through his nose. As soon as he learned a marker had been placed on Henry Stoner's grave, he insisted upon seeing it for himself.

Jacob shook his head, but took up the reins and continued at a slow pace. He knew there was no point in putting up a fight. When Nicholas Stoner set his mind to something, no matter how rattled it might be, there was no changing it or talking him out of his decision.

The day was cool, making his friend shiver. Jacob didn't like the look of him. Stoner's face was tight, the scratches like scarlet bolts of lightning across his temple all the way to his ear. He'd lost weight, something Nicholas could not afford to do, and his color was bad. Jacob suspected grief was the culprit.

"You can stop staring at me. I know I'm not the most appealing thing to look at right now." Stoner jabbed him in the ribs, forcing Jacob to look away.

They continued on in silence for the considerable journey to Tribes Hill. As they approached his father's farm, Nicholas drew himself up in his seat, his jaw clenched. His dark eyes burned with sorrow and anger, like coals in the fireplace, still giving off enough heat to easily erupt into flames. The man was like tinder. One spark and Stoner would be ablaze.

Hoping to extinguish the fire and be a balm to a son bereft of his

127

father, Jacob pulled the wagon to a halt in front of the large hemlock at the far end of the property. He jumped down and offered Nicholas his hand. After a moment's hesitation, Stoner squared his shoulders, set his jaw, and accepted.

The moment his feet hit the ground, Nicholas' legs trembled and he pressed a hand to the side of his head. "Sorry. I think my old injury has made this worse. Dizzy spells get the best of me from time to time."

Jacob didn't say anything, simply holding his friend's arm until he was ready. A few minutes passed and Nicholas drew a deep breath. With a nod, he stepped forward, his feet slowing the closer he came to the place where his father lay sleeping beneath the surface. At his first close-up glimpse of the marker, his knees gave and he dropped down on the grass. His face caved in upon itself as his hand reached out to trace the letters on the iron cross. Henry Stoner. Beloved father. Died 1782.

Jacob knelt beside his friend and bowed his head, his own emotions hanging by a thread. He had held Nicholas' father in the greatest esteem and could easily imagine how difficult it would be to lose the man who had been his everything.

A hand reached out and squeezed the nape of his neck. "It is a fine marker. Your work?"

"Mine and William's. He forged it. I did the engraving. It will last a good while. None of us will forget your father. He was a fine man and a true Patriot. This is only a small gesture to sum up a man's life. I wish we could have done more for him." The words died and Jacob stared at the ground, his eyes burning.

"It is enough." Nicholas shook him gently.

They stayed until the sun sank in the sky, climbing back in the wagon for the return journey. Stoner craned his neck to gaze at the marker casting a long shadow in the dying light. Jacob looked grimly ahead.

Not enough. Not even close. Nothing could be.

15 March, 1782

JACOB THOUGHT HE COULD BE CHARLOTTE'S FRIEND. He was wrong. With each minute under the same roof, sharing the same table, lying side by side, her nearness became impossible to bear. His frustration, anger, and passion for his wife only grew. Add his fury over Henry Stoner's fate, festering like an infection that spread its tendrils deeper into his heart with each passing day, and his grip on control was slipping. If he ever let loose his emotions, it would be like unleashing a hurricane.

Jacob had to do something before he was filled with regret and remorse. Something with his hands and back. Something outdoors. Away from the house. Away from the source of his inner turmoil. Away from Charlotte.

The ax swung through the air with a whoosh and a satisfying *thunk* as it bit into the tree. Again—again—and again, the vibrations traveling from the hickory handle to his hands, up his arms, to his shoulder. The joint burned and Jacob welcomed the pain. He focused on anything that would pull his thoughts astray from Charlotte.

A loud creak echoed in the woods, practically a scream, forcing him to back away. Jacob tipped his head back and watched the mighty oak sway back and forth as if fighting against surrender. The hardwood tree wavered several times before toppling to the ground with a crash. The ground's shaking traveled to his bones.

He closed his eyes and reveled in the feeling. Then to the work of trimming, cutting off all the extras, getting it down to just a log. Jacob hefted the remains of the tree to the side to join a mounting pile of trees, pushing his body to the limits to make the wood budge. He stopped to catch his breath, hands pressed to his knees.

He sucked in air, straightened up, and picked out another one. Started all over again. A few more and he would be able to begin framing out their log home. Another tree came down and Jacob's legs nearly caved. He dropped down and let the tree catch him. His body needed a break, like it or not.

A few weeks before, seeing his son's misery, Abraham gave him the gift of a piece of property outside of town. Jacob saw an outlet for his frustration, somewhere that he could find release. Besides, they couldn't stay with William forever and Charlotte deserved a place of her own before the baby was born. He plunged into the task of clearing the land, preparing to build. To get a fresh start and come to terms with the path he had chosen for his future.

His life took on a new routine. Up early in the morning to help his father, putting in the rest of the day until daylight was gone working on his house. Their house. If Jacob was weary to the bone, so tired his heart and mind were numb, he could make it through the few hours of lying by Charlotte's side feeling like there was an ocean between them.

She might as well be across the Atlantic in England, because he could not—would not—touch her. Hold her. Have her in his arms. Jacob was losing hope that he ever would. Spring was here, the snow gone, buds appearing on the trees as sprouts poked their way through the soil. The season of rebirth, yet he was dying inside.

Shying away from a train of thought that only served to darken his mood, Jacob stood and picked up the ax again. He made it sing through the air and the trees continued to drop. At least here, he could accomplish something, feel useful. Jacob's heart swelled with pride as he surveyed the scene before him, the cleared patch of land, the mountain of felled trees, and the image in his mind of what it could be.

A flash of movement caught the corner of his eye and he turned quickly, fighting the automatic clenching of his jaw. Charlotte picked her way through the forest, inspecting his efforts with a basket on her arm.

Her hair was up, twisted into a bun at the back of her head, but uncovered on a relatively mild day on the brink of spring. The sunlight caught the golden strands, made them shine bright enough to blind him. She'd chosen a simple, homespun dress in a pale rose that only brought out the color in her cheeks and glow in her eyes. Something that only reminded him once again how irresistible she was.

Jacob turned and picked up the ax. "What are you doing here? It's a long way to walk. You should be resting."

She had four months to go and the extra weight she carried was wearing her down. He often found her sitting by the fire to catch her breath, rubbing at the small of her back. Even now, one hand was pressed to the dip at the base of her spine. How he wanted to place his hand there. Knead the muscles gone tight. Feel her go loose in his arms as she found comfort in him.

"I brought you food and cider before you drop in your tracks. You've been pushing yourself at an unbelievable pace, Jacob. At this rate, you'll drive yourself into the ground." Charlotte set her basket down and rested her hands on her hips. "Besides, I'm not an invalid, for goodness sake. The walking is good for me, I'm sure—and the baby."

He nodded and turned back to his work, hoping to hide the telltale flush that rose in his face each time she was near. Jacob took down another tree, trimmed it, and dragged it across the clearing. He could feel her eyes on him the entire time. Jacob turned to see her holding herself, arms wrapped tightly around her middle. Her eyes were troubled as she chewed on her lip, her cheeks stained crimson. Why did she have to torment him so?

"Jacob, I can't stand this wall that has come up between us. It's getting to the point that I will never be able to climb to the top to find my way to you unless I tear it down. I'm sorry about what happened that night that you helped me. On Valentine's? I did not mean to hurt you. I just—I'm so confused sometimes and I feel like—"

"You feel you're betraying Benjamin. Benjamin is gone, Charlotte. He's not coming back. I'm here. I'm alive. I have feelings

131

and needs. You push me past the point of no return. Forgive me, but my body is not always my own and I am weary of waiting for something that may never happen."

He looked down at the ground, struggling to rein in his temper. More and more often of late, he found himself at war with his anger and it was a losing battle. His hands balled into tight fists, his shoulders trembling at the strain to contain himself, to not explode and tell her about all the matters that pressed so heavily on his mind.

Jacob glanced up and caught Charlotte with her eyes squeezed shut, as if in pain. He sighed wearily and squeezed her arm. "Never mind. Don't worry yourself. I know you can't give any more than you already are. That will have to be enough. Thank you for thinking of me. You should go back home now before it gets too late. I don't want you walking in the dark."

The sun would touch down on the horizon in a matter of an hour or so. Time. There was never enough time. To build a home. To close the gap between them. To mend hearts.

"I'll wait for you." She told him softly and settled herself on a trimmed log while Jacob continued to work.

When the last tree was down, he sat beside her, hands on his knees, tired to the bone. Her hand settled on his and her warmth, her nearness seeped inside, made his stomach tighten, and his heart hammer.

"It's hard for me, Jacob, but I will try to give you more of myself. I promise. Please be patient. Don't give up on me." She grazed his cheek with a kiss. He covered it with his palm and nodded.

"Anything you offer me will be enough."

She reached into her basket and pulled out bread, cheese, and some apples that had been saved in the root cellar since the fall. They divvied it up and munched quietly together, passing a jug of cider back and forth. The cool, sweet drink tasted good, the breeze of late March refreshing, lightening his spirits. Jacob glanced at Charlotte and couldn't help but smile. So pretty. She was so pretty it hurt and made him catch his breath every time.

Her hand found a home in his, easing the ache in his heart, and then she took him unawares, resting her head against his shoulder. Jacob shifted to wrap an arm around her when she let out a gasp, her hands clasping her stomach. He dropped his food and clutched her arm.

"What is it? What's wrong?" An undertow of panic threatened to pull him under. Not here, not so far from everything with nothing but his two hands. *Please God, not here, not now, much too early.* July. She should make it until July.

Charlotte's eyes lit with wonder. "It kicked!"

Jacob stared at the swelling of her belly. He jumped when it went up and down in a slow roll. She grabbed his hand and pressed it to the surprisingly firm, warmth that contained her baby.

They both held their breath until it happened again. Jacob burst out laughing, buoyed by Charlotte's delight. Swept up in the moment, she leaned in and kissed him, a tremulous smile tugging at her mouth. "Let's go home and tell Papa. Maybe it will happen again."

Jacob couldn't argue with her, couldn't tell her no. He nodded and tucked his tools away in a sack. Charlotte stood patiently and waited for him, her hand massaging her belly round and round. As he surveyed the scene once more, the sunset rooted him to the spot.

Jacob turned slowly to see his wife framed in a wash of color as day gave way to night, turning her into a shadowy silhouette. His legs went weak at the sight of her. If he could've grabbed a tree, he would have, but they were all too far away. The rest were stacked, ready to shape a house.

Charlotte went to him and rested her palm on his cheek. "Where did you go? You look so far away."

"I'm just done in, that's all. Nothing your cooking and company can't fix."

Jacob wrapped an arm around her waist, expecting her to pull away. If anything, she moved in closer, keeping pace with him on the journey back to the Ross homestead. Several times, they stopped as the baby continued to kick up a storm. Every time Jacob watched the marvel that was his wife and shared her wonder, the more deeply in love he fell for her. Much harder of a fall and he'd tumble right over the edge with no chance of saving himself.

18 April, 1782

JACOB SIGHTED IN HIS KENTUCKY LONG RIFLE, took aim, and fired. With a loud *crack* that set his heart to beating wildly every time, he waited in eager anticipation and gave a shout of victory. The bullet hit its mark, dead center, in the block of wood set up against a tree. His reason for celebration—every successful shot brought him a step closer to banishing the nightmares that continued to plague him and rob him of his sleep.

As had become her daily ritual, Charlotte emerged from the forest with a basket of refreshments on her arm. He suspected it was her attempt to get closer to him under the guise of checking on the cabin. She was cautious, like the animals that hovered on the fringe of the clearing, eying the stranger in their midst. The progress between them was slow, often two steps forward and three steps back, but it was progress nonetheless. Like their cabin.

The work was slow and backbreaking, but the house was taking form, an empty shell reaching toward the sky. A source of great pride, but another mountain to climb all the same. When he became crushed with weariness, his rifle was on hand until Jacob could take up the work again. He raised his chin in acknowledgement of Charlotte and fired again. She flinched.

Jacob brushed aside her skittishness and fired again. Out of the corner of his eye, he saw her jerk, her hands clenching into fists in her lap. His good mood started to evaporate. When a jolt ran through her the third time, he was ready to snap.

"Charlotte, if you can't bear the sound of the rifle, don't come along anymore," he told her impatiently. The gun shots were a reminder—for Charlotte, for all of them—of the war, the loss, the pain, but they were his livelihood as well. "You married a gunsmith, remember? What did you expect?"

"Why are you still out here? It's getting late and you stay later each night." Her voice dropped to a whisper and he had to strain to hear her.

Jacob lowered his rifle, planting the butt on the ground, and stared her down. "Do you really want to know why I come here as often as I do, why I work such long hours?" At her nod, he exploded. "To get away from his ghost! To get away from the fact that I look at you every day and I know that you wish someone else was in my place! There are too many memories in that house! Sometimes, I feel as if I must howl at the moon." He turned away. "So I come here to find a little peace."

"Do you want to leave me? I wouldn't blame you." Charlotte held on to her basket, the warm wind of April tugging at her hair, pulling it from the knot at the base of her neck. Snagging his heart. Threatening to tear him apart.

"I'd cut my own arm off before I did that, and if you think I'm capable of such a thing you don't know me at all." Jacob rested the gun against a tree with a curse, stomping back and forth. Finally, he grabbed hold of Charlotte by the shoulders and kissed her until she was breathless. "I don't want to leave! But sometimes I feel like I can't breathe. So I come here, I work, and I shoot. Understand?"

She leaned against him, her head on his chest. Jacob let out a gust of air, pent up in aggravation, and rested his chin on the soft tumble of her curls. The baby gave a kick, thumping him in the abdomen, making them pull apart. Laughter spilled over, the tension between them dissipating. Charlotte took Jacob's hand.

"Can we go back now? I'll put on tea and Papa will be home soon, in time for dinner. It will be just the three of us tonight." She stood on tiptoe and kissed his cheek.

"No ghosts?" He asked softly, with a hint of a grin.

Her smile faded. "No ghosts." Except for those inside of the both of them and a past that could not let go. Would never let go.

As they began a slow, meandering stroll back to her father's house, Charlotte glanced over her shoulder. She stopped to set her hand on his shoulder. "It will be a beautiful home, Jacob."

He turned and took her face in his hands, gazing deeply into her eyes. "Don't you understand, Charlotte? You are my home. I cannot come close to offering you what you offer me, but I must do my best. With my back. My hands and my heart."

She stepped in to trail her fingers through his hair. "Your poor heart, Jacob. You deserve so much better."

He shook his head. "You underestimate your value. It is I who am not worthy of you."

She couldn't persuade him otherwise, no matter what arguments were raised for the rest of the walk home. Jacob felt her eyes following him all evening in the Ross homestead. Often, he found her forehead creased in thought, eyes shadowed. What could be going through that head of hers?

That night, as he wrestled with the ghosts that haunted his sleep, Charlotte tossed and turned. Neither was well-rested come morning. Jacob wanted to stay in bed, but that was unheard of unless he was ill or dying. With a shudder, he pulled himself out of the haven of their covers, having come too close for comfort to both.

Charlotte paced back and forth after her father left for the smithy, taking up her chores, aimlessly walking from window to window, cleaning with more vigor than was needed, the steam practically rising off the top of her head. At one point, she actually stomped her foot and stopped, rubbing at her side.

Jacob stood from the table where he had been lingering over his cup of coffee. He just couldn't find the drive to go to the gunsmith shop and his heart wasn't in going to the house. All his muscles were sore. He wasn't sure he could lift the ax or another log and his hands smarted, filled with splinters.

Cautiously, he approached Charlotte and tipped her chin up. Her eyes flashed dangerously. Perhaps it was best to cast his lot with the ax and splinters. "Whatever is troubling you?"

She whipped around and crossed her arms over her chest. "I am so tired of being trapped in these four walls. In my body! I feel like I can't go anywhere or do anything, except the same thing every, single day. At least you and William get out, go to work. I am always here! Cooped up like a chicken in a pen!"

Jacob stood behind her and wrapped his arms around her growing waist. The baby shifted beneath his touch. *Do you know me?* What if the little one did not accept him as a father? It didn't bear thinking upon.

"You need to get out. Let me hitch the wagon with Bonnie and Powder. We'll take a ride into town."

Charlotte's body gave and she leaned back against him. "I do need a few things in the marketplace." She glanced up and slid him a smile. "How do you put up with me?"

He grazed her knuckles with a kiss. "Sometimes I think you will be the death of me, but I know no greater pleasure than being by your side." She held on a moment longer and Jacob felt as if the crack down the middle of his heart was beginning to heal. Gift him with more of her smiles, her touch and the gap would close completely.

He caught himself whistling, surprising himself, while hitching Powder and Bonnie to the wagon. A pat to Belle, who stood lazily munching her oats in contentment, and Jacob was ready. *Oh, to have the life of a milk cow.* The thought had him smiling, something that had been much too rare since the Battle of Johnstown. For all of them.

Charlotte waited on the top step with a basket on her arm. The sun touched her hair and lit her eyes, making her cheeks glow. Her mouth tilted up at the corners as he pulled up in front of her. He couldn't breathe. If Jacob lived to be a hundred, he could never take his fill of this woman.

He sprang down with agility and took her hand, leading her to the other side of the wagon. With his hands placed at her waist, Jacob gave her a boost up to the seat. The baby kicked in answer, making her laughter bubble over.

He couldn't help but join her. "Well, hello to you too. Are you looking forward to a ride?"

His hand grazed the hard, firm swelling of her belly and Charlotte caught it, held fast. "Thank you for being so attentive to me, Jacob. I would have gone out of my mind if not for you after Benjamin died."

He gazed up at her, gave her a nod. Charlotte had a way of making his emotions rise to the surface, especially when she graced him with her touch. His voice was hoarse when he spoke. "It goes both ways, Charlotte. Without you, I would be cast adrift with no purpose. War changes a man, makes him lose his way. You've been a compass."

He brushed her hand with a kiss and pulled away. How he longed to carry her inside to experience her wonders in their bed. With each passing day, she drove him to distraction. He wanted her—no, *needed* her. Like the air that filled his lungs or the water that he splashed over his face, trying to cool the fire in his blood. Charlotte was softening toward him, might even accept his advances—but the advanced state of her pregnancy slammed another door in his face. Biting back his disappointment, he walked around the horses and pretended to check the harness while he gathered his composure. Jacob would not allow himself to take advantage of her. Not now. When that day came—if it ever did—it would be on her terms.

He took up his seat and the reins with a whistle. With a shout of encouragement, the wagon lurched forward and they set off for town. The sun was surprisingly warm, beating down on their heads. Charlotte pulled off her bonnet and fanned at her face.

"I get overheated so easily now. I can only imagine what would happen if I tried to walk the whole way in like I used to. I don't know what's wrong with me." Annoyed, she clenched the small, white cap in her lap and twisted it into a wad.

"You're pregnant. There's nothing wrong with you. You're going through changes. That's no surprise what with the work of growing a new person inside of you. As for walking to town, don't you dare. I see how tired you get at home. You'd probably end up in a heap at the side of the road and then what would I do with you?"

Charlotte slid him a smile. "What indeed? I suppose I'd best listen to the voice of reason, although I must admit that sometimes I'm so tired of being reasonable I just want to scream. Do you ever feel that way, Jacob?"

His hands tightened on the reins as her words did strange things to his insides. Looking at the flush creeping from her chest to her cheeks and the way her eyes glittered, catching sight of the curl resting on her cheek, he could barely restrain himself from taking her in his arms and kissing her senseless.

"I think I understand what you mean," he told her gruffly and turned his attention back to the road.

They continued to take a meandering, slow pace, enjoying the ride as the wagon wheels rumbled beneath them, the noise and vibration soothing. The world was coming back to life after the long, cold winter, the grass turning a vibrant green once again as the leaves unfurled on the trees. Insects buzzed about and wild flowers poked up in the meadows.

Jacob mused on them. He'd have to gather a bouquet for Charlotte's table. He scanned the woods on either side with a keen eye. The hunting would be good now that the food was plentiful. Perhaps Stoner and Dodge would want to go on an expedition.

They rounded the bend when Charlotte gripped his shoulder, making him pull up. "Jacob, look. There's smoke, billowing up. It looks like it's in town."

At that, he slapped the reins hard, pushing the horses to move along at a fast clip until they reached the main street running through town to the market square. Several stands had been torched, starting a blaze, and an angry mob of men continued down the street, working their way toward the courthouse, bent on destruction. Jacob could see many familiar faces, one and the same as those who were grumbling their discontent in the tavern a few months before. They'd moved beyond talk to action.

"Hyah!" Jacob urged the team on, flying down the middle of the street, making the crowd part, and stopped at William's smithy. Charlotte's father stood outside in his heavy apron, tools of his trade in hand, ready to fight. Once a militia member, always a militia member.

Jacob leapt to the ground and rushed to lift Charlotte down, placing her in her father's hands. "William, stay here and guard Charlotte. I don't trust them to have the sense to leave her alone. When the madness of a crowd sets in, all niceties and proper ways of society break down. I'm going to see what I can do to make them see reason."

Charlotte clutched his hand in hers, her grip desperate. "No, please don't, Jacob! You've done enough. You don't need to risk yourself for the likes of this lot."

He bent his head and kissed her swiftly. If something happened, he would have one more taste of the sweet honey of her lips. "Someone has to, Charlotte. I'd never be able to live with myself if I just stood by and watched as someone else's dreams were destroyed or another life was taken. I must do something!"

Her breath caught on a sob. "Just like Benjamin." She leaned in, cupped his face with both hands, and kissed him again. "Come back safe to me."

William gave him a hug and ordered him to do the same, wrapping his arm around his daughter as Jacob turned and ran toward the chaos, instead of away like a sane person would do. More stands went up in flames.

One man stepped in front of the mob, arms raised, sheltering his young son behind him. "Do not do this! This is our livelihood. You can't ruin everything we've worked for!"

"The British already have! We have nothing, no money, nothing to show after all those years of fighting. We might as well tear it all down and admit we haven't won anything. We are defeated, ground down to dust!" The ring leader, a tall farmer at the front of the pack, moved forward and knocked the man down. The merchant's son let out a cry and knelt to tend to his father.

Jacob had enough. He sprinted ahead of the masses and stood his ground. "Enough! All of you! Go back home to your wives and your families! Be grateful you are alive. This isn't solving anything! You need to be patient, let the Continental Congress work out a solution. Destruction isn't the answer!"

The farmer, filthy, worn down, and frustrated, spit at Jacob's feet. Fire, fueled by despair, glowed in his eyes. "It may not be the answer, but at least it gives us some sort of satisfaction. Now, get out of the way. We've a courthouse to dismantle. There's no justice for us anyway." He stepped forward with a menacing sneer, wielding a pitchfork in his hands.

Jacob met him and shoved him back with both hands on his chest. "I said enough! We've paid enough! This has to stop now!"

"It will stop when we say it stops!" With that, the disgruntled man took the pitchfork and whacked Jacob upside the head with all his might, a considerable force from a man who worked the land.

The metal tines struck, making Jacob's ears ring. His knees gave and he dropped to the ground, his hand coming up to touch the side of his head. He pulled it away to find his fingers slick with blood. He started to sway as the world began to spin around him.

"Jacob! Hold on!" A voice called as if from far away.

Through a haze, he saw figures approaching the horde of angry men, heard more shouts. Stoner, Dodge, Edwards and more members of the Tryon County Militia come to the rescue. There were rumbles throughout the crowd, shots fired into the air, and Jacob's face hit the ground. A crimson river flowed over his eyes and he knew no more.

~

"JACOB! CAN YOU HEAR ME? WAKE UP, LAD!" Someone was shaking his shoulder, setting his skull to throbbing.

142

He groaned and reached up to make sure his head was still attached to find a hand pressing a cloth to his forehead. Slowly, his eyes opened to see William hovering over him, a move he instantly regretted when the light stabbed at his brain. He squeezed his eyes closed and clamped his mouth shut, swallowing a moan.

"Let's get him home, William." Jacob recognized Richard Dodge's voice. Nicholas Stoner voiced his agreement. Someone was crying softly. Charlotte.

A soft, gentle hand held his. He forced himself to open his eyes again to see her kneeling beside him. Her bonnet was pressed to the wound at his temple and it was red, soaked with his blood. Her tears rained down on his face.

He swallowed hard and whispered, "Don't cry, Charlotte. Please. Your crying hurts more than anything else."

She forced a shaky smile and leaned in to kiss his cheek. Jacob smelled the scent of flowers from her homemade soap and almost drifted off until he was jarred to painful awareness when his friends picked him up with a grunt. As his head was jostled from side to side, he thought it would split apart. He closed his eyes and prayed for unconsciousness, anything to make his headache go away.

He had no idea how far they carried him, jolting him as they stumbled from time to time, but it felt like half the way home before his friends loaded him into the back of William's wagon. Again, a gentle touch pushed the hair from his face. Charlotte would not be parted from his side. Her loyalty knew no bounds.

"What about—the—mob?" He mumbled, his words beginning to slur. The wagon moved forward with a lurch and he clutched her hand to hold her steady. To keep from slipping away. To stop everything from whirling round and round.

"They caused no more harm and went on home. Your friends and the Tryon County Militia put them in their place. As for the farmer with the pitchfork? You need not worry about him. Justice has been served." Charlotte's voice became choked and she shifted to cover her

143

consternation, settling Jacob's head in her lap.

Out of the corner of his eye, he could see the blood dripping down, covering her hand in a brilliant red. How much blood could come out of his head? She leaned down and kissed his forehead. "What were you thinking, trying to take them all on by yourself?"

Jacob shrugged, groaning as his head bounced after a particularly rough patch of road. "It's in my nature. Benjamin's too. Perhaps some of his courage rubbed off on me."

Charlotte stroked his cheek, soothing him with her touch. "You have always had a healthy supply of your own. It is your sense of caution that I fear is lacking at times."

"I second that opinion." William glanced over his shoulder at the couple from the driver's perch. "My Blessing, do your best to keep him still as possible, otherwise you might not be able to control the bleeding. I have seen many head injuries in the war and they are tricky. If you do not take care, Jacob could have more than a headache."

"He has a very thick skull," Nicholas called from his horse, flanking the wagon.

He wore a grin, but Jacob could see the shadows in his eyes. Richard and Talmadge rode beside him. All of them were covered in dust and dirt from the commotion, blood on their clothes and hands. His blood.

The pressure of Charlotte's hand on the side of his head became too much to bear. Jacob reached for her, nearly overcome by weakness, but managed to push her away. "Jacob, no! You must let me stop the bleeding! Papa, help me!"

"Richard, take Washington!" Nicholas shouted, springing from his horse and climbing up into the back of the wagon. He grabbed Charlotte's bonnet and pressed it to Jacob's head. "My turn to take care of you, old friend."

There was no point in arguing. Stoner was too strong, fully recovered from his injuries although his scars were livid reminders of their close scrape with the bear.

"We'll accompany you home, William, and bring Raven along with Nicholas' horse. You'll need help bringing Jacob in the house." Talmadge moved ahead of the others to talk with Charlotte's father. Their words became a jumble as the wagon hit a bump, making everything around Jacob start to fade in and out.

"Jacob! Stay with me!" Charlotte called to him.

He tried, but his body wouldn't listen. Everything seemed far away. Jacob couldn't make out anything that the others were trying to say. He strained to focus, to make sense of it all when his body began to shake uncontrollably, so hard that his teeth clacked together. He tasted blood from biting his tongue. He was vaguely aware of someone crying and someone else trying to provide comfort.

After what seemed like an eternity, his body grew still. It felt as if a heavy weight was pressing down on him and he couldn't move even if it was life or death. Charlotte continued to cry beside him, her head pressed to his hand. He could smell the scent of her sweet soap drifting from her hair. He wanted to tell her it was okay, but no words would come to the surface.

"Charlotte, it will be all right. It's called a seizure. They're common with head injuries. I had them regularly after Saratoga. This may be the only one." Nicholas' voice was soothing as he continued to hold the cloth to the side of Jacob's head.

Jacob slowly opened his eyes and finally managed to speak, although words were elusive. "I'm—so, so—tired."

"Just close your eyes and rest." Nicholas held his head in his lap. He continued to hold Charlotte's bonnet against Jacob's wound. What once was white was now scarlet, as were his friend's hands. Charlotte's tears wet his sleeve, her soft sobs tugging at him, trying to pull him back. He slipped away.

~

145

"PAPA! I CAN'T STOP THE BLEEDING!" A frantic voice rose in pitch, shredding the darkness that had been a welcome escape from the pain for all too brief a time. The beast was back, in full force, now. Try as he might, Jacob couldn't hold back a moan.

"Try to remain calm, Charlotte. You will only agitate him and aggravate his condition." Nicholas spoke in a hushed voice from somewhere close at hand.

Through the cracked slits of his eyelids, he saw the fireplace in the Ross homestead. Everything was blurred and doubled, making his stomach pitch. He was on his bed, propped up against Stoner's chest as his friend held him steady. Charlotte stood at his side, her hand pressing down on his head. Hard. Too hard. "Could you—ease up—a bit—please?"

"Let's trade places, My Blessing. You get your sewing kit while I apply pressure." William stepped in and placed his palm over his daughter's. She glanced up at him, questions in her eyes. "You need to stitch it now before he loses any more blood."

She nodded and pulled away, swiping at her tears. Jacob wanted to hold her, to tell her everything would be all right, but the words kept slipping out of his grasp. His thoughts were muddled, tumbling round and round in his mind. He heard a flurry of footsteps and then Charlotte was at his side again.

She sat down on the edge of the bed and attempted to thread a needle, her hands shaking so hard she nearly dropped it. William squeezed the nape of her neck and she paused. A deep breath and she tried again. This time she managed and her hand became steady.

She looked up at her father. "All right, Papa. Take the cloth away. Nicholas, please do your best to hold his head still while I close up his wound."

William lifted the cloth on the side of Jacob's head and held his arms while Stoner took a firm hold of his head, clamping down with considerable strength. The outdoorsman let a curse slip from between gritted teeth, revealing how dire the situation was. Nicholas had

146

learned the hard way on a distant battlefield in Saratoga.

The blood, hot and slick, ran down Jacob's face. As Charlotte leaned in closer with grim determination, he closed his eyes and clenched his jaw. The thin, sharp bit of metal cut into his skin, once, twice. Too many times to keep count. Jacob wasn't sure which was worse, the pounding inside of his head or the angry stinging each time the needle pierced him and the thread yanked at his temple. Each tug made his stomach clench. He was trembling when Charlotte stopped and rested her hands on his chest for a moment. Jacob forced himself to meet her gaze, to help her take heart.

She gazed at him and her eyes filled. "I'm so sorry."

He shook his head slightly, wincing at the movement. One hand slowly raised in the air. Why was his hand so heavy and why did it take so long to make it move? Finally, he managed to touch her cheek. "You have nothing to be sorry about."

Nicholas cleared his throat. "Don't stop now. Get on with it as quickly as possible. Head wounds are nasty things. They hurt something awful. He's fighting so hard to keep it together, his entire body is quivering."

Charlotte nodded, the tears trickling down her face, and pressed a kiss to Jacob's lips. William moved away for a moment, returning with a rag dampened in hot water. She accepted the cloth and gently swabbed Jacob's face, wiping away the blood. Each touch to the side of his head, no matter if it was a light as a butterfly, made him want to scream with the pain. He buried his fists in the covers and breathed hard through his nose, waiting for the agony to be over, but it was only the beginning.

"Hold on, Jacob. She's nearly done now." Nicholas spoke in a hushed whisper, giving his shoulder a gentle squeeze.

Charlotte finished and began to tidy up, William assisting her. As Jacob followed their movements, the thunder in his head grew louder, the pain making him feel as if a crack ran through his skull. Perhaps it did. Jacob thought back to the moment the heavy tines of the pitchfork struck him. The noise, the pounding in his brain, had been horrendous. Breaking his head wasn't that far-fetched.

Pushing away unpleasant thoughts, he tried concentrating on Charlotte, but his eyes kept playing tricks with him, making him feel nauseated. With another moan, he closed his eyes and rolled on to his side. A major mistake. *The pain!* Jacob thought his shoulder was unbearable. He was wrong. This. This was worse.

"Jacob, sip a little whiskey to ease you, help you sleep." William was at his side again, his hand resting on his shoulder. Nicholas gently laid his friend down on his pillow and took the jug from Charlotte's father. With a wink, he took a quick swallow, swiped his sleeve across his mouth, and held it to Jacob's lips.

Jacob's face twisted as he hitched himself up on one elbow and everything started spinning like a top around him. "God help me."

"By no means can I compete with our Lord, but I will lend you my strength any time you have a need for it. Try and take some of this." William braced an arm around his shoulders while Nicholas poured the whiskey down, some of it dribbling down Jacob's jaw.

Jacob managed a few swallows before his stomach heaved. He covered his mouth, took pause, whispered hoarsely. "No more—or I will be sick."

Troubled, William nodded and eased his patient back down to the pillows. Unwilling to touch his head and cause him any more discomfort, Charlotte's father rested a hand on Jacob's shoulder and gave a light squeeze. "Try to sleep now and it will soon be better."

"I am going to take my leave now and allow you to rest." Nicholas tipped his hat and turned to shake William's hand, saving a kiss for Charlotte's cheek last. "If you need anything, anything at all, do not hesitate to send for me. Understand?"

Charlotte gave him a tearful hug and escorted their good friend to the door. The sound of retreating hoof beats faded into the distance. Jacob fought to keep his eyes open, but fell into a fitful sleep. The intense throbbing in his head never let him drift far from the surface.

148

Lights flashed behind his eyes and stabs of pain streaked through his skull. As darkness fell and everyone prepared for bed, Jacob readied himself for battle. It was going to be a long night.

He turned on his side and a burst of lights, like sparks shooting from a musket or a fireplace, nearly blinded him even though his eyes were closed. Jacob closed his eyes tightly and concentrated on his breathing in an effort to beat down the wave of pain crashing in. Vaguely, he was aware of the movements of the others in the house, a log being tossed on the fire, the bar lowered across the door to keep them safe. There was a low moan and a sigh from William, one who rarely made any sign of complaint, followed by the soft murmurings of his daughter.

"Papa, what is wrong?"

Jacob chanced a glance and saw Charlotte standing behind her father, hands resting on his shoulders. She was such a source of comfort and support for all of them, no matter how she felt. The foundation of their lives. Jacob realized without her, he'd be cast adrift.

William reached back to cover her hand with his. "I'm just weary in my soul, My Blessing, so tired of the fighting, the anger, the discontent. Every night, I pray that we will finally live peacefully as we did before the war began."

Charlotte leaned against him and rested her head on his back. "We will, Papa. We must have faith that all of this will be worth it, however dear the price and sacrifice."

Jacob squeezed his eyes shut. At the moment, he had doubts that their world would ever be set right and the agony in his head didn't help any when it came to thinking clearly. He rolled on to his back and his head started to pound, sending a cry of pain from the pit of his stomach, but he refused to give Charlotte one more burden to bear. She carried enough for all of them.

The house fell silent. Minutes passed, some more soft murmuring between father and daughter, bolstering each other's spirits. At least they had that. Jacob drifted into a haze.

~

"WHAT CAN I DO FOR YOU? YOU'RE RIGID AS A BOARD." Charlotte whispered in his ear. He hadn't felt her slide into bed next to him, had no idea how long she had been at his side.

He moved, ever so slightly, and it was as if someone had sent him out on a boat on a storm-tossed sea. With each heave of the waves, his stomach rolled unpleasantly. If only sleep would give him some relief, no matter how short-lived. A gentle squeeze of his hand reminded him that he was not alone. No matter what happened, no matter how things were between them, Jacob would never be alone.

"It feels as if I am cast out to sea, pitching up and down. The bed won't stop swaying or spinning. Whether my eyes are open or closed." He had to stop as his stomach began to protest, waiting for it to settle. "Nothing helps."

Charlotte turned on her side. Even that slight jostling made him sink his teeth into his bottom lip. She began to stroke his hair, then his temples. Her soft breathing, her warmth, her mere presence gave him something to focus on, something other than whatever was going on in his head.

"Better?" She whispered.

"Yes." A fog had clouded his mind since the blow to the side of his head sent him off kilter. It became thicker, so dense he couldn't find his way out. Jacob was lost.

~

MAKE IT STOP. PLEASE GOD. MAKE—IT—STOP. Morning came, whether Jacob willed it or no, and with it a blazing sun. The light beat on his eyelids, beat on his brain, made the pain a hammer blow that should have knocked him into kingdom come. Pressure was

150

building inside his head to the point that he thought it might explode like one of the militia's cannons.

He pressed his palms to his temples and the room pitched so hard he rolled to his side, vomiting onto the floor. There was nothing in his stomach and so a dry retching began. Worse. So much worse to the point that a loud ringing sounded in his ears, sure to drive him to distraction.

"God—please," was all he managed to utter.

A cool touch, so soothing it nearly brought tears, came next and the swish of long skirts. "Dear God! You're drenched!"

A cloth dabbed at his face, his neck, and his chest. Jacob let loose another moan. The pain! When would the pain go away? Much more and he would go completely out of his mind. He gripped his head with both hands, rolling from side to side. The momentum sent him to the floor with a thud. "Jacob!"

William knelt beside him and scooped Jacob up in his arms. With a mighty thrust, he tucked him back in bed and laid his hands on Jacob's chest. "You need to be still. Each time you move, you aggravate your condition. You need to rest and heal. That is all there is to be done right now. That, and pray." His father-in-law gave him a weary grin.

"I—can't get any—rest. There is a thunderstorm in my head and blasts of lightning that threaten to tear me apart." Jacob raised an arm and pressed it to his eyes. The room continued to spin, making him so dizzy, he couldn't stand if his life depended on it.

Charlotte sat beside him and began her magic with massaging his hair, his head, and his shoulders. If only she could touch him at all times. That would be distraction enough and could see him through. Slowly, his body went loose, a gradual unraveling. "I want you to try and take a little broth. Not eating anything for two days can only make your recovery more difficult."

Two days?! Jacob didn't argue, didn't have the strength to do so. It felt as if he only closed his eyes for a few minutes. William carefully lifted him up, bolstering him with pillows, and his head felt like it would fall clean off his body.

Charlotte picked up a bowl and spoon, smiling at him with encouragement, but he could see right through her. To her ghost-white skin. Her red eyes. The lines of worry creasing her forehead. She brought the broth to his lips and he made a valiant effort to eat every drop, but his stomach revolted and Jacob lost everything over the side of the bed. He fell back on to the pillow and pressed the heels of his hands to his eyes, praying for unconsciousness. God was merciful and listened.

~

A RED FOG CROWDED IN, MAKING IT NEAR IMPOSSIBLE TO SEE. Jacob's heart became a rapid staccato, ready to burst from his chest. What if he became blind? A gunsmith without eyes? They might as well take his hands.

He sat up fast, panic-stricken, and the cabin appeared to tilt on its side as if picked up by a fierce windstorm. His head ached so badly he gripped his temples, hands balled into fists, and became sick. Frightfully sick. So sick, Jacob feared his insides would be turned out. The dry heaves took over as he hung over the side of the bed. Death would be an improvement.

A cool hand touched his forehead, pulled away as if burned, returned with a damp cloth. Sweet heaven. "Hush now." A woman's voice drifted through the layers of pain. "You've got to try to stop moving so fast, take things slow. Don't touch your head anymore. You'll only make it worse."

Music. She sounded like music. He opened his eyes slowly and the haze cleared to reveal an auburn-haired woman with a mass of heavy curls and green eyes that snapped, a smattering of freckles dusting her cheeks. So pretty with her gentle smile that Jacob wanted to cry.

"Mama?" He whispered hoarsely and began to fade. The darkness was calling his name.

Her breath caught and her hand stroked the hair from his face. "It's me, Charlotte. Look at me, Jacob. Look at me!"

There was an urgency tainted with fear that forced him to snap back from the edge of consciousness. He peeked through a slit in one eyelid and groaned. No auburn hair. No emerald eyes. Only an ache deep inside and a scar ripped away from his heart. Jacob longed for just one more minute with the woman who vanished from his life over twenty years before.

Charlotte's hand drifted through his hair and rested on his cheek. "What is it? Is the pain that bad? I can give you some whiskey."

He shook his head, only to regret it. His stomach rebelled, but he managed to maintain control. Barely. "I am sorry. I mistook you for my mother," he said gruffly.

Her hand trembled and she dipped down, her lips grazing his mouth. "I consider it an honor. I wish I had known her."

Jacob caught her hand and held on. She was his anchor. "You are like her. Beautiful. Strong. With such a big heart and great capacity to love. Like your own mother, I have no doubt."

Charlotte's eyes gleamed brightly, on the verge of overflowing. Her weariness was plain as she sank into the chair at the side of the bed, her station while tending him. She would not leave her post. Her loyalty to those she loved knew no bounds.

Her breath came out in a rush and her hand trailed to her stomach. "I pray every night and every morning that I will be a good mother. There are times when I fear I will be completely inadequate. After all, I had no mother as an example and I—" Her words drifted off. She began to chew on her lip, her brows gathered together in consternation.

"What is it?" Jacob rolled toward her, his body shifting on the bed as if riding a wave on the ocean. He choked down the bile that surged up in his throat, pushing back the fierce throbbing in his head, giving her something in return. Such a small gesture after all she had done for him. His hand hovered in the air and she took it.

One tear trailed down her cheek. If only he had the strength and equilibrium, Jacob would sit up and kiss it away. He could only hold on as it splashed down on his fingers and nearly scalded him with her pain.

"I have been damaged. By the war. By Benjamin's loss. I do not know if I am capable of being a mother." Her voice dropped down to a whisper and he had to strain to hear her. "If I dare even try."

Jacob's fingers tightened their hold and he raised himself up on one elbow. "You will be an amazing mother. You've been practicing all your life, first tending your father, then Benjamin. Now me. I could not ask for a better caretaker."

With his head fit to split down the middle, he dropped back and rested an arm across his eyes. The firelight hurt, stabbing into his brain. Thinking hurt. He just wanted to tumble into oblivion until the pain went away.

Water sloshed in a basin. For one instant, Jacob was mired in confusion, wondering if he was actually floating on a boat. If so, he wanted to get off. Find a deserted island. Stay there for the rest of his days, removed from all reminders of his past.

Charlotte's gentle fingers skimmed over his feverish brow once again. "Let me cover your eyes with this cloth. Perhaps it will help. You have a fever. That isn't helping any."

Again, sweet heaven. His mind drifted, gray floating in at the edges as a soft humming penetrated the wall of pain, wrapping him in a blanket. Easing him at a time when he so badly needed peace.

"My mother hummed that song. I still remember." Jacob murmured, his words becoming tangled. Sleep was coming for him. He was ready for it.

"You always will. Your heart will forever hold a place for her." Charlotte slid her hand into his.

Jacob's fingers slowly tightened around hers like a flower closing its petals in the moonlight. When he awoke in the morning, the thunder in his head had throttled down to a dull roar. Charlotte was asleep in her chair drawn up so close to the bed that her knees touched the mattress.

Their hands were still linked.

~

SOMEONE WAS ROCKING, THE RHYTHMIC SOUND OF THE CHAIR soothing as it made the floorboards creak. Jacob cautiously opened his eyes and let out a pent-up breath. Darkness had fallen. The only light came from the small blaze burning in the hearth. If he did not stare directly into the flames, his head was bearable.

Charlotte was seated beside their bed, sewing something small and white. Something for the baby. Her belly rose and fell, making her breathless. She set the garment down and rested her hands on the rounded mound, closing her eyes as her thoughts turned inward. A soft humming filled the room, his mother's song again. Perhaps every mother's song.

Jacob reached out and laid his hand on hers. Startled, her eyes flew open. He gave her a ghost of a grin. Her smile answered him in kind and she rested a palm on his cheek. Unshed tears brightened her eyes.

"You frightened us. You've been dead to the world for two days. I feared you would never wake up. I don't know what I would do if I lost you too, Jacob Cooper."

He turned his face into her palm and his eyes slid closed. Jacob pressed a kiss to the smooth, warm surface of her hand. She cared for him and that was a balm to his spirit.

"It would appear that I am not going anywhere. Too stubborn to die."

"Too precious. Benjamin was stolen much too soon. I could not bear to go through that again, Jacob. The only reason I have had the strength to make it this far is because you have been by my side. I know that this is not how you pictured winning me as your bride. You are a man above measure."

Her hand shifted, her fingers pressing the beating pulse at the base of his neck. At her touch, even in his condition, his breath grew short, his head light, and the rush of blood in his veins set his heart to pounding.

"I am but a flickering candle to the torch that burns within your spirit."

Jacob's hand skimmed up her arm to feel her pulse, found hers was racing as well. Tripping so fast that he feared for her health. There was a hectic color to her cheeks, her eyes bright. Winning his bride's affections became more of a likelihood with every day they spent in each other's company.

She bowed her head, flustered by his praise. "You speak too highly of me, Jacob."

He closed his eyes, suddenly crushed by a wave of fatigue. "I am too weary to argue the point with you right now, but I will never concede. Do you think . . . ." His breath came out in a rush. His thoughts were becoming muddled. Soon his speech would be garbled. "Would you—lie—" He gritted his teeth together, tried again. "Lie by my side for a while? Your company is all I need."

She didn't hesitate. Setting aside her sewing, Charlotte went around to the other side of the bed, removed her shoes, and slid in beside him. Her rounded belly pressed into the small of his back, a surprising comfort, as her arm stretched across his body to embrace him.

"I am tired too. With each passing day, this little one saps more of my energy. Go to sleep, Jacob. I will join you. The world will be waiting for us when we awaken."

As his eyes drooped shut, he only hoped that it would stop spinning like the tops his father bought him as a child.

Heidi Sprouse

~

THE ROOM TILTED, FORCING JACOB TO SIT DOWN
HARD. A week had passed since his injury. He could be up for short
stretches of time, but the dizzy spells put him down every time. If he
didn't give in, an unbearable headache would be next; they were
something to endure at least once a day. Aggravated, he fought his
way to the bed and stretched out. His head demanded a rest, no matter
what plans Jacob had. Unable to do work. Confined to the cottage.
Feeling worthless, so worthless. The darkness took over again.

When he awoke, Charlotte was bathing. She'd brought the
wooden tub from the barn—or William had. He prayed his father-in-
law had seen to the heavy lifting. She had enough on her plate without
straining herself, what with running the household, seeing to the
animals, and putting up with Jacob.

She sat in the tub, leaning back, her knees drawn up while
combing her hair. The mound of her belly was growing, getting larger
as if by the day. As she continued to work the comb through the long
strands, using her fingers to help untangle her curls, the baby moved.
With a gasp, the comb slid out of her hand and clattered on the floor,
her palms moving to massage the tiny occupant.

Jacob swung his legs over the side of the bed and stood slowly,
testing the waters. If he took his time, he was less likely to fall over.
Inexplicably shy, drawn to his wife, he knelt beside her where her
hands were cupping her belly in wonder.

"May I feel it for myself?" He whispered.

She nodded and took his hand, pressing it to the hard, firm
warmth of her body. It felt like a melon. A slow roll began as the baby
shifted from side to side. He could almost see the outline of a fist.

"Amazing, simply amazing," Jacob told her, laughing while the
tears burned in his eyes. It was a moment so pure, so sweet, Charlotte
forgot to be self-conscious about baring herself to him and Jacob
forgot everything, his pain, frustration, and weariness. His whole

157

world was here. In his hands.

"Like you." Caught in Charlotte's gaze, a fly in her web, he leaned in and brushed her lips lightly. His head began to swim and it had nothing to do with his injury.

"You're rather extraordinary yourself, Jacob. You kept Benjamin's promise. Every time I feel this little one inside of me, I am reminded. We are here because of you."

She let go of his hand to cup his face and bless him with the miracle of her kiss. A kiss that spun out, stole his breath away, and made his heart pound. A kiss that nearly knocked him flat as his love for her welled up inside of him and threatened to sweep him away. No matter what happened in the future, it would continue to flow, taking Charlotte and her child wherever they needed to go.

Before things went too far, Jacob pulled back, a hand pressed to his forehead. "I'd best take myself back to my bed before I'm passed out on the floor. I wouldn't want you to strain yourself trying to drag me back and that would be quite a story to tell William."

His eye caught the comb lying near the hearth. He picked it up and placed it in her palm. Charlotte's fingers closed around his hand, pinning him there. She bent over and kissed his hand. Jacob nearly dropped on the spot.

She chuckled softly as he turned to cross the room, swaying like a sapling caught in a windstorm. He took two steps toward the bed only to return to her side, taking her in his arms, kissing her senseless.

"Jacob . . . ." she whispered breathlessly, her fingers threaded through his hair, tugging insistently. "We—must stop. I hear hoofbeats—Papa can't find us like this, husband and wife or no."

She blushed, the color so becoming on her. He noticed that she was flushed more often than not now, the more advanced the stage of her pregnancy. Temptation. Temptation was fierce, tugging at his insides, making him want to climb into the tub with her or carry her across the room to their bed.

Reason told him otherwise. William would not be pleased. There was that argument and the fact that he would collapse if he tried to carry her that far. He kissed her once more and slid under the covers, feigning sleep, just in time as the door opened. Charlotte gave him a smile, one that kept their secret safe.

~

"WHAT ON EARTH DO YOU THINK YOU'RE DOING?" Charlotte stood in the doorway of the barn and there was fire in her eyes. She'd drifted off to sleep in the rocker while doing her mending. Jacob chose that moment to escape and he was paying for it.

At that moment, he couldn't get up if his life depended on it. Taking care of Bonnie and Belle, mucking their stalls, filling their water, bringing them food, proved to be too much. The spell of dizziness, the hammer blow of a headache came on fast and furious, bringing him to his hands and knees. Emptying his stomach. Sending him spinning into unconsciousness.

At the sound of Charlotte's voice, he pulled himself up into a sitting position and instantly regretted it. The light and the movement were more than he could bear. Jacob pressed his palms to his eyes and prayed for the thunder in his head to stop rolling.

A hand gripped his shoulder and gave him something to latch on to. "You overdid it again. When will you learn that sometimes you need to be patient, Jacob? I truly appreciate the fact that you're trying to help me with my chores, but now I have a much bigger problem on my hands. How am I going to get you back into bed?"

Hearing the fear mingled with frustration, Jacob forced himself to look at her. "One—step at—a time."

Curse his words for slurring. From time to time, whether he was tired or plagued with a headache, his speech would play tricks on him. He held out his hand and Charlotte offered him an anchor, lending him her strength, drawing him to his feet. Everything went topsy-turvy around him and he grabbed at the gate of a stall. Otherwise,

159

he'd take Charlotte down.

"I—I can't. Can't make it that far." He pressed his forehead to the unforgiving wood and squeezed his eyes shut.

"Your head hurts that badly?" At his nod, she began to stroke his hair, moving on to knead the nape of his neck and his shoulders. When the pain came crashing in, everything tensed into knots, making it worse. Time spun out and the headache continued to be a selfish, uninvited guest. "Any better?"

"No." His head was about to split in two. With each wave that rolled through his skull, a darkness crept in at the corners. He was fading. "Charlotte—I'm—I'm going to—pass—out."

Alarmed, she ducked under his shoulder. Together, they staggered as far as the bed of straw on the other side of the barn. The world tilted and Jacob toppled over, Charlotte's scream the last thing he heard.

~

SOMETHING WAS TICKLING HIS NOSE. He sneezed and reached up to investigate, found a piece of straw poking at him. As Jacob brushed it away, he became conscious of a weight resting against him. He opened his eyes to find himself lying in the straw, the sunlight streaming in, lighting up the woman who slept beside him. When Charlotte couldn't bring him to the house, she chose to stay at his side. Such devotion. Such a big heart. Enough to hold the world. The baby to come. Her father. Her first love. Jacob.

His throat closed at the thought and his eyes burned. He turned on his side to get a better look at her and lose himself in the view. Unable to resist, Jacob undid the pins that tamed her hair and let the heavy strands form a curtain around her face. He ran his fingers through the glory of it, his breath catching as it began to glow in the sun's rays. Her eyes opened and he couldn't breathe.

The corner of her mouth turned up and she let out a sigh of relief.

"You're feeling better?"

Jacob returned her smile. "I just might live." His hand trailed down her body, resting on her hip. The baby shifted in that moment, making her giggle. "Won't let us forget you're there, will you?" On an impulse, he slid down and kissed her belly. "I can't wait for us to become acquainted."

Charlotte's fingers grazed over his hair, pulling Jacob back up to her. He leaned in close, felt her breath on his face, felt the fluttering of her heart as his palm rested on her chest. "I can't wait to become better acquainted with you either, if it is meant to be."

She kissed him, a kiss with a promise. "Someday."

They lay still, gazing at one another until the barn door swung open. William stood in the opening, eyebrow raised in surprise, his expression quite comical. "Taking a roll in the hay at Charlotte's advanced stage of pregnancy? Do you think that's wise?"

Flustered, Charlotte pulled herself to her feet, her cheeks gone crimson. "Jacob passed out after doing chores out here. I couldn't move him so I stayed with him to make sure he was all right."

All humor fled as William bridged the gap between them with great strides. "Let me help. I'll get you to the house."

"I'm all right now. I can manage." Overcome with a rush of heat, embarrassed to no end, Jacob came up fast and the vertigo came back with a vengeance, making him start to sway.

William stepped in and caught him, draping his arm across his shoulders. "No arguments. To bed with you. I told you that head injuries can be tricky, Jacob. You've got to give yourself time. If you fall and hit your head again, it could kill you and I can't stand to lose another young man for whom I care so deeply."

His voice became choked and he was silent the rest of the way to the house, Charlotte trailing close behind. He helped Jacob to the bed and pressed a hand to his shoulder. "Rest now. You will be well soon enough if you listen to what your body is trying to tell you."

Jacob nodded. "I will, sir. Thank you for helping me."

William kissed the crown of his head. "That is my duty and it does not require thanks. You will find out soon enough when you and Charlotte are raising your little one."

He moved away, accepting a hot cup of tea from his daughter. Charlotte brought another to Jacob, helping him to sit up, holding the cup steady when his hands shook. "There's plenty of milk and sugar in it. Perhaps that will ease you," she told him softly.

Jacob pressed a finger under her chin. "You do. Every minute that you are mine."

14 May, 1782

"THAT'S IT. LET'S GO. OUT OF THIS HOUSE. NOW."
Charlotte held the door, pointing imperiously to the outdoors. She was
dressed to go out, her bonnet covering her shining cap of hair, a filled
basket on her arm.

Jacob couldn't help but grin at her. "I like it when you take
charge. You're like a general." As he walked past her, it was
impossible to keep going without stepping in to kiss her. His fingers
itched to snatch her bonnet and free her hair. He closed his eyes for an
instant, leaning against her. "Where are we going?"

She pressed her hand to the center of his chest and gave a little
push. "That's for me to know and you to find out."

He stepped away and gave a courtly bow. "Ladies first." Jacob
made the mistake of coming back up too fast and the vertigo, a
lingering effect from the blow to his head, set the world on tilt.

Charlotte turned back and took his hand. "Just wait a moment.
Breathe in. Breathe out. You will set yourself right again."

He didn't even have to tell her. She knew him so well. In the
months that they'd lived together, they were becoming interwoven in
the fabric of each other, forming a tight mesh. Jacob likened her to his
other half. If they were ever parted, he would never be whole again.
She squeezed hard and forced him to gaze into her eyes. "Go on. Do
what I told you."

He focused on her, his world, and inhaled deeply. A breath out
and the ground became level beneath his feet, settling his stomach
along with it. Jacob gave her a reassuring nod. "All right."

They began to walk hand in hand, going slow, with no reason to
hurry. The sun was warm enough to make the sweat bead on his
forehead. Jacob swiped at his forehead and saw Charlotte doing the
same with a handkerchief. The color had intensified in her cheeks, as
if she'd been out for hours. He paused and gestured to a rock. "Would

you like to sit a moment? It looks as if the heat is getting to you."

She gratefully accepted his offer and they settled together. Jacob tipped his head back and closed his eyes. His recovery had been long and hard. Getting out again felt good. If only he could get back to his normal routine of the gunsmith shop and work on the house. A few hours in the morning with his father was about all he could take. Then, mentally wrung out, his head starting to throb, he'd be forced to go home and lie down. The house was out of the question. The only good thing to come out of the mess?

Charlotte was always waiting for him.

Her hand stroked his forehead between his brows. "You've got that line between your eyes again. Thinking too hard. What is troubling you on such a lovely day?"

He blew hard, a puff of air pushing his hair from his eyes. "I can't stand not being able to work on our house. I can't even pull my weight as a gunsmith. I'm such a sorry excuse for a man."

Charlotte drew herself up in indignation, her eyes flashing as her finger drove into his chest. "I'll not hear of anyone throwing insults at those I love. That includes you."

She reached out to stroke his hair, her hand becoming still at his temple as her fingers traced the ragged, raised scar that was an inescapable reminder of Jacob's run in with an angry mob. A symbol of the discontentment that lingered in the United States, proving they were not united. Not yet.

Charlotte's teeth pinned her bottom lip as she felt the raised ridge of skin and a tremble ran through her, traveling straight to his heart. "You may not realize it, but you are not invincible, Jacob Cooper. Twice the Revolution has gravely wounded you. Twice it has nearly stolen you away from me. I do not care if you are unable to stray from the Ross homestead, by my side, for the rest of your days. At least you will be alive and I will know that you are safe. I couldn't keep Benjamin safe. I will move heaven and earth to do so for you."

The tears, never far from the surface, began to spill. With only a

164

month and a half or so left of her pregnancy, Charlotte was in a heightened emotional state. Anything could set her off, taking her from joy's highest peaks and dashing her on the cliffs of sorrow. Jacob pulled her against his chest and began to rock her. Her heart hammered against his.

"Don't cry. The last thing I want to do is to upset you. I will try to be patient. It's a troublesome virtue for me."

Charlotte's laughter bubbled up as she swabbed at the tears on her face. Back to happiness again, an emotion she wore well and not nearly enough since losing Benjamin. "Don't I know it? I remember when you came to our house with your father when you were just a boy, maybe ten or so. Papa had a horse he was selling and your father wanted you to try it first because the stallion was meant to be yours. He said he wouldn't buy it unless you could handle it."

Jacob winced at the memory and began to chuckle. He reached back and rubbed at his backside. "My bottom still aches sometimes from all of those falls. That beast threw me at least ten times that day and I probably broke my tailbone and a few ribs, not to mention my pride."

Charlotte smiled and her voice dropped down, so soft and low it was like the gentle breeze that tugged at their clothes. "You never gave up. You kept getting back on that horse again and every time you became angrier, more impatient. You were filthy and bruised, your nose and mouth bleeding after you went face-first once or twice. You refused to stop or go home because by God, that horse was going to be yours and you would be its master."

Her hand trailed through the mess of copper curls that went every which way no matter how hard he tried to tame it into some semblance of order. "Perhaps it is because of this fiery head of hair that matches your temper."

Jacob tucked her under his arm as her hand traveled to his shoulder, working at muscles and joints that still ached, would always ache, but they didn't matter. Nothing mattered except her. "I did it.

The sun was dipping down below the horizon when I finally rode Devil—the only name a black demon like that could have—around your father's field. I was so sore the next day I couldn't even walk."

"Patience is still a problem for you, but I'm sure we'll have many years ahead of us to work on it. Do you feel up to some more walking now? If I sit here much longer, I won't be able to get up." Charlotte patted her protruding belly to emphasize her point.

Jacob stood and offered her his hand. As she stooped for her basket, he snatched it first. "I'll get that for you. It's the least I can do."

He held out his arm and she accepted, placing her fingers in the crook. They resumed their journey, Charlotte leading the way. Jacob didn't realize where she was steering him until he glanced up and could glimpse a clearing through the stretch of forest ahead of them. He planted his feet.

"I don't want to go to the house, Charlotte, not yet, not until I can take up my work again." He turned away, intent on going back.

Undeterred, she held fast and pulled him forward. "Oh, no you don't. It will be good to see it again. You haven't been here since you were hurt. That's been nearly a month."

Jacob set his shoulders and his jaw clenched. "It's just a reminder that it won't be ready for you to move in before the baby arrives. I don't want to see it."

"I do."

End of story. Seeing the crimson streaks in her cheeks and the gleam in her honey eyes, he knew better than to argue or there might be more crying. He had better sense than to upset a pregnant woman. Besides, if Jacob hated anything most in the world, it was seeing Charlotte cry.

Reluctantly, he allowed her to tow him along. His feet dragged every step of the way. What had been a great source of pride and pleasure was only a thorn digging into his side now. They probably wouldn't be able to move in until the end of summer, at a time when

Charlotte would have her hands full with a newborn. He couldn't bear the thought of heaping more work on her. The last thing she would want to do was establish a household and put her personal stamp on it while caring for the baby.

Twenty paces, give or take, and they reached the edge of the forest to emerge into what should have been a peaceful, quiet clearing. Nothing could be further from the truth. The house and surrounding area were abuzz with activity, and the bees were all Jacob's closest friends. Abraham and William pitched in their efforts alongside the younger set, carting supplies, splitting wood, and stacking logs.

Nicholas was first to catch sight of the couple and let out a whoop in greeting. "Look! The lovebirds are finally here."

His words sent a warm glow straight to Jacob's heart and made his stomach tighten in anticipation. The description fit. At some point, their relationship had changed, moving beyond companionship to something deeper. Jacob knew that they would never have the same bond Charlotte had shared with Benjamin, nor would he want to, but they had something equally as meaningful. They had a shared past. God willing, they'd share the future.

Before either Charlotte or Jacob could protest, they were raised up on the shoulders of the work crew which included Talmadge Edwards, Richard Dodge, John Little, and at least ten more members of the militia. Jacob nearly fell off his perch in the air when a mountain of a man stepped through the doorway of his house.

Tall. Broad of shoulder. Brawny. His mane of dark hair tangled by the wind, stubble covering his cheeks, his black eyes sharp as flint. The farmer who nearly split Jacob's head open like a ripe melon. Alexander Jones.

The group set the couple on the newly finished porch and Jacob's assailant extended his hand, callused and filled with splinters. Tough and prickly, like the man. "I'm here to make amends, Cooper. I was wrong, what I did to you that day. A madness descended upon all of us, trampling all sense of reason. I'm sorry that you fell victim to my fury, and unjustly so. I've done what I can here to make up for it." Pulling out a rusty grin from a man who did not smile often, he stepped aside and waved them into the cottage.

On the spur of the moment, Jacob picked Charlotte up and carried her over the threshold. He set her down quickly because the sight before him made him weak in the knees. The cottage was finished. All that remained were some finishing bits, the doors, and a woman's touch, such as the dishware and the linens. In the center of the room, a simple table and benches waited, carved from the same trees that formed his house. Two chairs flanked the fieldstone hearth. A bed stood in the corner.

Jacob could not find words.

Alexander ducked his head, his eyes cast down at the floor. "My father was a farmer first, a carpenter second. He said it was best that a man have two trades. I could say the same about you, a gunsmith and a soldier. You are also a peacekeeper. I hope you'll forgive me."

Charlotte was crying, clinging to Jacob, her smile beaming through her tears. Jacob held fast to her, sure he would unravel if he let go. Too much. It was too much to comprehend. All those he held dear, and a man who should have been his enemy, had labored countless hours to give him and his bride a gift beyond measure.

At Charlotte's prompting, Jacob stepped forward and held out his hand so that Jones could see it. "You're right about being a peacekeeper. I have had my fill of war for a lifetime. I do not want to hold a grudge against you. It is too wearisome and I can no longer be weighed down by such a burden on my heart. You have my forgiveness—and my gratitude." Jacob raised his voice. "That goes for all of you. You've done too much."

Alexander took him completely by surprise, wrapping Jacob in a bear hug. The giant of a man picked up Charlotte next, her peals of laughter ringing out as cheerful as bells, a pure, musical sound that Jacob could never get enough of. A round of handshakes went from there, friends clapping the proud owner on the back, kissing Charlotte on the cheek, making her blush deepen. She began to fan at her face, the heat getting the best of her as it so often did of late.

Nicholas and Richard took her by the arms and settled her in one of the chairs by the fireplace, making her laugh. "She's as pretty as one of those peaches we see from time to time in the market, Jacob. Charlotte wears motherhood well. You are a lucky man," Richard called out.

Nicholas gripped Jacob at the nape of the neck, his smile wide. "She's been coming to inspect here every other day or so while you were at the gunsmith shop with your father. A tough taskmaster if I do say myself." The outdoorsman gave him a wink and sought out a refill of his tankard of ale.

Jacob caught Charlotte's eye at his friend's loud declaration. The crimson streaks on her cheeks became more brilliant as her eyes skittered away. An amazing woman. He would thank God for the rest of his days for bringing them together, no matter what the circumstances.

A few steps closed the distance between them, and he bent to snatch a kiss. A cheer and applause was the response of the boisterous group enjoying a bubble of happiness for a change. Perhaps the clouds of war were finally parting, giving them a glimpse of a bright future shining through.

Amidst all the celebrating, Abraham did not speak. He simply hugged his son in a rib-bruising grip, making him breathless. William was equally enthusiastic. Soon, the singing began. Whiskey, ale, and cider made the rounds. Talmadge brought in a load of wood and set the fireplace to crackling, only adding to the festive spirit. Charlotte's basket was filled with baked goods, enough to give everyone a tasty morsel.

Abigail Andrews, her good friend and neighbor, brought linens, baby clothes, and other goods to make the house a home. As she wrapped Charlotte in her arms, her green eyes filled with love for her best friend. Jacob and his wife were blessed with good company.

Jacob was sitting by his wife's side, enjoying her fresh bread and a bit of cheese when Nicholas sat down beside him. Thanks to Anna's attentive ministrations, his marks had faded to the point that it was impossible to tell where the bear's claw marks left off and the scars from Saratoga began. There were still shadows in his eyes, remnants from his father's death. Jacob saw the same any time he looked at his own reflection. They would all bear their inner scars, but the gathering today was a symbol of hope for the future and the fact that they would go on.

Jacob handed a jug of whiskey and half of his meal to his good friend. "Thank you for all you did for me here. It is too much."

Nicholas took a long draw on the bottle before nudging Jacob's arm. "There is no such thing between friends. You saved me that day with the bear and again when I was out of my mind with grief after my father was killed. If I could have built the whole thing myself, I would have. Now it is time for you to enjoy the fruits of everyone's labor, including yours."

He stayed with them until the jug was empty and the food was gone before moving on to mingle with the others. As he walked away, Nicholas turned back to catch Jacob's eye and give him the gift of a genuine smile. A true friend indeed.

As the day wound to a close, Charlotte held fast to Jacob's hands. "Let's stay here tonight, Jacob, and christen our new home by sleeping in our new bed."

That sent up a wild cheer amongst those gathered together. Someone had the forethought to bring a mattress, sweet with the scent of cedar chips, and a quilt as housewarming gifts. Courtesy of Grannie Brown, God bless her, the dear woman from the market who had passed her grandson's militia uniform and Brown Bess to Benjamin before the Battle of Johnstown.

Jacob couldn't deny his wife. His heart grew light at the very idea of a night to themselves in the home that he had framed out with his own two hands. He could've been bothered that others had stepped in, but he accepted their efforts for what they were: a gift of love and affection. Because of such generosity of spirit, they would be settled in well before the baby came.

The couple stood in the doorway and waved farewell to their friends and family, shielding their eyes from a fiery sunset. Jacob gestured to the top step of the porch and helped Charlotte to sit. They remained there, her head on his shoulder as the sun went down and the moon illuminated the night, the stars shining more brightly than ever before.

"I feel as if I could catch a star and hold it in my hands," Charlotte marveled, her eyes filled with wonder, reflecting the sparkles that hung in the black canvas above.

Jacob turned to stare at her face and imprint it on his brain. Here. Right now. This moment. He did not want to ever forget because the instant she chose to stay here with him Charlotte Elizabeth Ross Cooper was truly his. "I already hold a star, right now, and she is the most glorious creature I have ever seen."

He cupped her cheeks in his palms, forming a cradle, and his thumb grazed her pulse as it beat frantically at the base of her jaw. "I love you, Charlotte. More than anything else on God's green earth. More than life itself. Everything I am. Everything I have. Everything you want. It is yours."

"You. You are the only thing I need, Jacob."

Her eyes slid closed, one tear slipping down her cheek. Jacob caught it with his fingertip and set his mouth to hers as gently as if she was the most fragile thing in existence. In truth, he believed she was. That she could shatter at his touch—and he along with her.

A sigh escaped her and she pressed her forehead to his chest. "Jacob, I do not know how I could have survived this troublesome time without you. When I lost Benjamin, something died inside of me. I never thought I'd find joy again or a reason to live. You have given that back to me, made me feel alive, made me look forward to a new day because you are in it. I can never thank you enough."

"There is no need to thank me. Having you in my home, by my side, in my heart. That is thanks enough."

He kissed her, a gentle kiss, to prove she was cherished. They turned and gazed up at the sky, listening to the wind sighing in the trees. The chirp of the crickets. The hoot of the owls, and the soft humming of the blood in their veins.

A burst of light streaked across the sky, heading down to earth. Charlotte lifted a hand and traced its path. "Look! A wishing star! What do you wish for?"

Jacob caught her hand and pressed her palm to his chest, to the steady beating of his heart. "For myself, I could not wish for anything more, but I do have one for you." His hands drifted to the great swelling of her belly and he bowed his head as if in benediction. "My wish, my prayer, is to see you safe and well as you bring a healthy, little one into a world that holds the promise of peace. Just think. You will bring a baby boy into the world in this house."

"A boy? How can you be so sure?" She chuckled softly as he kissed her belly, tickling her sensitive skin in the process.

"I'm absolutely certain of it. Benjamin Willson promised he would find you and he has, right here, growing inside of you." Her occupant chose that moment to shift from one side to the other, a marvel Jacob would never tire of seeing.

Her breath caught and her hands covered his, tears splashing down. "I love you, Jacob Cooper."

He looked up and swiftly pressed a kiss to her lips. "I have loved you since that distant day when I fell on the floor at your feet. My heart has been at your feet ever since."

Wonder sparked in her eyes, filled with moon glow. "Such a long time you have waited."

He drew her into his arms and set his chin on the top of her head. "You are worth the wait." A strong breeze blew, sending a shiver through her. "You're cold. Let's go in and sit by the hearth a while before going to sleep."

Hand in hand, they stepped into their living quarters. The fire continued to crackle, casting light and warmth in the small space. Jacob grabbed the blanket from the bed and set it on the floor as close to the blaze as they dared to take full advantage of its heat. He sat down, his back propped against a chair and reached up for Charlotte. Getting down was difficult for her as her body grew heavier and clumsier. Getting up would be harder, but she indulged him. Jacob nestled her in between his legs, his chest perfect for propping her head. His hand stroked her hair soothingly and in minutes, her body went loose.

His feelings for her grew strong as the rush of the river after the winter's snows melted away. He kissed the nest of her shining hair and blinked hard against the stinging in his eyes. It took a bit of finagling, but Jacob managed to scoop her up and set her in their bed. As he pulled the covers up around them, she turned and tucked herself in closer. "'Night, Love," she murmured. Words he never expected to hear from her, words he handed back.

Jacob would give those words back to her every night until there was no breath left in his body.

28 June, 1782

"WHOA, TEAM, WHOA!" JACOB PULLED HARD ON THE REINS, bringing the wagon to a standstill in front of the house. His house. Her house. Their house. The Cooper homestead.

His chest puffed up with pride and satisfaction with every load. This was the last. Over the last six weeks or so, they'd brought supplies, Charlotte's handiwork, William's gifts from town, and more from a steady stream of well-wishers. The small community of Johnstown had banded together to share in their happiness. Today, he brought his guns and the tools of his trade to do his work from their home. Charlotte's time was close. The baby would arrive any day now and he would not leave her alone, not during her labor or in the days that followed.

His bride was on her hands and knees in a small patch of ground where Jacob had turned up the soil for her herb garden. She'd brought plants from the Ross homestead, harvested others in the wild, and rounded out her assortment with offerings from the women in town. Charlotte said it gave her pleasure to help things grow and calmed her as her body became less her own with each passing day. Every morning, she watered, weeded, and dipped her hands in the dirt.

Today was no different, but her face was an alarming shade of red, her hair and dress damp with sweat as the sun beat down on her. She drew herself up on her knees, one hand pressed to her back, the other cupping her belly that nearly dipped to the ground. A grimace rippled across her face and she started to sway.

Jacob jumped down from the wagon and rushed to her side, taking her arm. "That's enough herb gardening for you today. It will keep. Get to your chair."

She didn't argue and that scared him. He picked her up and carried her to the rocker that sat in the shade on their tiny porch. William had brought the gift himself and Charlotte rested in it more and more each day.

As Jacob set her down, she slumped back, the heat of her body rolling off her in waves. He hurried to the stoneware pitcher in the kitchen and poured a large mug of water for her, pouring more on a cloth. He returned to her side and wiped her brow, her cheeks, her neck, and her shoulders. Jacob finished with her arms and wrists.

She let out a soft moan as he held the mug to her lips. Her hand drifted up to take it, but trembled so badly that he couldn't let go. Jacob squatted down beside her and cupped her cheek, his forehead creased in worry.

"You are overheated. You must be more careful, especially now, so close to your time. Imagine if you collapsed and I wasn't here. You could hurt yourself or the babe."

Charlotte nodded, her eyes drifting closed. "You're right. I'm so tired, Jacob, and my back aches so, like a throbbing toothache. I just want to lie down."

"Then that is what you should do. You have to listen to what your body is trying to tell you as it gets ready. Carrying another person around all the time must be the hardest work anyone could ever do."

Jacob offered her his hand. She smiled wearily up at him and slowly stood, moaning again as her fingers kneaded at her back. That was all he needed to hear, pushing him to lift her up again and carry her to their bed. He carefully laid her down. "Sleep now, Charlotte. The world won't stop turning while you do, I promise."

Reassured that she was settled and could be no harm to herself, Jacob set about emptying the wagon. Only when his Brown Bess and Kentucky long rifle were hanging on hooks over the hearth with his tools neatly stored away did he feel as if their home was finally complete. A glance outside set him at ease to see Powder and Bonnie in the field. A small barn and corral had been raised in only a matter of weeks, thanks to the teamwork of his best friends. So much accomplished in so short a time.

Unexpected and unwelcome, a wave of exhaustion washed over

him as he propped his arm on the stone hearth. The work, the heat, the anticipation, and the lingering annoyances from his head injury all conspired, making it difficult to stay on his feet. Jacob glanced at Charlotte and smiled gently. *When in Rome.* He stretched out beside her and laid his hand on her hip. A long, drawn-out sigh, and he tumbled into a deep slumber.

A fly was buzzing through the room, skimming over his face. Jacob's nose twitched and he brushed at it. As he did, his hand brushed against the other side of the bed. The empty side of the bed. His eyes shot open and he scanned the room. The rest of the house was empty too. He stood up too fast, something that wasn't wise, setting him on tilt. Jacob grabbed the bed and held on until the floor stopped heaving. His heart pounded erratically. The angle of the sun had changed and Charlotte was nowhere in sight. What could've happened to her?

Unable to get past the terrible imaginings that crowded his mind, he rushed outside to find her standing in the shade of a mighty oak tree, hanging clothes of all things. The blasted woman did not know how to rest! Jacob's fists clenched and the blood thundered in his ears as he contemplated how she had managed to get the tub of heavy, wet clothes out by the tree, not to mention accomplishing the chore of washing in the first place.

Her wheezing laughter drifted his way. What with the weight of the baby pressing against her stomach and lungs, it was difficult for her to draw a full breath. "You're red as the devil, Jacob. Calm yourself before your head explodes. I didn't carry this out here. Papa was here while you were napping."

The tension eased up. He even managed a smile, joining her to help finish the job. As she continued to bend down and rise again, Jacob found himself mesmerized by the fullness in her face, the blush on her cheeks, and the roundness of her body.

Charlotte stopped and placed her hands on her hips. "Just what are you staring at?"

"I've never seen anyone so beautiful as a mother-to-be." He stepped in and cupped the back of her head, catching her in a kiss.

She swatted at his chest playfully. "The heat has obviously made you go out of your mind. Are you plagued by another attack of the vertigo, playing tricks on your senses?"

He could only grin at her. "The only thing clouding my mind is you."

They hung the last items together. Charlotte leaned back, both hands pressed to the small of her back. Bow much further and Jacob feared it would snap. He formed a fist with his hand and began to knead the base of her spine until a groan rose from her toes and she leaned back against him. "You do not know how good that feels. It aches like the dickens, all of the time now."

Jacob kissed her cheek, the side of her neck, and finally stopped at her collarbone, watching her blush prettily the more that he touched her. "You need to get off your feet. You do too much." He led her back to her rocker and set her to rocking before going out to take care of his chores in the barn. All the while, his mind was with his bride.

The sun was touching the horizon, marking the close to a long day, when Jacob walked out of the barn. Charlotte rocked back and forth in her chair, both hands circling round and round her belly. Every now and then, she'd stop and stare, as if in intense concentration, only to start rubbing again.

He rested a hand on the arm of the chair to stop her motion, staring down with questions in his eyes. She answered him with a tired smile. "Soon, but not yet."

Jacob understood. He kissed the top of her head and went back to work, chopping wood for their fireplace. Although the days were warm, the nights were cool, not to mention there was cooking to do. He felt a new sense of urgency when tackling every task. Soon. The baby would be coming soon and the thought terrified him. Jacob knew nothing about delivering babies, but he would soon find out.

He swiped a sleeve across his forehead and felt her eyes on him.

177

Jacob turned back and froze, transfixed. By her smile. By the tilt of her head. By the curl against her cheek in the fiery glow of sunset. His feet carried him to her side. His knees went down. His head rested on her lap. "I am so blessed to have you."

Her fingers threaded through his hair. "The blessings are mine." They sat there until the stars came out, finally going inside hand and hand. No little one made an appearance that night, a brief respite, but the anticipation was building.

Charlotte sighed, her hand clasped in his. They'd moved to the steps to sit side by side. Jacob didn't care if they never stood up. "You chose well for our home. It is a lovely view here."

"Yes, it is," he whispered softly, his gaze unwavering from her face. She was the only view that mattered to him. His lips brushed her fingers, calloused from the hard work that a woman endured day in and day out. "The fourth of July is nearly here. Dance with me in celebration of all the gifts we share."

Her eyes became bright with unshed tears as she smiled and stood up with a clumsy curtsy. There had not been much occasion for dancing and this would be a first for them as a couple. Jacob led her on to the tall grasses, surrounded by wildflowers, the scent of the nearby pines filling their lungs. Nothing could be sweeter than this moment. As he swayed with his love, the stars shone bright above. A beacon. For their future.

3 July, 1782

SHE COULD BARELY MOVE. EVERYTHING WAS
SWOLLEN. HER FINGERS. HER ANKLES. HER FEET. So heavy
and ungainly that the smallest task was a struggle. Jacob did not stray
far from her side, on hand in case she needed him. At the moment, her
needs were few. Charlotte spent most of her time in her rocker,
sewing garments for the baby or nodding off. She was so tired—and
fretful.

"I am useless. I am so sick of sitting in this chair! I should be
doing chores and cooking dinner!"

She crossed her arms with a huff. Even that simple act proved to
be a challenge. Her belly bulged out so far now that there was no sight
of her toes and she had to prop her arms on the swollen mound. Her
eyes glittered dangerously, her cheeks streaked with crimson. Jacob
had to tread lightly. Beware a woman on the brink of giving birth.

He hooked her at the nape of her neck and started to work at
muscles gone tight. The line between her eyes, etched deep with her
irritation, faded. She let out a sigh and her mouth turned up in a smile.
"That's better."

Jacob bent over and tipped her face to his to drop a kiss on her
lips. "There's nothing for you to do. I've hung the wash. The stew is
bubbling on the hearth. It may not be as tasty as yours, but it's not
likely to kill us. Grannie Brown dropped off that crusty bread we love
so much and a jug of cider. I know you can't stand it, but you need to
take some of your own advice. It's your turn to rest and let me take
care of you. Lord knows you do more than enough for me."

Charlotte covered his hand with her own and gave it a squeeze,
her expression softening. "I would do so again without complaint.
Thank you for being so good to me, Jacob. I don't know how you put
up with me."

His hands cupped her face, forcing her to focus on him. "It has

179

always been and always will be my greatest pleasure." He bent to kiss her again and felt her body go tight. Jacob pulled back. "What's wrong?"

She waved off his concern. "Just a muscle spasm. Carrying around this boulder is quite a strain on a body. Do you think . . . ." Her breath came out in a rush as a ripple of pain crossed over her face. "I want to lie down for a spell. Do you think you could help me to the bed?"

"Of course." Stamping down his fears, he wrapped an arm around her waist and helped her to her feet. She groaned with the effort. Her poor, swollen feet pained her and walking was a struggle. Jacob guided her to the bed, pulled back the covers, and helped her to stretch out. He took her hand. "Is there anything else that I can get for you?"

Charlotte patted his cheek. "Stop worrying so. I can see it in the shadows in your eyes. I'm just tired. A little nap and I'll sit and eat with you."

One more kiss and her eyes drifted shut. Her body went slack, sleep pulling her under faster than he would have thought possible.

Jacob paced through their cottage, at odds with himself. He felt trapped in a waiting game, the tension mounting, ready to snap in an instant. When? When would her time come? As darkness fell and she continued to sleep, he dished out a bowl of stew, but had no appetite for it. He pushed it aside and sat in a chair by the fireplace, head in his hands, waiting for something to happen.

A soft cry pulled him to his feet and to her bedside, his heart fluttering madly. Her hands were gripping the blankets, her knuckles white, her face twisted in pain. "Charlotte, is it time?"

He stroked her hair from her face. She looked up at him, pain darkening her eyes. A hard exhalation and she nodded. "I think—it's begun. The pains—they woke me up some time ago. They come in waves—like that time before but much harder—stronger." Her words were cut off by a gasp. "Dear God, help me!"

"I'm not God, but I will do what I can and leave the rest in His hands." Jacob continued to run his fingers through her hair, murmuring softly, gentling her. Slowly, her tension eased and she let out a sigh.

He sat by her side, holding her hand. Ticking off the space between her pains. They began at ten minutes or so apart. As the night wore on and the hours passed, they shortened to five minutes apart with no signs of stopping this time. No false alarm, they only became more fierce.

"Jacob, I want to get out of bed—to walk. Help me, please." She reached for him, her eyes heavy with the pain and fatigue, her face drawn.

He obliged her wishes, giving her a strong arm around her waist as they began to pace the length of the room. Each time a pain hit, hectic bursts of color exploded in her cheeks, her breath became strangled, and she nearly doubled over. As soon as the contraction ended, her face went white. She trembled in his arms.

"I'm so tired, Jacob." Charlotte was exhausted, on the verge of crying.

"Come back to bed and try to rest a bit," he told her, his voice hoarse with fatigue.

Watching the woman he loved go through such a trial was the hardest thing Jacob had endured in his life. The sun burst over the horizon, light painting the walls and illuminating her face. As Charlotte squeezed her eyes shut, her jaw tightened, and she gave a nod in surrender. He installed her back in bed where she turned on her side and closed her eyes. She drifted off to sleep, weariness winning until another pain slammed into her, tightening its fist. Two minutes apart now.

"I think . . . ." Her voice was reedy, her breath faint. "I think—it will soon be time to push." Her face scrunched up and she groaned as another pain hit. "My back—there is such a pounding in my back."

Jacob joined her on the bed and pressed his fist at the base of her spine. Her whole body went tight and then relaxed as the pain eased up. She held out her hand and he took it, marveling at her strength as her fingers clasped his tight enough to grind his bones to powder. She was strong. Steel strong, stronger than men or the iron forged in her father's smithy, stronger than the guns that had been made by his own hands.

He bent down and kissed her cheek. "What can I do for you?" Damn the catch in his voice!

"Help—help me to sit up. I feel—Something is happening! Oh Lord, I must push!" Her whole face went red and she grunted, her body gone rigid with the effort and her breath came out in a rush.

Jacob sprang into action. He had spoken with Grannie Brown and a few of the women in town for advice at this pivotal moment in their lives. He began by stripping the blankets off Charlotte and propping her back up with pillows to give her desperately needed support. Next, to gather supplies with hands that shook. Clean cloths, a basin of boiling water, scissors, a soft blanket for the moment the little one came. Last, in a moment of inspiration, he tore off two rags and tied them to the bed, placing them in her hands.

"Here now. Hold these whenever you need to push and don't forget to breathe!"

She gave him a ghost of a smile, her hair damp with perspiration when her face went white. "Oh Lord! Here comes another!"

Again, she pushed, the color rising up to her hairline, only to fade away, leaving her white as her sheets as her body slumped against the pillows. The knots in Jacob's stomach tightened. How much longer? How much more could she take and how did women survive this?

Charlotte's mother didn't. He viciously shoved that thought to the back of his mind and stationed himself at the foot of the bed. Jacob threw back her nightgown and shook his head. No sign of the baby yet. Again, her body went tight and with a scream that rang in his ears, she pushed. Still nothing. What if something was wrong? He could not leave her, could not even go for help.

Stamping on his fears, he swiped at his forehead and smiled at her. "Hold on. Try and rest in between. Save your strength."

Easier said than done. Her pains were a minute apart now, lasting a minute at a time. Giving her hardly a moment to breathe. Wave after wave rolled in until she was crying and he could do nothing, except wipe the sweat from her brow. Hold a cup of water to her lips to wet a mouth and throat gone dry. Resume his post and pray something would happen.

4 July, 1782

HIS WHOLE BODY WAS WOUND TIGHT, intent on her progress when he caught a glimpse of something dark between her legs. Voice gone hoarse with a throat worn raw, it was a strain to be heard. "Now, Charlotte! Push! Push with all your might!"

God love her, she did as he asked. With a valiant effort, like a soldier going to battle, she gritted her teeth together, grabbed hold of the rags tied to the headboard, and pushed. The material tore with the strain and there was a gush of fluid between her legs. Jacob was at the ready, his hands catching the warm, wriggling life that had been inside her all this time. Covered in Lord knows what, red as the tomatoes in the market, and one of the most beautiful sights he'd ever laid eyes on—except for one. Charlotte, her smile lighting up the room brighter than the sun as a loud wail filled the house.

With hands that were trembling uncontrollably, Jacob managed to snip the umbilical cord with the scissors and swaddle the baby in the blanket. A quick glance down and he confirmed what had been suspected all along in his mind. "What do you want to call your son?"

He placed the baby in her arms, striving to give her a wobbly smile. At any moment, he would be flat on the floor, but a mother and baby had to be tended to first. There would be time and enough for his needs.

Charlotte tucked her wee one against her breast and he began to suckle hungrily, a strong, little man if ever there was one. Her smile cracked and faded away as she began to cry. "Benjamin."

Bathed in light, steeped in hope, tangled with sorrow. Jacob laid a hand on her head and her son's. "Benjamin Willson Cooper, welcome to the world. I will protect you, care for you, and love you until the day that I die."

Blinded by a river of tears, the new mother reached out and her hand fumbled for his. He kissed every finger, the love rising in his

184

heart, threatening to drown him. "You have my promise to do the same for you, Charlotte. I know that I can never replace Benjamin, nor would I try. I know you may never come to love me in the same way, although you care for me deeply. Know that my love is strong enough for the both of us."

The room became flooded with light, the sun's rays intensifying. Warm air brushed against Jacob's body, made Charlotte's hair flutter, and the baby's blanket shifted, yet no window was open. "Go with God, Benjamin," she whispered raggedly. In an instant, it was gone.

Jacob's knees gave and he sat down by her side, leaning his head against her knuckles. At a touch, he could shatter. A knock sounded at the door and he came up quickly, swabbing at his face with his sleeve.

"Good morning to My Blessings," William shouted from their doorstep. Jacob hurried to lift the bar across the door and let in his father-in-law, shielding his eyes from the full blast of daylight that met him.

William stepped in, hands full with wild flowers and a basket of food. He set them down quickly and grabbed hold of Jacob in a hearty hug. "It is the fourth of July, a day that must not be forgotten. We are the United States of America because of it!" He stepped back and his eyes widened in alarm. "My son, you are covered in blood! Whatever has happened?"

Jacob gestured to the bed. "Your grandson decided to make his appearance on this most memorable of days." Exhaustion forced him to lean against the door before his body gave out. "Go ahead. Make your acquaintances."

Charlotte continued to feed her little one, the sun bringing out the gold in her hair, her cheek blushing prettily as her father bent over her to kiss her forehead first, then the baby's. Jacob's eyes began to burn. *Beautiful.* He'd never seen anything so beautiful in his life.

"What a fine, handsome lad. It is no wonder, with a mother like you." William's tears began to fall, splashing down on Charlotte and the baby, making the wee one's face scrunch up. Father and daughter

185

laughed softly until she moaned, pressing a hand to her stomach.

Jacob stepped forward, worry never far from the surface threatening to choke him, but he spoke lightly. "She must pass the afterbirth. William, will you take the baby so I can take care of her?"

His father-in-law willingly gathered the tiny bundle into his arms, cooing softly, beaming with pride. He'd had a great deal of experience what with raising Charlotte after losing his wife in childbirth. Time had not made him forget what to do.

Thankful he could concentrate on the new mother, Jacob took her hands in his. "Your womb is trying to pass the afterbirth. Let me try and help you."

At her nod, he rested his hands on her distended belly and began to massage at the swelling. She moaned softly, her body still wracked with pain after her labor. Jacob clamped his jaw shut and continued to gently knead her swollen abdomen, blinking hard to fight the stinging in his eyes. There was no term more fitting than labor for what this woman had endured for so many long hours. A grunt, a loosening of her body, and a large, bloody sac attached to the other end of the umbilical cord was released from Charlotte's body. She sagged back in relief, her eyes drooping shut.

"There. Your work is done," Jacob murmured softly, smiling even as his body began to shake from the letdown—until the blood began to gush between her legs. "Dear God, no!" He whispered and grabbed hold of a pile of clean rags at the side of the bed. He packed them between her legs and applied pressure.

Charlotte's eyes flew open and she cried out, reaching weakly for him. "No, please stop, Jacob. It hurts so!"

Grimly, he pulled the wad of cloth away. Sopping wet with blood without a bit of white to be seen. "I'm sorry, but there's some bleeding. Do not worry yourself. I just need to make it stop." *Dear God, help me make it stop!*

The color faded from her face and her eyes slid shut again as the blood continued to pump out of her body. William stood from his chair by the fire, gone rigid with fear. "No. Dear God, not again. Not My Blessing!" He began to pray, his words a soft litany.

Jacob focused on one thing and one thing alone. Saving Charlotte. What a fragile life he held in his hands. He grabbed rag after rag, continued to pack it between her legs, to press hard. She did not move, did not make a sound. The pulse fluttering at her neck slowed. Fading. She was fading away from him.

"Please God. Help me."

He pulled more, drenched cloths away, his hands as red as if he'd painted them with blood. Too much blood. Jacob grabbed the last of the rags he had, all the while searching about the room. He used the blanket next. He pushed it between her legs, closing his eyes as his hand traveled into the loose, warm birth canal, slick with bleeding. A place his hand did not belong, but Jacob would do anything, anything in his power to help her.

His hand remained in place, pressing hard, a soft pulsing beating against his fist. Precious minutes ticked away until it stopped. The whole room was hushed, the only noise his ragged breathing and the quiet suckling of the baby on his grandfather's finger. Slowly, Jacob opened his eyes, fearful of what he would see.

Charlotte's chest continued a slow, gentle rise and fall as she fell into a deep slumber. Jacob pulled his hand out of the damp warmth of her body to find that the bloody flow had stopped. His face crumpled and he dropped to his knees, weeping shaking him to the core. Gasp after gasp, taking in gulps of air, it still felt as if his lungs could not be filled. So close. He'd come so close to losing her. To losing his world.

A sturdy hand squeezed his shoulder. "God bless you, Jacob."

William kissed the crown of his head, unable to say anything more. His father-in-law set his grandson in the cradle he'd made as a gift for the little family and went about the task of straightening up the cottage, allowing Jacob time.

To fall apart.

Ever since the Battle of Johnstown, even before then if Jacob was honest with himself, he'd been like a rope that was frayed. Benjamin's birth and the prospect of losing Charlotte were enough to make it snap. He rested his head on the foot of the bed and unleashed the storm of emotions that had been pent up inside of him for too long.

"Jacob." Her voice was soft as the lightest breeze on a summer morning, her touch that of a butterfly's wings. Tentatively, her hand reached him, her fingers trailing through his hair.

He choked down a sob and rushed to Charlotte's side, grabbing hold of her hand, lacing his fingers with hers so hard she winced, but offered him the sweetest smile. "I was so afraid of losing you, that once the baby arrived you would feel as if you had no reason to stay."

Her hand drifted to his cheek. Jacob pressed his face into her palm. There was no place he'd rather be, nothing more life had to offer him. "I very nearly did slip away," she whispered. Her eyes grew distant. Had she glimpsed the other side? "I knew that Benjamin was waiting for me, so close. If I reached out, he would lead me home. I knew it in my soul, but I heard my father. How could I leave him and cause him such sorrow? I thought of my little Benjamin and couldn't bear to leave him without a mother." She paused, turned her honey gaze on Jacob. "I thought of you."

The crack in his heart grew wider and he bowed his head to shield her from the force of his feelings. Her finger moved to his chin, pressing lightly. She did not have strength to do more, but her slightest touch was enough to lay him flat at her feet. He met her eyes and could not look away.

"I heard you. Felt your strong, capable hands on my body, keeping liberty's promise with your will alone. I came back for you."

He dropped down by her side and buried his head against her. He couldn't have held back his sobs if his life depended upon it. Charlotte's fingers threaded through his hair, keeping his soul tethered with hers.

Where it belonged.

~

SHE MIGHT AS WELL HAVE BEEN MADE FROM SPUN GLASS. Jacob treated Charlotte like something fragile enough to shatter at his touch. He carried her to the privy and back, from her bed to her rocking chair. Cleaned, cooked, and tended to the animals. He even helped in caring for Benjamin, changing him when his clothing was soiled, bathing him with great care in a basin of warm water, so afraid that he would break.

"You're doing just fine, Jacob. He's not as delicate as you think," Charlotte told him softly from her bed, following all of the proceedings, upset that she could not do it herself. Not yet. Her strength had not returned and she was as weak as a kitten.

Jacob watched her like a hawk as a parade of women visited from town, the latest being Grannie Brown. He met her at the door and kissed her cheek as she tilted her flushed face his way. She waved a handkerchief and dabbed at her damp brow, waiting patiently. Reluctantly, he ushered her inside. The good woman was the third that morning and Charlotte was beginning to fade.

"Oh, my, but it is a cooker of a day out there, an absolute cooker. I feel as if I have just walked off the surface of the sun after the walk from town." She smiled and patted Jacob's arm. "Now, now, young one, do not fret so. I know sweet Charlotte is plumb worn out. I'll only visit a few minutes." Impulsively, she leaned in and gave him a hug, her eyes bright. "I heard how you saved her life. God bless you, Jacob."

He didn't have the heart to be aggravated with her as she bustled over to Charlotte's side and fussed over the new mother. "My child, just look at you! Absolutely glowing! I do not think I have ever seen you look more lovely." The elderly woman kissed her brow, her face softening as she gazed at the infant nestled against Charlotte's chest. "May I hold your precious one?"

Charlotte nodded and lifted him up. It pained Jacob to see how her arms trembled at the strain. Grannie Brown tucked the baby against her ample chest and began to rock with the expertise born of years of experience, first with her children, then her grandchildren, and many members of the community in between.

She sank down in the chair at the side of the bed with a contented sigh. "What a fine young man." Her penetrating gaze swept over Benjamin's face before focusing on Charlotte. "I see you in him—and I see your Patriot too. In his eyes. In his dark cap of hair. Your Benjamin lives in your little one."

Charlotte's eyes widened in alarm and Jacob's breath came out in a rush, as if he'd been punched in the gut. His legs wobbled and he pressed his back against the door for support. No one knew about the depth of her relationship with Benjamin Willson except William and Jacob.

Grannie took her hand. "I see better than most, child. I knew about the bond between you two, saw it instantly that day I met him in the market for the first time. I know that you grieve, Charlotte, but you must remember something."

She leaned in closer, staring at the young mother with an intensity that could not be ignored. "I know that you grieve as so many of us do. I understood you better than most. My Nathanial sleeps in that cemetery with your beloved." Her voice became thick with tears and the old woman bowed her head. She swabbed her eyes with her handkerchief and cleared her throat, forcing herself to go on.

"My grandson is gone, only a memory, but you have this precious one." Grannie Brown kissed Benjamin's fine swirl of hair. She lifted her head and looked across the room at Jacob. "And you have your gunsmith, a man whose love for you is as deep as the mighty Atlantic. You must promise me that you will not let yesterday darken today or your tomorrows. Hold on tight to all of your blessings right now."

Charlotte's hand tightened around the matronly woman who was like a grandmother to all of them, the tears that were never far from the surface spilling over once again. "I promise," she whispered.

She reached out to embrace their kindly neighbor, sagging back against her pillow. Completely drained by the effort, her face lost all its color. All the visiting was simply too much for her.

Jacob stepped forward, intent on sending Grannie Brown on her way as politely as possible. He needn't have worried. She handed the sleeping infant to him and gave him a warm smile. "Don't get yourself all flustered, Jacob. I can see how anxious you are about your bride. I'll show myself out now. If there's anything you two need, anything at all, you be sure to send word my way."

She rose up on tiptoe to give him a peck on the cheek before turning back to Charlotte, placing a work-roughened palm gently against her fair skin. "I must go now. Your Jacob is simply beside himself, and with good reason. When you are recovered, I expect all of you to come for a visit. I will cook dinner, including the best apple cobbler you have ever had. You rest now."

A nod of her head and Grannie Brown left without fanfare, the same way that she came in. Jacob dropped the bar over the door and pressed his back against it. No one else would disturb Charlotte if he had to take down his Brown Bess to frighten them off.

"Jacob, you're being impossibly rude." Her disapproval was clear in the way her lips turned down and her forehead creased. He didn't care.

He crossed the room in great strides and stood at her side, gazing down at her head tipped to the baby as Benjamin suckled hungrily. Awakened by the commotion, the voracious child could not get enough. Sometimes Jacob feared he would drain his mother dry.

Charlotte gazed at him and shook her head. "You look as if you are about to erupt. The top of your head is going to blow off at any instant."

Jacob placed his hands on his hips and breathed out hard through his nose. "You nearly died, Charlotte. You may not take that fact seriously, but I do. I am the one who desperately struggled to keep you here with me. You almost slipped through my hands. I think that gives me just cause to send people away when you have had enough—and you have had enough today."

His voice grew soft. He didn't like the look of her, her skin white as paper, the lines of weariness etched deep around her eyes and her mouth. What little strength Charlotte had was waning quickly, draining her dry. Any moment and she would drift away, forcing Jacob to remain at her side until she woke. An irrational part of him feared she would go to sleep one day and never come back to him.

Benjamin had nodded off at her breast. Gently, Jacob gathered him up and laid him in the wooden cradle by the bed. The little one didn't even stir. God bless him but he was a good baby, spending the majority of his time eating and sleeping. He rarely fussed.

Charlotte's hand rested lightly on Jacob's arm, making him wince. She was much too weak. "I am so very tired. All the time. Why am I so tired?"

He bent over her and kissed her brow. "You lost a great deal of blood. Your body needs time to restore itself and heal. You must listen to what it is trying to tell you. If it calls for rest, that is what you need to do."

She nodded and her eyes slid shut for a moment, opened again to focus on him. "Lie down with me. You are tired too. You've been doing so much and haven't stopped for a minute since Benjamin was born."

All too true. At her words, Jacob suddenly felt as if a sack of stones had been tossed on his shoulders and they were driving him into the ground. He squeezed her hand. "Perhaps—perhaps I could, just for a little while."

He climbed over her and stretched out with a groan. Everything ached and nothing wanted to move. Lifting his hand to rest it on her hip was a challenge. She turned to him and did the same.

"Jacob?" She whispered. He nodded in acknowledgment. "You

can stop worrying so. I know I scared you terribly and I am sorry I put you through such a trial. I'm not going anywhere."

He moved in closer and grazed her lips with a kiss. "Neither am I," he said with a catch in his voice.

She pulled at him, tugged at his heart, every minute of the day. During his waking and his sleeping hours, Charlotte was the spark that burned inside of him. Gave him a reason to draw breath. To dream. To believe in a better world. As he felt her sink into him and her body went loose, he wasn't far behind.

In the quiet of their house, bathed in sunshine on a warm summer's day, Jacob felt as if his heart had finally made its way home. Charlotte's was there as well. She had found her way. Together, they could finally bind the wounds of war and look ahead to whatever life may have in store for them. For the nation.

28 August, 1782

THE DAY WAS FINE, THE SUN SHINING OVERHEAD, the breeze a gentle caress that kept the heat from being unbearable. Standing at the wood pile, gazing out at the surrounding forest that closed in around their cottage, Jacob inhaled deeply. Smelled autumn, saw a few leaves dusted with gold, orange, red. A medley of colors, like Charlotte's hair. Yes, the cool, crisp days would soon arrive and he welcomed them. Soon enough, winter would come and they'd be wrapped up in the Cooper homestead. Snug. Warm. Together.

He'd become selfish. Jacob didn't want to share Charlotte and Benjamin with the rest of the world. In the seven weeks or so since the babe's birth, it had been a marvel to watch his transformation. He was growing like the weeds that sprouted in his mother's herb garden. Charlotte would carry him out in a large basket, another gift from Grannie Brown who had been a regular visitor, and set him nearby while she did her chores. Whether she was hanging clothes, tending her garden, or taking care of the animals, her little Benjamin was never far. He'd planted seeds of love in all their hearts, seeds that sprouted, flourished, and bloomed, spreading everywhere his smile or tiny fingers touched.

Right now, the baby was in his mother's arms, in the rocker on the porch. The day was too pleasant to be wasted indoors. Unable to concentrate on his latest project, another rifle that was sure to be a sensation, Jacob had come outside to chop wood. Mesmerized by the sight of his wife and adopted son, he didn't even notice that she was staring at him intently.

"That wood isn't going to split itself, you know. I would like to cook dinner tonight." Her voice drifted on the air, forcing him to snap to attention.

Jacob gave her a sheepish grin and took up the ax again. With a mighty swing, he brought it down, splitting the large log into two, manageable pieces. He fell into a steady rhythm, log after log, until the pile began to mount beside him. Feeling the intense sun beating down on his shoulders, he peeled off his shirt and continued, swiping at the sweat on his brow as it ran in rivulets down his face. Something—the slightest cry, a movement—made him look up, become transfixed.

Charlotte had set the baby in the basket by her side. Her hands gripped the rocker, so hard he could see every knuckle defined. Her whole body was tight, her gaze focused on him alone. A flush had traveled from her chest to her cheeks and her eyes glittered like gemstones. Jacob imagined the pulse at the base of her neck was beating wildly, so hard and fast that he wanted to close the gap between them and place his thumb there. His lips there. Take her in his arms and never let her go.

Finding it hard to breathe, to resist temptation, he tore his gaze away. Resumed his work. Chopped fast and furious before he couldn't stop himself from ravaging her. It was a losing battle.

"Jacob." It was a whisper, only a few feet away, but might as well have been a shout, the way the sound of Charlotte's voice stopped his heart. He dropped the ax and her hands were on his shoulders, her face pressed to his back. "I want you."

Three, simple words. Words he never expected to hear. Slowly, he pivoted and gathered her into his arms, his mouth coming down to claim hers. The world began to spin and time stopped. There was only this woman. This instant. Right now. Give him time to come up for air and he would lay her down on a carpet of wood chips. Inside or out, Jacob had to have her.

"Good afternoon, My Blessings!" William's voice carried from a distance as he approached on Raven. He grinned knowingly as Jacob pulled away, breathing hard, squashing a groan of frustration. He loved his father-in-law. It was simply a matter of poor timing.

Charlotte slid Jacob a smile, tucked at a strand of hair that had come down when his hand became embedded in her curls, and

195

approached her father. "Papa! What a pleasant surprise. What brings you?"

He dismounted smoothly, handing the reins to Jacob. The blacksmith stepped forward and gathered her into his arms. "I missed you. After twenty-three years under my roof, it seems quite empty. I thought I'd pay you a visit." His gaze traveled between the two, a grin tugging at his lips. "I have a gift for you two as well. After you put Raven in the barn, I'll tell you all about it."

Charlotte took his hand and led her father to the porch where he fawned over his grandson. The man was head over heels for the little one. Charlotte gestured to the bench beside the rockers. Jacob had expanded their porch so that they could enjoy it as a family. By the time he settled Raven in a stall and hastily pulled on his shirt, his father-in-law was indulging in a tankard of Grannie Brown's cider, the talk of the town.

Jacob joined them, accepting a mug of his own, and clapped William on the back. "It's a hot day. The temperatures are rising. You've got to take care not to spend too much time out in the sun."

William waved him off. "I'm not that old and feeble yet, son." He glanced in the basket by Charlotte's feet. "Let me get my hands on that big, brawny boy of yours."

She carefully scooped the baby up. An expert in such a short period of time, she knew exactly how to pick him up without disturbing him. When Benjamin was restless, no one could put him at ease like Charlotte. She was a gifted mother. The realization pained Jacob to think she had never known the touch of her mother except for one brief instant as she held her little girl—and then bled to death before her father's eyes.

Jacob shook off his grim turn of thought and focused on the moment. He took a deep swallow of his cider and let out a great sigh. "This is a bit of heaven on earth."

William rocked the baby, his gaze fixed on Benjamin. "Yes, it is." He cleared his throat. When he looked up, there was a sheen of tears that made his eyes shine brilliantly. "Such gifts you have been given, that you share with me. That's why I have one for you. I want you two to take the afternoon to go where you would like and do what you would. Neither one of you has been away from this place since weeks before Benjamin's birth. Go enjoy this day that God has given you."

Charlotte's forehead creased in doubt, her arms wrapped around her middle. "Papa, are you sure about that? I would not want to burden you."

He smiled gently and reached out to pat her arm. "You could never burden me, Charlotte. I will give anything I have to give for you, Jacob, and my grandson. If you recall, I have had some experience with babies. You pack yourself a basket and take a walk. Take some time to yourselves."

Her eyes darted from the baby to Jacob and he became trapped in her gaze. Time alone. With Charlotte. Now, as the tidal wave of her affections threatened to sweep him away. He wanted nothing more. The blood thundered in his ears, the heat flooding through his body. Jacob thought he would burst into flames. Could William hear his heart pounding?

She nodded almost imperceptibly. "I'll be only a minute." Charlotte went inside, the door swinging shut behind her. Jacob turned and gripped the railing, inhaling deeply through his nose. *Hold on. Only a few minutes more. Hold on!*

"You are strung so tight you are about to snap in two, Jacob. Breathe. Remember. She is yours." William's voice was warm with barely contained laughter.

Charlotte stepped outside, a basket on her arm. She went to her father and kissed him lightly, lingering over the baby. William touched her cheek and murmured softly, "I will tend to your son, My Blessing. It is time that you tended to Jacob."

She squeezed his hand and stepped away. Jacob hugged his father-in-law in thanks, grazing Benjamin's shining cap of hair with a kiss. His heart swelled. How he loved this child. It did not matter that Jacob did not plant the seed. He would help Benjamin to grow to his full potential, to ensure that this boy would be all that he could possibly be.

Charlotte waited at the steps, her hand extended to Jacob's. He took it and they began to walk. He had to give her credit. She didn't look back. Her fingers threaded through his and gave a tug.

Jacob let her lead the way. Into the woods. Up a small incline. Down below to a meadow exploding with lush grasses, wildflowers, butterflies and bees. A veritable paradise on earth. They'd stumbled upon the small patch of wonder one day on a walk with Benjamin.

Today there was only the woman by his side. His hand floated on the air with a will of its own, traveled to her cap, and slid it from her hair. Jacob closed his fist around it, pressed it to his nose, breathed in the scent of her soap. Honey. Lavender. Sunshine. Jacob tucked the slip of material in his pocket and went for the pins next, slipping them all from the heavy strands of her hair and letting it fall down in full waves. To her shoulders, down her back, to the dip at her waist. A river of gold

Unable to wait another minute, he took the basket from her hand, wrapped Charlotte in his arms, and sank to a carpet of greenery on the ground. They were surrounded by the tall strands of wild grass waving in the wind, a banner of blue unfurling overhead. Jacob raised up on both arms, bracing them by her head, and pressed his lips to hers. He gave himself to the kiss and tried to take his fill of her. Realized he could never get enough of this woman. He'd waited. So long. An eternity. Most of his life. Jacob bowed his head as a groan rose from his gut. The wanting was fast becoming a need he could not resist.

"Jacob, you don't have to wait anymore. You don't have to suffer. I want to share myself with you." Charlotte took his face in her hands and he saw nothing but truth and trust in her eyes. No fear. No regret. No pain. Only promises. "It's time."

He laid down beside her, his chest heaving. She rested a palm on his hammering heart as he threw an arm over his eyes. "Are you sure, truly sure? I will not take advantage of you or force you to do anything you do not want to do. I know how you felt about Benjamin. I am but a candle compared to that bonfire."

Her finger touched his lip, effectively silencing him. "Enough. It is true that I what I had with Benjamin was like a wildfire, uncontrollable, raging through my life. He consumed me and his death reduced me to ashes." Her eyes filled with tears and Jacob cursed himself for causing her pain. She paused a moment and composed herself. "You are my hearth fire, steady, warm, and safe. Right now, I need a hearth fire. I need you."

His hand covered hers. He could feel Charlotte quaking, a leaf tossed by life's storms. His voice was hushed. "You're certain? Once we cross this line, we can never go back. Things will be irrevocably changed."

She raised her chin, her jaw set. He saw the fire of determination in her eyes. God, what was there not to love about this woman? "You kept liberty's promise for all of us. It's time I did the same for you. You have given everything you have for little Benjamin and me. The least I can do is share the gift of myself."

Jacob nodded and turned to her. Slow and gentle, that was the only way he could be with her. Charlotte was fragile. It would not take much to break her into a million pieces, scattered on the wind. He ran his hands up and down her body and felt her respond to him, drawing herself closer, not pulling away.

Start small. It had been nearly a year since she had shared herself and that had been with only one other. Jacob focused on her hair, lost himself in the heavy strands, first with his hands, then pressing his face into the thick curls. His breath tickled her ear and she laughed.

He thrilled to that sound, brought his lips to her jaw next and the frantic beating of her pulse, felt the reassuring throb of her life force running through her. So much more precious considering how fleeting life could be, that twice Charlotte had nearly slipped through his hands.

His fingers traveled to her shoulder, pushing the sleeve away, allowing him to graze her warm skin with his mouth. She was a cinder in his hands, getting hotter by the second. His fingers continued to trail down her side, cataloging every rib, then to her hip where his hand found a home. Since Benjamin's birth, she had a new softness to her, a roundness that drew him in like a spider in a web. The war, grief, and influenza had whittled her down, made her sharp around the edges. Not anymore. She was a full, warm place to fall.

Jacob's head dropped to the cushion of her chest, made more ample with feeding the baby, and he couldn't hold back a moan. His body began to shake with the tension.

Charlotte grabbed hold of his shoulders, her fingernails digging in deep. "Now. Don't make me wait any longer. This is torture!"

She was breathless, her heart a steady beating beneath his ear. Echoing through his body. Tugging at his gut. Making his insides twist and turn.

He rose to his knees and pulled her up, his fingers fumbling with the laces that ran down the front of her bodice, containing the fullness of her beautiful body. He nearly began to cry with frustration, his hands were shaking so badly. Charlotte laid her fingers on his and made him go still. She took over, her knowing touch quickly releasing her stays. The dress dropped, leaving her plain, white shift. She stood, a puddle of fabric forming at her feet. Jacob grabbed hold of her legs and pressed his face to her shins for a moment. To collect himself. To gather his strength. To keep his heart from exploding.

Her hand rested on his head, skimmed over his shoulder, down to his hand. Pressed urgently. He took the hint and stood, catching her shift and bringing the plain, white shirt over her head. Revealing the body God had given her for only heaven above, nature, and Jacob to see. His breath caught and he was frozen.

"Jacob, please!" She begged.

He nodded and placed her hands on his chest in invitation. Shyly, she lifted his shirt over his head and her hands went to the lacing at his waist. A few, deft tugs and he was freed from the bonds of his clothes. She stared at him, eyes wide. Her color rose and her pulse rivaled the thrumming in his veins.

Jacob stepped forward and took her in his arms, took her to the ground, made her body one with his. Fell over the brink and Charlotte went with him.

~

"WE'D BEST GO BACK." THEY LAY ON A FLAT, WIDE STONE in the middle of a creek.

After sharing one another, they'd been overcome with a ravenous hunger and thirst. The contents of Charlotte's basket had been devoured within minutes. They had another taste of each other and began to scavenge to bolster their strength, finding energy for more. An explosion of wild blackberries filled their rumbling bellies, the creek sating their thirst. The warm rock was a perfect bed. Cushioned by their clothes, they found no better spot to delve into the treasure of each other. No longer a secret, they couldn't experience one another enough.

Jacob squeezed Charlotte's hand in acknowledgment even though he wanted to bat her words away like a fly. The sun was low in the sky, the trees beginning to look like dark skeletons stretching imploring fingers to the heavens above. He could sympathize, wanting nothing more than to pray to all that was holy to give them a few more hours. Days. Years in this place that was all their own, sealed off from everyone else.

"Jacob, I mean it! It's getting late. Benjamin will be hungry and my breasts are so heavy, they are starting to hurt." He heard the aching in her voice and turned, saw the fullness, knew that the lightest touch would set the milk to flowing.

With a heavy sigh of regret, he sat up and gathered her clothes. "I know that you're right, but what I want to do is make love to you until our bones go soft and the heat nearly reduces us to nothing. Then I'll carry you into the creek, dousing the flames, and I will have you again."

Charlotte held her arms up, allowing him to slip her shirt over her head, followed by her dress. As soon as the bodice was tied tightly, ensconcing her in clothing once again, she looped her arms over his head.

"That will have to wait for another day. Isn't it good to know that we have no end of days before us and a bed waiting for us tonight? We've been blessed with a baby that sleeps well. He might even sleep until dawn." She dipped in and graced him with a kiss.

Jacob couldn't help but grin. "Until dawn? Hmm, there's something to look forward to. I believe you are giving me a challenge. I will do my best to rise to the occasion."

He fought his way back into his clothes, even though he'd much rather stay there with her. Freezing time, as he'd found out the hard way, was not an option. Charlotte took up her skirts, tossing them over her arm, while he pulled his breeches up past his knees. He tossed his stockings and hers over his shoulder. Slowly, they picked their way across when unable to resist her, he scooped her into his arms. Charlotte cried out in surprise, her laughter bubbling up and spilling over. Contagious. Her joy, her spirit, her fire was contagious.

They made it to the shoreline and tumbled to the ground. Jacob lost himself in one more kiss before he reluctantly pulled away and helped her with her stockings. She returned the favor and they slipped their shoes on their feet. Hand in hand, they made their way through the forest. To the cottage. To their hearth where William sat by the fireplace, rocking his grandson in his wooden cradle. Dinner waited on the table as well as his smile. A more welcome homecoming no one could ever ask for.

William stayed until darkness fell. Try as they might, he would not spend the night. With one of Jacob's lanterns in hand and a promise to be careful, he made the half hour journey home. As Jacob stood by Charlotte's side on the porch, marveling at the glory of her bathed in moonlight, he couldn't wonder if his father-in-law left because of the leaves embedded in her hair. Or the redness in her cheeks. Or the way Jacob couldn't take his eyes off her the entire evening.

They were not long in preparing for bed that night, building a hearty fire so that clothes—and bed covers—were not necessary. As for the challenge, Jacob did not close his eyes until the first rays of daylight splashed the walls of their cottage, Charlotte nestled in against his side. Blessings upon blessings, little Benjamin slept late.

25 October, 1782

"I FEEL LIKE A RIDE, JACOB." Charlotte stood at the window, gazing outside with a wistful expression. Benjamin was in her arms, waving his fist. Healthy, brawny, and lively, the baby continued to light up their lives.

Jacob stepped in behind her and wrapped an arm around her waist, more generous since Benjamin's birth. One more reason she was irresistible. He kissed the top of the baby's head, then her cheek. She smiled and leaned into him.

"Where do you want to go?" Jacob already knew. He'd take her anywhere. To the ends of the earth. Back to Mother England. To the bottom of the ocean or the top of the highest peak. *You're getting carried away, Cooper. Come back down to earth.* His mouth turned up in a grin at his wayward turn of thoughts.

Charlotte shrugged. "I don't really care. I am just tired of staying inside."

The weather had taken a turn for the worse the past few days as rain fell and the harsh winds blew, giving them a hint of what was to come. This day had brought a respite. Sunshine. Mild temperatures. Not a cloud in the sky. No matter how brief, they had to enjoy every minute for soon they would be trapped indoors by the cold and snow.

"All right. I'll get the wagon ready."

As much as he'd like to take Charlotte with him on Powder, that wasn't an option with the baby. Besides, Jacob had already given his stallion a workout that morning. A slow, easy amble with Bonnie by his steed's side would be for the best for all involved.

He whistled while hitching the horses, stopping in awe as he stepped out into the sunlight to marvel at the view before him. Charlotte stood on the porch, her hair left loose for a change, tangled around her face in the breeze. She'd chosen one of his favorite dresses, one in a blue that matched the sky and brought out the golden honey in her eyes. Her gaze was clear, her smile wide. Happiness looked good on his wife.

Jacob's heart was light, his spirit free, no longer burdened by the sorrow that had been a dark shadow hovering over them for so long. No more nightmares had haunted him since the night Charlotte faced his demons with him. Since then, in her arms, she chased them away.

His wife was like no other. Unwavering in the storm. With such an endless capacity to love. Staring at her from the barn, his breath caught in his throat and his heart pounded in his chest. Jacob didn't know how he'd come to deserve her, but he'd never tire of trying to rise to the challenge of being worthy.

He pulled up in front of her, locked the wheels in place, and jumped down to the ground with a resounding *thud!* With a bow, he kissed her hand and winked at her. "Ready, my lady?'

She nodded, little Benjamin waving his arms and chortling in agreement. Soon, the boy would be talking up a storm. Without giving her time to argue, Jacob grabbed hold of Charlotte by the waist and gave her a boost into the seat. The baby's peals of laughter made the day even brighter.

Jacob went around to the driver's side and climbed back up. With a *hyah*, they were off. The wagon rumbled slowly over the dirt lane, jostling them against each other, sending a vibration from his head to his toes. At one particularly rough jolt, Charlotte grabbed hold of his arm, her breath coming out in a gasp. He slid her a grin, wondering if she knew of her effect on him. Charlotte Ross Cooper was stronger and more intoxicating than any whiskey or ale a man could drink.

"Which way, Charlotte?"

She gestured to the left or to the right as they plodded along. Jacob didn't question her. She had an excellent sense of direction. He did not fear they'd get lost. Except in each other. A good half hour's ride passed and the wagon rolled to a halt in a place Jacob never planned on laying eyes on again.

A lonely field stretched before them, interspersed with trees here and there. The weeds had grown tall, browning with the change of the seasons, and a medley of colors floated down from the trees. Jacob only saw a river of blood. Heard agonized screams. Smelled smoke and death.

He closed his eyes, his body gone rigid. "Not here, Charlotte. Anyplace but here. The memories are still too fresh—too dark."

Her hand took his, pressing until he met her gaze. Pure honey. Strong. Fearless. "If we are going to have a future and make the most of everything it holds, we must bury the past." Her eyes filled, but she blinked her tears away. "Benjamin should know from a young age where his father fell, where so many, including you paid such a dear price. It is time we laid our ghosts to rest, my love." A shiver went up Jacob's back. He wasn't sure if she spoke to him or to Benjamin Willson.

Although the very thought of touching the tainted soil filled him with dread, Jacob did as she bid him. He leapt from his seat and helped her to the ground. Sensing his turmoil, she offered him her hand. A few steps on to the field and her trembling traveled through her fingers to his heart. This was not easy by any means for Charlotte either. Bravely, she forged ahead, closer to the site where her Benjamin fell. Where Jacob nearly died, fighting his way to a militia uniform with a ragged hole in the chest and a thick braid of golden hair in the pocket. His knees gave and he landed on the heels of his hands, head hung low, sucking in air as if for dear life.

Charlotte knelt with him, her hand traveling to the nape of his neck to soothe him when she froze. "Jacob! Dear God, Jacob, look, will you?"

He beat down his sorrow, his fear, and the sick feeling in the pit of his stomach. Jacob forced himself to lift his head, to follow where she pointed with fingers that shook. A small oak sapling had sprung from the earth in the same spot where Benjamin fell. Such a small but profound sign of hope, a light in the darkness.

Jacob took Charlotte in his arms, giving the baby shelter as well.

Little Benjamin always put him at ease and lightened any burden he carried. Today was no different. A rush of warm air swirled around them, kicking up leaves and making them dance around the tiny family. Charlotte closed her eyes and sighed softly as a wave of scarlet washed over her cheeks, her hair dancing around her face. The baby's hair became tousled as well. Jacob didn't question it. It was fitting that Benjamin Willson chose that day to visit.

Jacob had to give him his due. "Liberty's promise was made. Liberty's promise has been kept. I'll take good care of them, Benjamin, until I have no breath left in my body. I love them both more than life itself."

Charlotte smiled even as a tear trailed down her cheek. She turned to give Jacob all her attention, focusing on him. "You have taught me how to love again, Jacob. I look forward to what this life will hold, for little Benjamin and us."

The wind rose once more, carrying the leaves high into the air. For an instant, Jacob could swear he could hear laughter and see the outline of a man before it was gone. All that remained was Charlotte, little Benjamin, and Jacob. A family. A torch burning bright for America's future.

June 24, 1812

I HAVE WALKED THAT LONELY FIELD, stood where my father fell. I have felt his presence and his valiant heart beats in me.

My father was liberty's son. Because of his love for my mother and his sacrifice, I came to be. Because of Jacob Cooper, I became the man I am supposed to be, the kind of son Benjamin Willson would be proud to call his own. Jacob taught me that someone must shine a light in the darkness. Even if I am only one candle amongst thousands, I will do my part to live up to the expectations of the men who went before me, born up by the love of a mother who was willing to fight the British and defy the bottomless pit of her grief to bring me into this world.

The drums of Madison's war are beating again and I must answer the call. Like my father before me. Like the man who raised me as his own. I am liberty's legacy.

December 24, 2015

I COULDN'T BREATHE, MY HAND GRIPPING BEN'S so tightly, my knuckles had gone white. It was as if all the blood drained from my body and poured out onto the floor. I expected to look down and see a scarlet puddle that would cover our feet. I gazed at my husband's face and couldn't suppress a shudder. He had lost all color and looked like death.

"Dear God! What do you think happened to him?" I wrapped my arms around my waist, but the knot deep inside did not loosen. If anything, it formed into a heavy, leaden ball in my stomach the moment the date in Benjamin Cooper's last entry sank in. June 1812. Just after the War of 1812 began. Another life entangled by war.

Benjamin Willson Cooper was not mine, but my mind, my distant memories, my body told a different story.

It felt like only yesterday when the whispers of liberty spoke in my ear, pulling me back to colonial times, the Battle of Johnstown, and the arms of my Patriot, Benjamin Willson. The last time I saw him, held him, and looked into his eyes in those days, I was on the battlefield and the fighting was underway. In the midst of the smoke, the gunfire, I fell into my Benjamin, the future—our unborn child—in my womb.

I pressed my stomach hard. Even though it was the present and I was no longer Charlotte Elizabeth Ross the First, I had dreamt of Benjamin Willson Cooper's birth, an impression that had been emblazoned vividly in my mind, made even more meaningful since I gave birth to Jacob Cooper Wilson in 2015. Ben and I had been reunited, the torch that was lit over two hundred and thirty years before still burning bright inside of us, and yet I wondered. What happened to liberty's legacy, to Benjamin and Charlotte's son, the son that I had known from his beginnings?

"I'll find him." Ben took my face in his hands, his fingers

threading into my hair, pulling the heavy strands hard enough to bring the tears to my eyes. I welcomed the pain, anything to distract me from my fear and the wound that had been torn open wide once again, the one that nearly killed me the day I lost Benjamin.

Here. I'm right here! My husband's eyes told the story, anchoring me, making it possible to breathe again. "He's mine too and I'll find out what happened. I promise, and—" I placed a finger on his lip before Ben could say more.

"You always keep your promises." I kissed him, proving my faith in his words, even as the tears rose and overflowed. Ben wrapped me in his arms, in liberty's promise. I held on tight.

The sound of the wind whispering in the trees set the snow to whipping past our window, a streak of white against the glass. In the distance, lights could be seen winking in the darkness. Our lone oak, the guardian of the field. It called to me, drawing me closer. I pressed my face and my palms against its cold surface. Somehow, it soothed my raw spirit. The journal had stirred up memories I would rather not recall.

Ben stepped up behind me and looped an arm around my neck. His face was reflected in the window, gone white as paper. The telling of Jacob Cooper's story had not been easy on him either. I leaned back against him and closed my eyes. He was my peace in the middle of the chaos and always had been.

"Let's visit the tree tonight. It's Christmas Eve. We should pay our respects." His voice dropped low. I could barely hear him, but his heart thudded against my back.

I turned and buried my face in Ben's chest. A part of me didn't want to set foot on that field. I had lost my Benjamin there over two centuries ago. Even though I won him back, on that same remote patch of earth that was the thread between past and present, I would never forget seeing my love's blood spill into that soil. Never erase the sight of the life fading from his eyes. Never allow the mental picture of his body falling to the ground to fade.

Ben rubbed my back and threaded his hands through my hair, tipping my face to his. As always, as it had been from the start, this man could not be ignored. "Get your coat. I'll get Jacob. I can hear him moving about on the monitor."

I swallowed hard and nodded. I rubbed at the tears that had slipped down my cheeks. My face was hot. Emotions were a hard burden to bear. I held on to the railing as I went down the stairs, my steps uncertain. At one point, I wavered and reached out for the wall to steady myself. It was late and the journal had consumed us for two days, I was completely drained.

I was leaning against the wall when I felt a strong arm wrap itself around my shoulders. "Charlotte, your coat?" Ben turned me to face him and grazed my cheek with a kiss. Jake was tucked into the cradle of his arm, peering out at the world with sleepy eyes. His father's eyes. Absolutely precious.

The sight of our son made me take heart. I smiled and went to the hooks by the door to slip into my coat and boots. I took my baby in my arms while his father put on his winter gear next. Finally, I grabbed a blanket off the back of the couch and swaddled Jake so well one could not tell where the blanket left off and the baby began.

Ben opened the door and gave a bow. I stepped out into a night that was bitter cold, but so clear it hurt my eyes with its beauty. The stars were shining high overhead and Jake giggled, reaching out and pointing, his little fingers trying to catch the light. I buried my face in the nape of his neck and inhaled the sweet scent of baby and powder. The light, Benjamin's light, ours was aglow within our boy.

Ben took my hand and we walked together, through snow at least three feet deep after the storm only two nights before. It felt like ages ago when my husband walked through the door, hounded by our past, carrying the bombshell of a book bound in faded leather. Several times I stumbled. Every time, a strong hand was there to steady me. We were both breathing hard by the time we finally stood before our sacred tree, ablaze with light. The snow sparkled around us and it was as if the whole world was waiting with us for the spirits of the field to rise up again.

We did not have long to wait as a rush of warm air swirled around us. I reached for Ben and entwined my fingers tightly with his as the breath was sucked from my lungs. The blood hummed in my veins and anticipation made my whole body go tight. Ben's figure went taut beside me. He could have been a statue. His head snapped up and he gasped, his gaze trained on a spot beside the tree. I didn't want to look away from the reassuring face of my husband, but it was as if a magnet pulled my head to the side. My breath caught in my throat.

A sturdy, brawny figure stood before us, crackling with vitality in the fire in his hair and bolt of blue eyes, hand extended to us. Jacob Cooper. I would know him anywhere, past or present. After all this time, buried in the dust of memories and past lives, he was stamped upon my heart.

A blink and the image began to fade, but a river of love ran through me and there was a whisper on the air, "I always loved you and baby Benjamin."

I loved you too, Jacob. I could not say the words aloud, could not betray my husband beside me and yet I think the other man who loved me so understood. There was no pain, no anger. Only acceptance and devotion.

Ben stiffened beside me, touching my arm in wonder, and little Jake's face lit up. They could see Jacob, too and my heart swelled with gratitude. This man had left such a mark on their lives. It was only fitting that they would know him in some way. Jake's arms waved in the air as my tears flowed down my cheeks. I could taste their salt on my lips. It seemed I would fill the world with my tears since my adventures in time began over a year before.

I reached for my husband and he stepped in closer, a wall that would never crumble, my lighthouse in any storm. Our story had not been an easy one, but meant all the more because we struggled for our happy ending. Ben gathered me close against his side, little Jake tucked in between us. A light blazing in the night for all of us, hope for the future. The first spark was lit in our past lives, by Benjamin Willson and Charlotte Elizabeth Ross the First. How remarkable that the flame continued to burn now. For all of us to see.

Ben's words were hushed, drifting into the air. "We'll find him, Jacob, find out what happened to Benjamin. Liberty's legacy doesn't end here."

The wind picked up in intensity, creating a miniature cyclone of snow that whipped around our oak. It set the branches to waving and the lights sparkled even more intensely, as if they winked at us. The moon and stars above seemed brighter than they ever had before, close enough for me to hold in my hands.

Ben's arms tightened around my waist and the music of Jake's cooing filled my ears as the tears welled in my eyes. Liberty's legacy didn't come to an end. It lived. In us.

Afterword

Ben, Benjamin, Charlotte, and William, as well as most of the events in Liberty's Promise, are fictional, inspired by a combination of "*The Sons of Liberty*," a miniseries on the History Channel, *Outlander*, and the colonial heritage that surrounds me here in the small, historic town of Johnstown. Tucked away in upstate New York, it is rich in history dating back to Sir William Johnson, an extremely influential figure who played a major role in the French and Indian War. It could be argued that we remained British colonies, not French, because of him. The Battle of Johnstown was one of the final battles of the American Revolution, taking place six days after Cornwallis' surrender at Yorktown. Other characters that, in fact, lived during the birth of our nation include Talmadge Edwards, Richard Dodge, Anna Mason Scarborough Stoner, and her daughter Mary.

As for Nick Stoner, this colorful figure is well-known throughout Fulton County. His larger than life statue stands watch over the land he loved and fought for, calling to mind Daniel Boone. He truly did serve at Oriskany and Saratoga where he was severely injured when a fellow soldier was killed by a cannonball. He served with Benedict Arnold, saw the surrender at Yorktown firsthand, and joined Colonel Marinus Willett when the British finally left New York City in 1783. Stoner was a trapper, guide, and outdoorsman. A bold figure, he also had a soft side. His sweetheart, Anna Mason Scarborough, married William Scarborough while Nicholas was engaged in battle far from home. During the Battle of Johnstown, William died. Nicholas married Anna, caring for her baby girl, Mary. How similar to Jacob, Charlotte—and Benjamin Willson Cooper. I did not know about Anna when I created Jacob and Charlotte, but I'd like to think Jacob was inspired by great men like Stoner and our forefathers.

As for Liberty's Promise, it lives on. In all who answer the call. Whenever we see the red, white, and blue waving high. Filling our hearts and eyes with pride. Let freedom ring.

Liberty's Promise

Whispers of Liberty
Book #1 in the *Liberty* series
And prequel to *Liberty's Promise*
by
Heidi Sprouse
(Preview)

.

Chapter 1

I HEAR THE WHISPERS of liberty every day and its ghosts pass me by. The rustling of heavy skirts. A tricorne hat, head and shoulders above the others ambling on the sidewalk. A smattering of red coats scrambling across a farmer's field with blue coats in hot pursuit before vanishing into the woods. The crackle of musket fire making me catch my breath. The boom of cannons waking me in the night from a sound sleep. It's not surprising really. I have lived in historic Johnstown all of my twenty-two years, steeped in colonial history like a tea bag in a dark, strong brew.

those patriotic times, thanks to my mother's brilliant imagination and skill with a sewing machine. My father's burning desire for historical accuracy ensured they were right. Each time I had to give a speech, my classmates began to place bets trying to figure out who I was before I opened my mouth and spilled the beans.

All of those outfits are carefully packed away in my hope chest, reminders of my school days. Betsy Ross, mother of our flag. Molly Pitcher, alias Mary Ludwig Hays, who tended the wounded, carried water, and helped load the cannons at the Battle of Monmouth. Sybil Ludington, the brave heroine who rode more than twice as far as Paul Revere at the young age of 16 to save the day after the British raided Danbury, Connecticut. Deborah Sampson, who posed as her brother and actually fought for the Americans. Courageous, strong women that are a part of me.

To say I'm entangled in colonial days is an understatement. I'm addicted to Assassin's Creed III, mainly because Sir William Johnson, founder of my town, is a character and his estate, only a few miles away from my home, has been recreated with incredible authenticity. When most people are watching the Walking Dead and an abundance of reality shows, I'm on the edge of my seat following "The Sons of Liberty" on the History Channel. I'm thinking about starting a petition because I can't live without a continuation. Instead of credit cards, I carry a mem I can climb my family tree all the way back to the 1760's and some of the original settlers in Sir William Johnson's colony. My father, Martin Ross, is a major, history buff, particularly US history, with a full-blown obsession for the American Revolution. While other children grew up with fairy tales, I heard "The Midnight Ride of Paul Revere" and the Declaration of Independence so many times the words are written on my heart.

Most kids went to Disney. Our family getaways and vacations took us to every point of interest in the battle for our independence. Boston. Breed's Hill. Lexington and Concord. Ticonderoga. Long Island. White Plains. Fort Washington. The Delaware. Trenton. Oriskany. Bennington. Valley Forge. Saratoga. Yorktown. I could rattle off more. The Battle of Johnstown holds a special place in my heart as my hometown's claim to fame; it was one of the final battles in the Northern theatre of war. I can spin off more details about that distant day than an encyclopedia. Believe it or not, our brave Patriots fought six days after Cornwallis' surrender. No cell phones to spread the word back then.

As a double whammy, my mother, Clara, is a social studies teacher at the junior high. Not nearly as passionate about colonial history as my dear father, she still managed to cheerfully humor and indulge his whims all of my life, which could be worse. Every costume, every oral presentation, every book report at school involved an important figure in full dress from bership card in my purse: *Charlotte Ross, proud member of the Daughters of the American Revolution*. I earned a history degree and opened a bookstore, the Colonial Book Nook, so I could indulge in my greatest loves, olden times in America and my own writing. I spend more time in a bygone era than in the 21st century.

I guess I shouldn't have been shocked that one day the past and present would collide.

October 25, 2014. The anniversary of the Battle of Johnstown and a ghost walk was taking place in town. With only six days until Halloween, it was an opportunity that couldn't be missed. The air was brisk, hinting of the onset of winter as the dead leaves skittered by my feet on the mile and a half walk from my snug, rental cottage. I figured the exercise would do me good. I buttoned up my coat and moved along at a steady pace as the sun finally dipped below the horizon over my sleepy town. A full moon blazed high in the sky and lit my path.

I'd walked the roads of my town so many times I could find my way with my eyes closed, first holding my father's hand as a child, then on my own, soaking up historical sites everywhere I turned. The James Burke Inn, originally established for Robert Picken, Johntown's surveyor, 1765. Fort Johnstown, aka. the Tryon County Jail, 1772. The Fulton County Courthouse, formerly known as the Tryon County Courthouse and the oldest working courthouse in New York, also dating back to 1772. Night or day, it comforted me to share my town with these enduring landmarks. I thought of them as old friends.

As I rounded the corner of St. John's Episcopal, I had to squash the perverse urge to spit on Sir William Johnson's grave. A major figure in pre-Revolutionary history, I could only think of him as a Loyalist through and through, a true British baron. I didn't care that the man was instrumental in ensuring we remained British colonies, not French, due to his part in the French and Indian War. It did not matter that he was the Great White Father to the Natives at the time. An insatiable imperialist, he just had to take everything and keep it all.

Thanks to *my* father, I had a rather partial view that favored the Americans, rational or no. I lengthened my stride and resolutely turned my gaze away, moving swiftly down West Green Street, past the Colonial Cemetery. I'd done rubbings of many of the stones where Revolutionary notables slept. My feet were tempted to turn inside the gate and visit those honorable grave markers, but the ghost walk was about to begin.

Maynard Hughes, town historian and old crony of my father's, was the host of the evening, quite dashing in a cape and cap that was in style over 250 years ago. He stood on the Drumm House steps. A fitting location, it was supposedly built in 1763 for the first school master, Edward Wall, and acted as a museum. I'd taken many a trip to the tiny, colonial house with my parents and teachers. I gave Maynard a wave and joined the small crowd that had gathered.

The elderly gentleman doffed his tricorne hat and bowed his snowy head, flashing me a grin, his eyes twinkling behind wire-rimmed glasses in the glow of the moon. The man was in his glory and reveled in drawing his audience into the past to find out who haunted our noble town. As the wind kicked up, making the branches of the trees creak eerily, the stage was set perfectly. Maynard launched into a long-winded tale that dragged on and on.

Get to the punchline, Maynard! God love him, but the man could talk. There was many an evening that I nodded off on our couch while my father and the historian talked about the olden days. Fighting the urge to snooze, I decided to browse the cemetery after all. I broke away from the others and had only taken a few steps when a masculine figure passed by me, sending a draft of cold air my way that made me shiver and set my tousled curls to fluttering around my face. Goosebumps rose up on my arms, the fine hairs on the back of my neck standing on end, and I couldn't take my eyes off of him.

He was tall, broad of back, his shoulders firmly set, the kind of man who stood out in a crowd and would turn heads everywhere. He wore Revolutionary garb, his dark hair tied back in a tail, brushing a collar that stood up straight. Breeches that went just below the knee, stockings, and leather shoes with buckles gleaming in the light completed the ensemble. The man called to mind Ichabod Crane from that new Sleepy Hollow series on TV. *Wow. Someone is really getting into the spirit tonight.*

The stranger made his way through the gates, between the stones, as Maynard's deep voice droned on in the distance. Inexplicably drawn to the back of the graveyard, I followed him. He paused in front of a tall stone, one I had seen the day before while wandering through the cemetery on my lunch break as I often did. I'd planned to come back to take a picture or do a rubbing, maybe do a genealogy search because it pulled at me. The writing was remarkably clear, the stone a pure white when others had been stained by time, yet I'd never noticed it before and the fire of curiosity started burning in the pit of my stomach. Tonight, it was a bonfire.

The man knelt on the dead grass in front of the stone and bowed his head. The clouds shifted as I approached, bathing him in a shaft of light, and the he looked up at me. His face was troubled, his dark eyes filled with longing. His hand lifted, palm up, and reached out for me. I couldn't resist his beckon, couldn't turn away. The sounds of the night, the low rumble of Maynard's voice, the rustling of the straggling, dry leaves scraping against the trees, the thundering of my heart, all faded away.

The man turned and rested his hand on the grave and I stared at the words that had already been etched in my mind. Here lies Benjamin Willson. Died October 25, 1781 at the Battle of Johnstown. Liberty's son, he bravely fought. To break tyranny's chains is what he sought.

Trembling, I slowly lowered myself to the ground beside him, hoping to give comfort, and pressed my hand to the pale sandstone. *"Remember…I said I would find you."* A low voice whispered softly in my ear. I felt like someone was tugging me into a deep, bottomless pit and I was falling pell-mell through the air into blackness.

Whispers of Liberty by Heidi Sprouse – available at most online retailers.

Whispers of Liberty

About Heidi Sprouse

Heidi Sprouse lives in upstate NY in historic Johnstown. She attended college at St. Rose in Albany, knowing all along her two loves were teaching and English. It took four years before she landed the teaching job of her dreams, but twenty years later she is still nurturing little ones in pre-K. She loves the privilege of watching brand-new little humans as they discover and begin to shape their own worlds.

Knowing what she wants and going after it in relentless pursuit is Heidi's gift. Deciding to become an author can be downright unnerving, but Heidi bit into the challenge, took off, and never looked back. Her perseverance proves success is not a matter of luck; it's a matter of finding what speaks to your heart, and committing to do that thing until it makes a difference.

When she isn't busy teaching or with her husband, Jim, her son, Patrick, and her canine kids Chuck and Dale, she's cooking up her next novel. She dabbles in sweet romances, historical fiction, and suspense thrillers, depending on what pleases her reader's eye at any given moment. Heidi is always in search of the extraordinary in the ordinary, writing about strong men with old-fashioned values and the women who pick them up when they fall. She'll tell anyone it's never too late to chase after your dreams, no dream is too small or insignificant, and any mountain can be moved with a proposal and a good plan.

Connect with Heidi:
At Salt Run Publishing: http://saltrunpub.com/heidi-sprouse/
Heidi Sprouse, Author: http://heidisprouse.wixsite.com/heidi-sprouse
Facebook: https://www.facebook.com/Heidi-Sprouse-Writer-194228980730069/
TWITTER Heidi Sprouse Author @heidi_sprouse

Made in the USA
Middletown, DE
02 July 2017